In the Depths of Winter

Winslo Brauer

Northshore Noir Press

Northshore Noir Press

Toronto, Canada

www.northshorenoir.com

ISBN: 978-1-7381518-7-5

eBook ISBN: 978-1-7381518-8-2

For more information visit www.northshorenoir.com

English is a beautiful monster.

~ Winslo

Contents

Chapter 1

The night was bitterly cold, but the fireplace crackled with warmth as I settled into bed. My idiot of a husband had neglected to chop wood, so I took it upon myself to do the job. The strenuous labour left me exhausted, but I refused to rely on anyone else.

Despite the risk, I found comfort in the dancing flames throughout the night. The fear of fire didn't faze me; the cozy heat was worth any danger. Besides, the carbon monoxide alarm stood guard in the kitchen.

Morning arrived just as serene as nightfall. Waking to find my husband already gone was a rare blessing. It meant I could savour a leisurely breakfast without his presence looming over me.

After tending to the fire, I indulged in a hearty meal of a toasted bacon and eggs sandwich. The rich yolk spilled out with each bite, a simple pleasure that never failed to satisfy. A steaming cup of coffee with milk and sugar accompanied my meal as I gazed out at the lightly falling snow.

The beauty outside was marred by thoughts of our neighbour, Ethel Smart. The woman who had once resided next door haunted my thoughts. She was a lovely woman. Quiet, kept to herself. Her family's lineage in that cabin stretched back generations until her passing left it empty and for sale. And it sold.

Then came Rike Volk, a German woman who dared to disrupt our tranquil town with her presence and that rainbow flag of hers. The mere memory of her incited anger within me, tarnishing what should have been a peaceful morning.

Finishing my coffee, I cleared away breakfast and prepared to chop more firewood. As I swung the axe behind me, an unsettling noise pierced through the crisp air. Ignoring it initially, assuming safety with an axe in hand, proved to be a grave mistake.

The rumbling grew louder before an ominous roar filled my ears. Pain seared through me as reality shifted; something dreadful loomed behind me. With one final swing of the axe, agony consumed me like never before. Collapsing to the ground, awareness faded into darkness.

In that moment of despair and realization that death loomed near, pain ebbed away into numbness until nothing remained but darkness.

Chapter 2

The first light of dawn painted Rike Volk's secluded cabin with a fragile glow, perched on the borderlands of Saint Berna Aux Étranger. Frost delicately traced elabourate designs on each window, while the forest loomed as a silent guardian, encircling her haven with a tranquil solitude. The brisk air carried the crisp fragrance of pine needles and the subtle hint of impending snowfall, a secret shared by the heavy clouds looming overhead.

Rike, her silver hair shimmering in the morning light, moved with a sense of ease that belied the turmoil within. Each step she took exuded purpose and tranquillity. The wooden floor groaned softly under her weight as she made her way to the simple kitchen, where the kettle had just started its hissing overture.

With a low hum resonating through the room, Rike's melodic voice intertwined with the kettle's song. Pouring the water into a waiting cup became a graceful performance, wisps of steam swirling upwards to meet the chilly air. Her hand, steady from years of meticulous police work, wrapped around the ceramic handle of her teacup as she allowed herself a fleeting smile. These routines held a serene joy, born from surviving life's storms.

Seated at the worn pine table scarred by time and use, Rike cradled the cup in her hands while her gaze drifted out of the window. Beyond the glass, she beheld a winter landscape painted in ethereal beauty. "Exquisite," she murmured, breath forming a delicate mist on the pane. The earth lay cloaked in pristine snow, interrupted only by skeletal trees reaching towards the sky. The sun, a timid orb of muted gold, crept along the horizon casting elongated shadows that grasped at the land like ghostly fingers.

Rike's tea embraced her with warmth, a stark contrast to the icy fingers of the chill that crept around her cabin. Through the window, she saw the snow-covered fields undulate gently, the evergreen trees standing steadfast against any howling wind that came calling. This serene landscape painted a picture of calm, a world untouched by the chaos of her former life in Berlin—a life she willingly traded for this solitary existence. Her heart, once burdened by the darkest cases, now found solace in solitude and the silent partnership with nature.

With practiced precision, Rike rose from her seat, carrying her empty cup as she made her way to the sink. Each movement deliberate, each action part of a well-worn routine that had become ritualistic. Cup washed and placed upside down to dry. In the small mudroom at the cabin's rear, her cross-country skis stood like loyal companions against the wall, beckoning for another day of exploration. Above them hung an array of outdoor gear—insulated jackets, fleece-lined gloves, and a weathered knit cap that bore witness to countless winter mornings. Beside the door rested her ski boots, their insulated linings promising comfort amidst the harsh bite of the cold awaiting outside.

Methodically dressing for the cold, Rike layered up against the winter's bite. Each garment she donned spoke of her reverence for nature's harsh embrace. She slung the rifle across her back, a familiar weight that brought comfort in its readiness. Next, her hand found the can of bear spray, a precautionary measure she holstered around her waist with practiced ease—her former life as a detective shining through in her preparedness and vigilance.

Swinging open the cabin door, a blast of icy air welcomed Rike as she ventured outside. Clicking into her skis with precision, she left behind the safety of her refuge. The snow whispered beneath her gliding skis, sharing secrets only it knew as she journeyed along the road. Her exhaled breath formed fleeting clouds that dissipated into the morning air, carrying with them a sense of tranquillity. Towering firs and pines flanked her path like silent guardians in the gentle dawn light.

The rhythmic crunch of snow underfoot became a comforting chant, lulling Rike into a state of detachment from the world she once inhabited—a world shadowed by death's constant presence. In this remote corner of Saint Berna Aux Étranger, isolation became Rike's solace. The sole spectators to her passage were occasional deer peeking curiously from among the trees before gracefully retreating into the wilderness beyond.

Today was a day meant for living, where the vast expanse of open spaces beckoned with freedom. The simplicity of existence revealed itself in the glide of ski over pristine snow, the icy air filling her lungs, and the steady thud of her heart—a heart now unburdened by the pains of murder, but awakened to the raw beauty of untouched wilderness.

She skied tirelessly, her pulse syncing with the scuff of ski against snow, each exhale forming wispy clouds that dissipated into the cobalt sky above. Despite the weak rays of the sun offering little warmth, she pressed on, squinting against its icy glare as she navigated through a mesmerizing play of shadows and light dancing beneath towering pines.

Her movements held a hypnotic rhythm, drawing her into a trance where only the crisp scrape of skis and the whispering symphony of wind through evergreen needles existed.

Rike stood at the ridge's edge, peering down at the frozen lake below, a pristine canvas of ice bordered by snow-draped evergreens. The morning sun climbed higher in the sky, signalling her to return. Opting for a shortcut along an abandoned logging trail, she plunged into the dense forest, its solemn hush a stark departure from the clamour of civilization she had forsaken. Abruptly, a murder of crows exploded from a nearby tree, their cacophonous cries rupturing the tranquillity. Startled, Rike's heart raced in her chest at the jarring eruption of noise and flurry of ebony wings. Despite a decade away from active duty, certain instincts remained etched in her very being. Silence returned until it fled again.

The morning's peace shattered abruptly with a sharp crack, a branch snapping underfoot—or so Rike believed. She froze, her breath suspended, scanning the tree line for any disturbance. It was too weighty for a small creature like a hare or fox, she noted with unease. She loved that she'd developed such wariness, but hated that it never left her.

Proceeding cautiously, her skiing cadence now disrupted by a heightened sense of vigilance, Rike navigated around a bend where the trees thinned out to reveal an open space. The scene before her anchored her in place, skis firmly planted in the snow as if they shared her reluctance to advance.

"What in the world..." she gasped softly, her hand automatically reaching for the bear spray nestled at her side. A stark splash of red against the pristine white snow caught her eye. Intrigued yet apprehensive, Rike edged closer, a familiar dread creeping over her skin.

Spread out before her like a macabre masterpiece was a vast pool of crimson staining the snow—a jarring contrast against the purity of the landscape. It resembled an open wound on the earth itself, bleeding into the snowy expanse and tainting it with the forbidden colour of blood; an unsettling presence in this sanctuary of solitude.

Her heart thundered in her chest, a drumbeat of alarm reverberating through her. The chilling familiarity of the grim scene unfolding before her triggered a visceral response she thought long buried with her past in Berlin. Despite years away from the force, her instincts surged back to life, though her hands betrayed a slight tremor—a silent testament to the haunting memories etched into her from years of pursuing darkness.

With deliberate movement, she closed the distance to the edge of the crimson stain marring her tranquil retreat. The pungent scent of copper mingled with the sharp pine aroma, a disquieting blend that twisted her gut. This intrusion upon nature felt like an ominous echo of her former life encroaching on her sanctuary. It was very fresh.

Remaining vigilant, she scanned the surroundings for any hint of movement, every sense attuned to potential danger. Without hesitation, she unslung the rifle from her back, its weight grounding her in this surreal moment.

Kneeling beside the pool of blood, she observed how it starkly contrasted against the pristine snow—a macabre painting etched by violence. The vivid red hue stood out defiantly against the winter landscape's purity; too fresh to have succumbed to the icy grip of nature just yet.

Her breath billowed out in rapid clouds, the icy air biting at her lungs as she stood frozen by the sight before her. The crimson stain on the pristine snow taunted her, a stark symbol of a life violently cut short. Rike's sharp eyes scanned the snowy landscape, honed by years of detective work, and immediately caught sight of the telltale signs that shattered the surrounding serenity—a trail of deep paw prints etched into the snow with purposeful strides. These were no ordinary tracks; they belonged to a predator, a wolf moving undisturbed through the scene of death like a ghost in the winter wilderness. The presence of the lone wolf only added to the ominous aura enveloping her, its silent journey intertwining with the grim reality she faced.

Bites, torn patches in the blood-stained snow, revealed the scavenger's feast. Nature's swift justice, erasing traces of violence. Shimmering amidst the crimson slush were glistening fragments of what seemed like flesh. The quiet landscape bore witness as Rike towered over the chilling scene, her silhouette casting a dark presence. While her mind grasped for routine procedures—observe, analyze, probe—a sinister memory clawed at her thoughts, a recollection she had long battled to suppress within these icy horizons.

A vivid recollection seized her, slicing through the tranquillity like a blade. In her mind's eye, a young woman lay lifeless in a pool of crimson, her vitality draining into the earth, leaving behind a gaping void of lost potential. The haunting image melded with the pristine snowscape before her, casting an eerie veil over reality that sent tremors racing through Rike's fingers. This wasn't just any memory; it was a spectre from her past in Berlin, etched with sorrow so deep it seemed to carve trenches in her very soul.

"Damn it," she muttered under her breath, a mantra against the encroaching darkness of death that threatened to engulf her. The tendrils of old traumas slithered uninvited and unwavering through her thoughts, coiling like vipers within the recesses of her consciousness. The once tranquil haven she sought refuge in now mocked her with its calm facade, heedless to the storm raging inside her.

She fought to steady her hands, the icy air stinging her lungs as she struggled to slow her breath. The forest stood eerily silent around her, a stark contrast to the whirlwind of memories raging inside her mind. Despite the tranquil beauty of the snowy landscape, her pulse raced uncontrollably, drowning out the serenity that had enveloped her just seconds before.

Rike's hands trembled as she reached for her jacket pocket, the zipper resisting her urgency before finally giving way. With unsteady fingers, she retrieved her cellphone, a tool now transformed into an extension of her investigative instincts. The camera lens morphed into her keen eye, the screen a canvas capturing the chilling tableau before her.

Each click of the camera was a heartbeat in the silent snow-covered landscape, freezing time to immortalize the jarring sight. She meticulously framed each shot: the scarlet stain stark against the pristine white backdrop, a haunting reminder of violence cutting through purity. The intersection of animal tracks with absence painted a grim narrative in nature's cruel handiwork, a macabre tapestry unfolding before her lens. Something died here very recently, and not enough of it remained. She wondered where the body was. Deer, fox, or human, something more should remain. Unless it was poachers.

In that frozen moment, Rike became not just an observer but a chronicler of horror, etching each detail with precision onto the digital canvas. The scene whispered secrets of loss and fear, drawing her deeper into its chilling embrace as she documented every nuance of the unsettling scene with unwavering focus.

Rike navigated the edge of the crimson pool with calculated precision, her movements akin to a silent dance on the snowy canvas. Her eyes, fixated on the scene before her, captured every detail with unwavering intensity. Not a single step was taken without purpose, each imprint in the snow a potential clue waiting to be unveiled. The chill in the air clawed at her skin, but she remained undeterred, determined to unravel the mystery that lay beneath the surface.

The woods enveloped her in a shroud of silence as she wrapped up her spontaneous investigation, the only audible sounds the gentle snow crunching beneath her boots and the soft click of the camera capturing the scene. Yet, this tranquillity masked the storm brewing within this remote setting and within Rike herself.

"Signal's dead," Rike muttered to herself, tucking away her phone. The frozen snapshots were now preserved. Her breath billowed out in wisps, mingling with the icy air, a visible reminder of the tension slowly easing from her chest. Despite this relief, the persistent throb of her pulse lingered in her ears like a haunting melody.

Chapter 3

Rike Volk's figure remained frozen against the winter backdrop, her exhalations forming ethereal clouds in the icy atmosphere. She saw more tracks. "A truck," she murmured softly as she delved into her jacket for her phone once more. Despite the slim odds, she angled her camera towards the road, where tire tracks almost vanished under the snow. The tracks in the snow resembled a series of interconnected diamonds, each imprint sharp and defined against the pristine white backdrop. Undoubtedly, someone would be able to identify at least the brand.

Her attention snapped to a vivid anomaly against the pristine snow—a discarded Sun Nut cigarette, its vibrant orange filter starkly contrasting the pure white landscape. Methodically, she captured it in a photograph and searched for any other traces of human presence. Finding no more, Rike stood upright, surveying the desolate surroundings. No dwellings, no indicators of life beyond her own existence. A gust of wind whispered through the towering pines, sending an eerie chill down her spine. This solitude had always been her sanctuary, where worldly distractions dissolved into nothingness. Yet, with the crimson stain at her feet, it transformed into a chilling tableau ripe with ominous possibilities.

In the heart of winter, the snow held tight to its chilling mysteries, revealing whispered secrets only to those with sharp senses. With a firm grip on her ski poles, she propelled herself forward, each glide across the untouched snow, leaving a trail behind her. The pool of blood now distant, she pressed on towards her isolated home, the absence of phone service amplifying her sense of isolation and unease.

The snowy forest enveloped Rike in a cocoon of silence, broken only by the swish of her skis slicing through the pristine snow. Each exhale materialized in the frosty air, a transient dance of mist that mingled with the icy breath of winter. The tranquillity was oppressive, amplifying the thud of her heartbeats like a drumbeat against nature's hush, a stark contrast to the vast uncertainty that loomed around her.

Navigating through the dense woods, she followed the old logging road reluctantly. The skeletal trees stood sentinel-like, their branches reaching out like frozen fingers clawing at the sky. Despite its eerie beauty, there was an undeniable sense of urgency that propelled her forward, leaving no room for admiration of nature's splendour.

A sudden burst of wind whipped through the trees, sending a flurry of snow cascading down from the heavy-laden branches, causing Rike to jolt in surprise. She came to an abrupt stop, her senses on high alert, straining to catch any sound—no crunch of boots on snow, no distant howl of animals. Only a chilling stillness enveloped her, creeping into her mind and body, magnifying every thought and twitch with a sinister intensity that threatened to unravel her nerves.

In a brief lapse from reality, Rike's thoughts wandered back to the winters of her youth. She envisioned a younger version of herself, carefree and full of laughter, creating snow angels with pure delight painting her cheeks. These recollections, once vivid but now shrouded by a lifetime of unraveling mysteries and battling demons, briefly emerged in the icy stillness like ethereal remnants of a lost serenity.

Muttering a curse, she banished the fleeting nostalgia, knowing there was no place for simple sentimentality in her world. Inhaling the crisp air, she propelled forward; the swish of her skis creating a hypnotic cadence, while the ghosts of her past ebbed away like wisps of frost melting under the clouded sun.

Driven by her unsettling find, Rike's hand dove into the deep pocket of her insulated parka, searching for her phone. The icy air stung her exposed fingertips as they emerged, struggling against the frost to tap on the screen. She realized there was still no signal. Under the dense cover of the snow-laden branches above, a muffled curse escaped her lips, dissipating into the wintry stillness around her.

"Let's go," she coaxed the silent gadget, a futile attempt to rouse it from its dormant state. Yet, amidst the stoic trees, technology remained powerless; nature reigned supreme, unmoved by her desire for contact. With a resigned sigh, Rike stowed the unresponsive phone away and pressed on with renewed determination. The serene glide of her skis morphed into an easy cadence, each swoosh now mirroring her de-escalating frustration, leaving behind the gnawing fear. "It was just poachers," she thought.

As Rike skied back to her cabin from the chilling discovery, the familiar solitary landscape now felt like a haunting companion. The bitter wind nipped at her cheeks, urging her to hasten her pace. With every backward glance, only the silent sentinel of the dense forest greeted her, intensifying the shivers that still gripped her.

Skiing harder, she couldn't shake the feeling that her former life in homicide was casting a shadow over her peaceful existence in Berna. She was bringing this on herself. Each laboured breath billowed out in misty puffs, the strain of the activity and the high altitude weaving together to make each inhale akin to pulling icy pins into her chest. She'd gone to cognitive behavioural therapy for a year shortly after leaving the force. It was not working for her right now. Now she has to decide whether to tell law enforcement, or leave it be.

A torrent of memories clouding her mind with uncertainty. She understood the intricate dance required when involving law enforcement, the tangled web of bureaucracy and conflicting interests that could entangle even the most well-meaning individual.

Lost in thought, Rike's recollection drifted to the day she had first crossed paths with Officer Horton years ago, thanks to Craig Griffith and his wife, Tammy. The scene mirrored the present moment—the pristine snow-covered expanse unfolding like a pristine canvas yearning to capture echoes of days long past.

Barely seven days into her new seclusion, the piercing echo of a rifle blast ruptured the tranquil isolation she had sought. Racing through the snow-covered landscape that made up her property, Rike's gaze locked onto Craig and Tammy as they loomed over a majestic deer sprawled in her pristine yard, their intrusion violating the sanctity of her snowy haven.

"Remove that carcass from my land!" Rike's voice sliced through the crisp air, a sharp command cutting into their conscience.

Craig pivoted, cheeks tinged red with more than just the biting cold, and argued, "We haven't dressed it yet—it'll spoil!" Towering over Craig, Rike exuded a quiet power that unsettled him. She observed Craig straighten his spine and surreptitiously rise on his toes in an attempt to match her height.

"That deer can't weigh more than forty-five kilos," she stated firmly, her disdain coating her words with frost. "Certainly not an insurmountable task for someone of even your...stature."

Craig's wounded pride was evident in the tight clench of his jaw, a silent admission of humiliation that brought a grim sense of satisfaction to Rike. They were hunting on her land after all. Standing firm and resolute, she crossed her arms like an impenetrable fortress, unwavering in her stance. Reluctantly, with faces twisted in sour expressions, Craig and Tammy begrudgingly obeyed, their hands moving with visible reluctance as they dragged the deer away. A trail of crimson blood marred the untouched white landscape, a vivid and haunting contrast that lingered as a chilling testament to their actions. It looked a little like the earlier blood pool.

The following morning unveiled a chilling sight: a macabre display awaited Rike as she stepped outside, a gruesome gut pile purposefully left on her doorstep. The putrid offering reeked of malice, unmistakably the handiwork of Craig and Tammy, a despicable act dripping with spite. Reluctantly, Rike made the difficult decision to mark her territory. While she allowed people the serene walks they craved and exhilarating ski trips across her property, the actions of Craig and Tammy left her with no choice but to bar them—and consequently everyone else—from trespassing on her land.

She shook snow off of her coat and memories out of her mind. She hated that those two kept coming to mind. She recalled the morning sun painting the snowy landscape in a soft golden hue as Rike stood outside that morning years ago, her breath forming misty clouds in the crisp air. The rhythmic thud of her axe biting into wood filled the serene surroundings, a comforting routine disrupted by an abrupt crack that shattered the tranquillity. Startled, Rike's gaze shot towards the source of the sound, her eyes narrowing as she pinpointed Craig and Tammy amidst the skeletal trees, rifles poised in their hands, brazenly encroaching on her land. Again.

Rike set down her axe with a resounding thud and reached for her phone. Dialling the local police force with swift precision, she wasted no time in conveying the urgency of the situation. "Officer Horton," she spoke firmly into the phone, her voice cutting through the frosty air, "This is Rike Volk. I require your immediate presence at my residence. My neighbours, Craig and Tammy, are trespassing on my property for hunting purposes despite clear postings prohibiting such actions. They shot a deer yesterday, and they are up to something again today." She headed out once more with her rifle. She had experience shooting a man. She hated that she was willing to do it again.

Rike stood firm, her gaze firm as she confronted Craig and Tammy in her backyard, the rifle heavy against her shoulder. Behind them, the vast expanse of her property stretched out, a silent witness to the unfolding standoff.

"Thought you could just help yourselves, again?" Rike's voice was laced with simmering anger, her finger twitching on the trigger of the rifle. "This is my land, and you had no right."

Craig's jaw tightened, his grip on his own rifle betraying his nervousness. "We always hunted the land," he muttered, a defiant edge creeping into his tone. "You've got plenty of deer."

Tammy, standing by his side, shot Rike a venomous glare. "We're just trying to survive out here," she spat. "You think you're better than us, with your fancy accent and your high and mighty attitude."

Rike's nostrils flared, her grip on the rifle tightening. "What? Nothing gives you the right to trespass and poach," she countered, her voice cold and unwavering. "You crossed a line, and now you're going to face the consequences." Tension hung heavy in the air, each of them locked in a silent standoff, the only sound the rustle of leaves in the breeze.

Officer Horton's arrival was like a sudden chill sweeping through the tense standoff with the poachers. His presence halted the standoff, and everyone lowered their weapons. "Hunting is strictly prohibited in this area. It's clearly posted. There is literally a sign a metre from your head," he stated firmly. With a swift motion, he retrieved his citation book, each stroke of his pen etching fines that loomed ominously in the air like heavy snow clouds.

Craig's fury radiated palpably, a visible wave of heat distorting the icy landscape around him. His accusatory complaints cut through the frosty air like sharpened icicles as he directed his blame towards Officer Horton and Rike. "You got no fuckin' right to come here and accuse me of shit!" Craig spat, his face contorted with rage as he glared at the police officer. "This is my fuckin' land too, and I'll do whatever the hell I want on it! You think you can just waltz in here and tell me what to do? Fuck you!"

"It's my land, not yours," Rike said.

"But I used to hunt here when Ethel lived here."

"Stop it, Craig. It's not your land, you don't have Ms. Volk's permission, and it's posted. You're getting citations, and you need to stop before I figure out more," Officer Horton said.

The clash between Rike and the Griffiths didn't stop. That night, Craig's voice thundered outside her cabin, his face not flushed by the cold but by a seething rage. Each knock on the door echoed like a warning drumbeat, demanding her retreat. "Leave!" he bellowed, his anger palpable in the frigid air.

Responding with unwavering composure, Rike stepped out into the biting chill, her initial bewilderment swiftly giving way to unyielding resolve. "Leave my home?" she asked, her tone cutting through the frosty atmosphere with icy precision.

"Go back to where you came from! You're robbing us of our livelihoods!" Craig's accusations sliced through the silence like a sharpened blade, dripping with animosity and resentment.

A sardonic chuckle slipped from Rike's lips, laden with bitterness. "I'm not taking jobs, I'm retired. And retired means retired," she retorted sharply, her voice carrying the weight of years spent facing far greater challenges. "Get the hell off my property."

Craig's hand casually extended out, showing her a middle finger. "Your kind aren't welcome here," he sneered, gesturing disdainfully towards a stained-glass rainbow adorning her window.

Silently, Rike pivoted and strode back into the cabin, each step purposeful and controlled. The echoes of Craig and Tammy's taunts lingered in the air, their harsh words rebounding off the wooden walls like hollow victories in a battleground of ideologies.

Rike emerged once more, and cradled in her arms was her trusted hunting rifle, its polished barrel glinting in the winter sun like a deadly promise. With unwavering determination etched on her face, she issued a single word that echoed through the icy air like a decree from on high: "Go," she ordered, each syllable heavy with authority and finality.

Craig and Tammy's eyes met, their overconfidence crumbling like a fragile balloon losing air. Without a word, they pivoted on their heels, conceding to the bitter taste of failure. However, Rike, the victor in this silent exchange, was not ready to conclude the confrontation just yet. She disappeared indoors momentarily, only to emerge carrying a vibrant LGBTQ flag. She had purchased the flags before arriving in Berna, but only now were they coming in handy. Against the snowy landscape, the colours stood out boldly. With unwavering determination, she fastened it to her front porch—a symbol of pride and resistance. There was no ambiguity in its message; it boldly challenged their prejudices and affirmed her unwavering beliefs with every flutter in the icy breeze.

With the break of dawn on the following day, a gentle luminescence bathed the snow-covered expanse as Rike emerged from her cabin to discover the absence of her cherished flag. The chill in the morning breeze failed to extinguish the smoldering ember of fury that ignited within her core. A silent vow to confront the culprit tightened her jaw as she clad herself in skis, each sinew responding instinctively to her seasoned movements.

Muscles honed by years of skiing propelled her forward with fluid grace, leaving a trail of determination etched upon the glistening snowscape.

Her rifle, a weighty companion, secured snugly against her back, ready for any unexpected encounter in the wilderness or the Griffiths. Skiing gracefully through the snow-covered woods, Rike's path guided her past Craig and Tammy's homestead. Rising from a burn barrel, a twisting column of smoke spiralled into the winter air. Within the crackling fire's dance, she spotted her flag being consumed by the flames, its once vivid hues now twisted and scorched.

"Hey!" Rike's voice sliced through the crisp morning air, her eyes locked on Craig by the crackling barrel. His response was immediate, a fiery defiance that shattered the peaceful surroundings. "Back off, you damn dyke!" Craig's words boomed, sending a nearby crow flapping into the sky in alarm.

Rike's movements were swift and calculated as she surged ahead, kicking off the skis. Her rifle came off her shoulder as she closed the distance to Craig with purpose, each step leaving imprints in the pristine snow. Letting out a primal cry, she brandished the rifle like a warrior's weapon, targeting his shoulder with violent intent.

Caught off guard, Craig stumbled back, his features contorted with a mix of shock and fury. In response, he lashed out with a punch aimed at Rike's abdomen, the force rippling through her core. Though winded, she stood her ground, channeling her resolve into a swift knee strike to his midsection.

Their confrontation unfolded like a chilling ballet of aggression, every action driven by fury and hate. With precision, Rike's fist connected with Craig's jaw, the impact causing him to reel backward unsteadily. Reacting swiftly, he scooped up a handful of icy snow, hurling it towards her face, momentarily obscuring her vision.

Seizing the split-second opening, Craig lunged forward with a reckless swing, but Rike gracefully sidestepped his attack and unleashed a forceful kick to his knee. She was wearing her ski boots. The sound of his pained cry filled the air as Craig crumbled to the ground, his expression twisted in agony.

Rike's breaths came in ragged gasps, the frigid air stinging her lungs as she loomed over him, her figure cast in stark relief against the snow-covered landscape. With a fierce glint in her eyes, she warned through clenched teeth, "Keep your distance." Her voice, a chilling whisper that cut through the silence like a blade.

Craig's gaze met hers from his place on the ground, a mix of defeat and simmering rage burning in his eyes. Through gritted teeth, he hissed a threat, "There will be consequences for this."

Disregarding his menacing words, Rike pivoted sharply on her boots, snapped into her skis, and left Craig splayed in the pristine snow, a tempest of powerless fury consuming him. Seeking refuge in the familiar embrace of skiing, she aimed to channel her frustration into purposeful motion. Her lithe frame attested to her dedication to fitness with adrenaline, propelling her onward with a fervour that teetered on the brink of desperation.

Rike Volk glided through the winter wonderland, her lithe form cutting through the pure, icy air with each purposeful movement. The sinewy muscles in her legs tingled with the effort, not from weariness but from the raw intensity of her feelings. As she navigated the snow-covered terrain, every push and slide on her skis became a cathartic release for the whirlwind of emotions swirling inside her. Each powerful stride was a testament to her resolve as she harnessed her anger and discontent into a driving force that propelled her relentlessly forward, leaving a trail of determination in her wake.

When she arrived back at her secluded abode, what remained of her torn flag lay strewn across the doorstep like remnants of a battle fought and lost. With steely resolve, Rike gritted her teeth and lifted a charred piece of fabric, its frayed edges resembling sneering lips of defiance. Fuelled by anger, she marched towards Craig's residence, only to find Tammy standing alone within.

"See the mess you've made!" Rike's tone sliced through the air like a frozen blade.

Tammy's fury rose to meet hers, her retort dripping with venom. "He's gotta put ice on his knee, you lesbo man-hater. You pervert!"

"I'd rather be a pervert than a fascist," Rike fired back, her revulsion palpable.

"Go!" Tammy's demand echoed sharply as she forcefully shut the door behind her. Rike stood for a moment, the weight of their confrontation heavy upon her shoulders. With a deep breath to steady herself, she turned on her heel and marched back towards her cabin, leaving behind the chaos of the argument, but not the burning anger that simmered within her.

Even now, years later, the wounds were deep. The echoes of their heated exchange reverberated in the recesses of Rike's mind, a constant reminder of an easily roiled anger.

Inside the sanctuary of her home, despite the physical warmth enveloping her, an icy chill settled in her heart.

With a heavy sigh, she sank into her favourite armchair, the crackling fire casting flickering shadows across the walls. In the silence that followed, Rike found herself grappling with the stark reality of fractured relationships and the enduring scars they left behind.

Chapter 4

Rike's breath caught in her chest, surprised she had been caught so long in machinations of the past. She still hadn't called about the blood. Delicately, she retrieved the cellphone nestled on the table beside her.

The soft glow of the screen illuminated Rike's determined expression as her finger pressed against the cold glass, dialling the number for the local police station. Her hesitation to call 911 lingered in her mind; there was no definitive proof that the blood staining the snow was human. Opting for the local police, she awaited a human voice at the other end. The phone rang incessantly until an automated message echoed through the line, "All our officers are currently occupied. Please leave a message after the tone." Disbelief etched across her features at the thought of resorting to a mere voicemail in such a crucial moment. What could she possibly say in a message? There's blood in the snow near some hidden forest spot? Probably poachers? Like the Griffiths? Frustration mingled with her growing concern that stir up the neighbourly fight. She hung up without leaving a message.

The only sound now was the soft click of the radio coming to life. Eager for weather information for the upcoming week, she tuned into the announcer's voice that resonated through the room. "Storm watch issued for Saint Berna," the voice warned, its message laced with static whispers. "Prepare for heavy snowfall and fierce winds." Rike's gaze drifted across the intricate patterns of her kitchen table, a heavy sigh escaping her lips. The impending storm threatened to shroud any lingering evidence of the blood in a blanket of white, concealing both tracks and secrets alike. She loved living in the snowbelt, and now, it was giving her a great excuse not to interact with Officer Horton.

With the sky outside darkening rapidly, casting shadows across the snow-covered landscape, she hurried to gather candles and flashlights in anticipation of the storm's impending isolation. Seated at the sturdy kitchen table, Rike's eyes traced the snow list:

her headlamps with extra batteries, bottled water, winterized sleeping bag and food. And gasoline.

Her thoughts drifted to the troublesome neighbours she despised. Memories of the night after the flag debacle flooded back. An overwhelming smell of gasoline. The chilly night air nipped at Rike's exposed skin as she ventured out, drawn by a disturbance that shattered the peace of her secluded haven. With practiced ease, her hand sought the reassuring chill of her rifle, a familiar weight in her grasp as she navigated through the moonlit snow shadows.

A man's silhouette, burdened with cans of gasoline, stealthily traversed her property boundary. A surge of fury ignited within her upon recognizing Craig's distinct form, his sinister intentions evident in the sloshing flammable liquid.

"Hey!" Rike's voice sliced through the tranquil air, shattering the quiet like glass. It reverberated through the stillness, a piercing sound in the vast expanse of snow. With swift precision, she hoisted her rifle onto her shoulder, prepared for any eventuality.

Craig's expression twisted in fear, his features momentarily frozen in the brilliant white landscape. Rike moved forward purposefully, the gun now aimed directly at him, emanating a commanding presence that brooked no defiance.

Rike unleashed a torrent of fury, her eyes ablaze with a primal rage that could make even the bravest shudder. "You sorry excuse for a coward! I've faced monsters bigger than you in my sleep! You think you can drive me out? Try me, you pathetic waste of oxygen! I've felt the breath of true evil on my neck. You gutless maggot, I've crushed bigger pests under my boot. You want a war? Trust me, you won't even be a footnote in the history of the battles I've won. Run, you spineless worm, before I start counting to three!"

"You're a freak, Rike! Always spewing your lying crap," Craig lashed out, his words dripping with venom. Each syllable sliced through the air, fuelled by an undercurrent of seething rage that threatened to boil over. "You strut around like you're better than us all, but let me set you straight—you're nothing in this town. Nothing." His voice quivered, the false bravado crumbling like fragile ice beneath the weight of her unwavering stare. In that moment, he resembled a petulant child on the brink of a tantrum.

Rike's lips curved into a wry smile, her eyes alive with a blend of amusement and contempt. "Oh, resorting to petty taunts now, are we, Craig?" she quipped, her tone heavy with mockery. "Grow the fuck up. "

Craig's face turned a violent shade of red, his hands balling into fists at his sides as he fought to keep his temper in check. "You think you're so damn tough, Rike, you aren't nothing! You need a balling by good man is all," he spat out, venom dripping from every word.

Rike's laughter sliced through the air like a blade, challenging Craig's fragile masculinity. "I'm more of a man than you'll ever be, you terrible excuse for a human," she shot back with unyielding determination. "Maybe what you really need is to grow a pair yourself."

Craig's anger flared, his features contorting with fury as he struggled to find a retort. "You're just a gutless bitch. You won't do nothing to me!" he spat, the bitterness evident in his tone.

Rike's unwavering gaze bore into Craig, her demeanour composed yet chilling. Without a flicker of fear, she squeezed the trigger, the gunshot echoing loudly above Craig's head, prompting him to yelp and hastily duck for cover.

"I was a detective once. Don't mistake my composure for hesitation in making this appear to be self-defence," Rike's voice cut through the tense air, her words sharp and decisive. She shot again, this time just missing his foot. "Leave my property... and take your cans with you. Do not cross me again. Ever. Next time, I won't miss." The words tasted bitter in her mouth, but they were spoken with conviction. Craig scoffed as he dragged the gasoline cans away from Rike's intense stare, his bravado faltering under her unyielding presence, and her excellent aim.

Upon her return from the next morning's ski, Rike was met with an unexpected sight at her cabin—Officer Horton's patrol car stationed in stark contrast to the tranquil snowy backdrop. Exhaling clouds of exertion, she approached, her skis crunching against the snow. Horton emerged from the vehicle, his expression a mix of official concern and curiosity. "Good morning, Ms. Volk," he greeted. "There's been a report of you aiming you gun at your neighbour, Craig. And shooting at him?"

Rike couldn't help but let out a humourless chuckle before retorting, "Did he come knocking with a hole in his head?" Horton's gaze bore into Rike's, searching for any flicker of deception. "I assure you, if I ever wanted to shoot someone, they wouldn't stand a ghost of a chance," Rike quipped with a hint of dry humour lacing her words. With a deliberate shift in her stance, she squarely faced the officer, her tone unwavering and precise. It was as though she challenged Horton to overlook the glaring truth. "Did he tell you why he was on my property?"

A reluctant sigh escaped Horton, signalling his unease at the turn their conversation had taken. "He mentioned something about needing to clean up a spill of gasoline," he finally disclosed, his discomfort evident in his voice.

Rike's steely gaze bore into Officer Horton, a flicker of rage dancing in her eyes, causing them to gleam like shards of ice under the winter sun. "So, he confessed to dousing my property with gasoline? Did he offer any explanation for his actions? Was he forthcoming about his attempt to set fire to my cabin? With me in it?"

Officer Horton tensed visibly at her pointed questions, a hint of unease shadowing his features. "Ms. Volk, these are grave allegations. Do you possess any substantiation for your claims?" Rike's lips pressed into a thin line as she gestured for him to accompany her, striding purposefully around the corner of her cabin. There, abandoned in a rush, lay a gas can discarded by Craig in his hurried departure — a tangible piece of evidence pointing to his malicious intentions.

Officer Horton's brow furrowed, his gaze shifting from the stained can to Rike. A silent understanding passed between them, the weight of Rike's revelations hanging heavy in the air. It was now undeniable that Craig harboured malicious intentions. Without a hint of triumph in her demeanour, Rike made a request, her voice tinged with weariness. "I'd rather not pursue this further at the moment. Can we let it be?" she inquired.

"I...If he withdraws his complaint. Of course," Horton acquiesced, concern etched on his face. "I'll talk to him. Just be cautious around them, Ms. Volk. Craig and Tammy... they're trouble," he cautioned gently, though his words merely echoed what Rike already knew all too well.

"Much obliged for the warning," she responded with a hint of sarcasm, her voice carrying a subtle edge. "Oh, and do call me Rike, should we have cause to meet again." As the lingering images of her conversation with Craig gradually ebbed away, Rike's thoughts shifted back to the immediate surroundings. She was suddenly recalled–she was almost out of her favourite tea.

As ominous clouds gathered on the horizon, the idea of being trapped indoors without her cherished tea felt utterly intolerable. While she had a hefty checklist of necessities to procure, it was the dwindling tea supply that stirred a sense of urgency within her. Determination etched on her features, Rike knew she couldn't delay any longer.

Donning her weathered leather boots and the down parka that shielded her from the biting cold, she snatched the jingling keys before stepping out into the crisp air. Each breath crystallized in front of her as she strode purposefully towards her trusty old truck. The vehicle, a relic of past journeys, stood steadfast in the icy morning, its robust engine rumbling to life with a reassuring growl that echoed through the frost-laden air.

The headlights pierced through the ethereal glow as she skillfully maneuvered the sturdy truck onto the winding road that led towards Saint Berna Aux Étranger. Her calloused hands gripped the worn steering wheel with an intimate familiarity, a companion on countless trips along this familiar path. As Rike navigated closer to town, the Griffiths' residence loomed into view, its windows veiled behind delicate curtains that seemed to shy away from acknowledging the world outside.

Rike's arm shot out instinctively, her middle finger defiantly raised as she glided past the residence. A silent message of resistance against the neighbours. Her mouth tightened into a determined line, the subtle gesture a quiet rebellion in the face of their disapproval.

Up ahead, the trees stood like sentinels, their majestic forms blanketed in thick layers of snow, framing a tranquil path through the untouched wilderness. The wheels of Rike's truck crunched rhythmically over the crisp snow covering the road, creating a harmonious symphony of winter sounds beneath her journey.

Serenity enveloped Rike briefly before being shattered by an unexpected sight. At the summit of a gentle rise, her gaze locked onto an impediment—a massive tree sprawled across the road, its imposing trunk casting a shadow in the fading daylight. Bringing her truck to a stop, she let the engine idle while she contemplated the fallen giant.

"Bother," Rike grumbled quietly as she silenced the engine and disembarked into the frigid air. She harboured hopes that with some strategic maneuvering, she could clear the path enough to continue her journey. Drawing closer, she assessed the situation with a seasoned eye. The tree stood as a colossal obstacle, likely succumbing to the weight of snow from recent storms.

Gripping the rugged bark firmly, Rike exerted all her strength to dislodge it. Her boots skidded on the icy ground, causing her to momentarily lose balance and flounder in search of stability. With a vexed huff, she tumbled backward onto the pristine snow, defeated by the unyielding tree that remained stoic and unmoved by her determined efforts.

"Alright then," she muttered under her breath, a cloud of snow swirling around her figure as she retreated to the shelter of her trusty truck. Rike's routine was disrupted by nature's whims once more; the fallen tree demanded respect and forced her onto an extended route. Grudgingly, she accepted the tree's silent challenge, knowing there was no room for negotiation in this wintry landscape.

Maneuvering the vehicle with practiced ease, Rike found herself passing by the Griffiths' residence again. This time, a gesture of defiance lingered longer in the frosty air as she raised a single finger in their direction before continuing on her altered path.

Passing by her cabin, Rike couldn't help but notice the warm glow emanating from the windows, a silent invitation she reluctantly left behind. She continued her journey, veering onto a different path that meandered towards Berna. This alternate route snaked through the forest, with trees looming closer together, their branches intertwining above like nature's own arched canopy.

She saw the gathering sky and feeling a sense of urgency propelling her forward, Rike navigated the narrow road as it twisted and turned among the dense woods. The impending storm loomed ominously on the horizon, threatening to unleash its wrath upon unsuspecting travelers. It was imperative for Rike to make her way to town, complete her errands swiftly, and return home before nature's fury descended upon the land.

In Saint Berna Aux Étranger, sudden storms were a common occurrence: it was in the snowbelt, and these storms were common in winter. Rike strained to remember if the forecast had mentioned anything about lake-effect snow. A wry chuckle escaped her lips at the thought–in this region, it seemed that lake-effect snow was almost a certainty: unpredictable, swift, and merciless in its intensity.

The winter's icy breath whispered through the trees, offering solace only to those sheltered from its chill. Each snowflake seemed like a spectral dancer twirling in the air, floating under the sturdy wheels of Rike's truck as she skillfully maneuvered along the winding road. The forest enveloped her like a hushed sanctuary, adorned with frosted pine trees standing tall like sentinels guarding their domain. Suddenly, as she negotiated a curve, a fleeting shadow perched on the ridge captured her attention, adding an element of beauty to the wintry scene.

Slowing the truck, Rike's heart quickened at the sight of a lone wolf against the dreary sky. Its fur, a blend of silver and white, blended seamlessly with the snow-covered terrain. Balanced elegantly on the ridge, it fixed her with a gaze that seemed to freeze time itself. The wolf exuded a majestic aura that demanded respect.

Locked in a silent exchange, Rike felt a primal connection with this untamed creature. The wolf's eyes, gleaming amber orbs in its rugged visage, held ancient knowledge of survival in the wilderness. Despite the absurdity, she whispered, "You belong here with me."

The tension thickened as she awaited the wolf's response, and finally came a sharp bark before it disappeared. A sense of unease crept over her.

The wolf, a majestic creature of the wild, pivoted effortlessly on strong, sinewy limbs, its fur dense and insulating against the biting cold. Its departure into the shadowed woods was silent, a ghostly retreat that melted seamlessly into the wintry landscape. As the truck pressed onward, distancing itself from this fleeting encounter, the only remnants of the wolf's presence were delicate imprints in the pristine snow. Amidst the serene hush of nature's embrace, the fading echoes of the wolf's passage resonated most profoundly, a wordless testament to its untamed essence.

Chapter 5

Down the winding road, Rike's sharp gaze scanned the snowy surroundings, half-expecting the shadow of a wolf to emerge again from the trees. Yet, the woods remained quiet spectators to her solitary journey. As she approached the town, a stark contrast unfolded before her eyes. The majestic pines gave way to squat buildings weathered by harsh winters. Amidst this rugged landscape, the local diner exhaled warmth, its windows misted with steam offering a glimpse of bustling life within. A group of children, bundled up against the biting cold, gleefully pursued a rogue soccer ball along the sidewalk, their laughter piercing through the frosty air like delicate chimes. A soft smile graced Rike's lips as she savoured these fleeting moments of ordinary joy that adorned this remote place.

She navigated her weather-beaten truck along the tranquil streets, the vibrant Canadian flag at the post office fluttering proudly in the crisp breeze. The hardware store stood stoically, its array of shovels poised for the impending snowfall, while the quaint library exuded a sense of community warmth. The comforting familiarity of these sights helped soothe the tight coil of tension in her chest.

After encountering the unsettling pool of blood earlier, she had to report it. Rike proceeded towards the makeshift police station. The faux clock on its door indicated a midday opening, prompting Rike to ponder why law enforcement here operated from noon until 8 p.m. Such hours seemed incongruous with peak crime times; perhaps a deliberate choice to deter criminal activity during those late afternoon and evening hours when emotions ran high and inhibitions were lowered by alcohol.

Arriving at the grocery store, Rike noticed the sun casting strangled shadows across the snow-covered lot. The air was crisp, making her breath visible in wispy clouds. She parked close to the entrance, where patches of ice glistened under the dimming light. Turning off the engine, she wrapped a hand-knitted scarf–a gift from a lover now long gone–snugly around her neck before stepping out onto the frozen ground.

Her boots crunched rhythmically on the icy pavement, a sound that echoed in the quiet surroundings. As she approached the automatic doors, they glided open effortlessly with a gentle whoosh, beckoning her into the welcoming glow of the bustling market.

The harsh, artificial buzz of the fluorescent lights overhead cut through the quiet ambiance of the grocery store like a sharp knife. Rike's fingers curled around the handle of the basket as she ventured down the narrow aisles, each step deliberate and methodical. Her gaze seemed distant, lost in the memory of crimson staining the pristine snow.

A persistent unease gnawed at her core, refusing to be ignored, akin to the relentless grip of winter's icy fingers on her skin. She begrudgingly acknowledged this unwelcome aspect of herself that refused to let go.

Amidst the soft hum of conversations that swirled around her in the dimly lit store, Rike moved past a pair of elderly women engaged in a spirited debate over canned versus frozen peas. Their voices carried a weight born from decades spent in kitchens, infusing their mundane discussion with an unexpected depth that mirrored Rike's own inner turmoil.

"Try the canned ones, Margaret. They're nearly as delightful as freshly picked from the garden," one woman insisted, her fingers adorned with sparkling rings that chimed against the cold metal of the can.

"They're too mushy for my taste. I prefer the crispness of frozen peas," Margaret countered, her knitted shawl draping over her stooped shoulders in a protective embrace.

Observing the exchange with a faint smile playing on her lips, Rike marvelled at the simplicity of their argument over peas. In this moment, it felt comforting to witness such mundane disagreements where no lives hung in the balance.

Turning towards the fruit section, Rike's gaze swept over rows of firm apples and flawless oranges, searching for perfection amidst imperfection. The chill from the refrigerated units brushed against her skin, prompting her to snugly wrap her scarf around her neck for warmth.

"Ah, the convenience is undeniable, but there's a certain charm to having a genuine butcher shop," a voice resonated behind her, laced with wistfulness and longing for the past.

"Craig, nowadays everything comes pre-packaged. Even the meat lacks that personal connection," another voice chimed in, their laughter masking a shared sense of dissatisfaction.

At the mention of the name, Rike felt a sudden tension grip her, causing the hairs on the nape of her neck to bristle. Slowly turning around, she found herself locking eyes with Craig Griffith amidst the neatly arranged packaged meats. His shopping cart was filled with items emblematic of rural life. Their gazes held for a fleeting moment as Craig conversed with Warren McDaniel, the amiable postal worker.

"Morning, Rike," Craig's voice sliced through the chilled air, his tone carrying a subtle edge. "Finding everything you need?"

Rike met his gaze with a forced politeness, her words measured. "Good morning, Craig. Just stocking up on some fruit. Gotta keep up appearances." Craig's lips twitched in a semblance of a smile as he reached for a package of ground beef, inspecting it with exaggerated interest.

"The eternal struggle," he mused lightly, as if sharing an inside joke only he understood. "This weather doesn't make it any easier to stay sane indoors." Rike's grip on the apples tightened imperceptibly as she agreed with a tight-lipped nod, tension crackling beneath the facade of civility.

Separated by the icy arrangement of butchered meats, Rike and Craig stood in silent opposition, their gazes like frosty blades cutting through the frigid air. A palpable tension simmered between them, a blend of animosity and suspicion that tainted even their most courteous words. In this small town where grudges ran deep beneath the surface, an unspoken war brewed between the two, casting a shadow over their encounter. The arrival of a stocker with a cart laden with fresh ribeye momentarily disrupted their standoff, his cheerful announcement slicing through the thick atmosphere like a knife.

In the midst of the bustling aisle, Warren's nonchalant voice cut through the air as he reached for a fresh package of ground beef. "It's unsettling, isn't it? This impending winter storm," he remarked, his gaze flickering towards the frost-covered meat counter.

Rike's fingers grazed a frost-veiled packet of chicken breasts, recoiling swiftly as if stung by an icy chill. "Indeed," she agreed with a tight-lipped nod, her eyes betraying a hint of unease. "There will be treachery soon enough."

Craig peered over his glasses, his eyebrows arching ever so slightly in a subtle display of interest that bordered on apprehension.

"Huh?" Warren grunted.

"Oh, ah, I meant, the roads will be treacherous. English is a funny language sometime," Rike said. "On the old logging road this morning, there was a pool of blood on the pristine snow, surrounded by wolf tracks. It felt eerie, out of place."

Craig's hazel eyes darkened momentarily, a fleeting shadow crossing his usual composure as he stood taller, clutching a packet of bacon with rigid fingers. "Blood, you say? Nature at work," he offered cautiously.

Warren chimed in. "I bet it was the Cumming twins, poaching. Those boys are always stirring shit up. Pardon my French," he added for Rike's sake.

"Yes. They started that fire last year in my back 40," Rike said. Asher and Aaron Cummings, 23-years-old and both notorious in Berna, had been arrested after a fire at Hollister & Devon Lumber Company and a fire that completely destroyed an abandoned home near neighbouring Leicester. The charges were dropped, and three more fires–including trees at the back of Rike's property–were set that night. They regularly poached deer, wild turkey and were rumoured to have hunted a cow.

"I swear those two are going to end up killing someone," Warren grumbled, "or getting themselves killed."

"Yes, they certainly are on the wrong path," Rike reluctantly admitted. She had met men like this. Usually while arresting for murder.

"Have you involved law enforcement? What did they say?" Craig probed, his voice tinged with a hint of urgency.

"No police yet. Just a pool of blood. Nothing new around these parts," Rike replied dismissively, but inside, her gut twisted with a sense of foreboding that refused to be ignored.

"Could be the twins. Reporting them might bring trouble your way," Craig suggested, his voice barely above a whisper, sending shivers down Rike's spine. As she inspected the fruits and vegetables, her mind raced like a blizzard, questioning Craig's wisdom. She hated that he was right.

"Where exactly did you stumble upon this?" Craig's words pierced through the ambient noise of cooling systems and chattering customers. His hand clumsily returned the bacon to its place.

"Half a mile north off Route 27, where the pines cluster thick," Rike's voice cut through the crisp air, her tone unwavering. She plucked an apple from the display, fingers tracing its smooth surface as she recounted the chilling scene. "I was on my skis. And, there it was."

Craig's throat worked visibly as he swallowed, his movements betraying a sudden unease. Shifting his weight uneasily, he attempted to mask his discomfort with rehearsed words. "The wilderness is full of dangers," he muttered, but his voice cracked like fragile ice under pressure, hinting at deeper uncertainties lurking beneath the surface.

"Danger, schmanger. Except when it comes to my wife. Now she is dangerous!" Warren laughed before excusing himself from the conversation to finish his shopping.

"Living in these parts does have its charms, though," Craig chimed, his tone feigning cheerfulness as he examined a package of ground beef as though it held secrets within. "The crisp air, vast expanses of untouched land, and the blissful absence of nosy neighbours prying into your affairs or judging your every move."

"What a jerk he is," Rike thought. Rike's eyes narrowed at Craig's words, a subtle frown creasing her brow as she carefully plucked a vibrant orange from the display, its citrusy scent momentarily distracting her from the unsettling conversation.

"Nah, you know what the problem is?" Katherine Washerman asked. "I couldn't help but overhear."

"Nosy neighbours prying," Rike thought.

A wistful smile tugged at the corners of Craig's lips, devoid of genuine mirth. "What?" he asked with a hollow chuckle that failed to reach his eyes.

"Jealousy. Living out here is like being trapped in a pressure cooker at times. And let me tell you, jealousy... it festers in these remote corners like nowhere else."

"Jealousy?" Rike's voice rang out, a hint of intrigue lacing her words as she furrowed her brow, her head tilting slightly in genuine interest.

Craig's hands deftly maneuvered the beef, returning one package to its place while selecting another with a more suitable expiration date. "I agree," he chimed in, his tone thoughtful.

"It's peculiar, isn't it? People believe they escape all that stuff out here. Yet here, in this remote expanse, jealousy seems to flourish. Joe down the road upgrades his snowmobile, and suddenly envy spreads like wildfire; everyone yearning for what they don't have," Katherine said.

"Pettiness at its finest," Rike remarked casually, her fingers lightly grazing the surface of a pear.

"A sin," Craig said as he pointedly looked at Rike. "A G.D. sin."

Despite her focus on the fruit selection before her, Craig's attention was unwelcome. *"Why can't he just let me be? All I want is some fruit,"* Rike thought. Katherine and Craig continued to chat and, like Warren before her, Rike quietly excused herself from the conversation.

The conversation had veered unexpectedly into the Bible and God. She pondered the intricate relationship between rural life, envy, and sin, recognizing how intolerance could distort motives and push individuals to extremes. Rike shook her head: there was still a long list of groceries awaiting her attention. And she still needed her ski wax, and her tea.

Chapter 6

The bell above the entrance of Saint Berna Aux Étranger Co-op chimed melodiously as Rike Volk gently nudged the door open, transitioning from the pristine snowscape outside into the welcoming embrace of warmth within. Wisps of her cropped hair peeked out from beneath the snug woolen beanie, creating a soft halo around a countenance accustomed to navigating shadows and suspicions, rather than the cozy interior of a small-town co-op. She clasped her hands together, savouring the ordinary yet comforting prospect that lay ahead–the quest for just the perfect ski wax amidst shelves lined with essentials for winter adventures.

Rike glided effortlessly through the winter sports store, maneuvering around racks filled with colourful snow gear. She paused in front of the meticulously arranged display of ski waxes, her keen eyes assessing each vibrant hue and precise label. From cold-weather formulas to those designed for wet snow, every block held the promise of a smooth glide tailored to specific conditions. Her fingertips brushed against a striking turquoise block marked for polar vortex snow.

"Finding everything you need?" The voice cut through the quiet hum of the store, belonging to a young man named Lucas whose tentative approach hinted at either respect for the self-sufficiency radiating from Rike or perhaps a touch of intimidation caused by her imposing height. It was possible he was just a shy employee diligently carrying out his duties.

"Yes, thank you," Rike acknowledged with a nod, her gaze fixed on the array of ski gear before her. The morning's unsettling discovery lingered in her mind, yet her exterior demeanour remained composed and collected. *Was there a wax for bloody snow?* she wondered.

Lucas, a weathered local, leaned against the wooden counter, his eyes flicking towards the darkening sky visible through the shop window. "Looks like a storm's brewing. Planning to tackle the storm?" he inquired casually, though his interest was evident.

A faint furrow creased Rike's brow briefly before she responded evenly, her voice carrying a hint of determination. "Indeed," she affirmed, deftly selecting a block of turquoise wax and adding it to her basket. "Preparation is key."

"Yeah, it can be awesome." Lucas, attempting to make conversation, struggled to engage her. "Exciting day?" he asked feebly.

Rike, with a nonchalant air but a glint of fascination in her eyes unrelated to the wax she held, replied, "Something of the sort. I crossed paths with a wolf amidst the towering pines this morning."

"Wolves," Lucas pondered thoughtfully as he leaned against the shelves. "They symbolize friendship, loyalty, and intuition, you know."

Overhearing their dialogue from the neighbouring aisle, a customer interjected. "Wolves," he pronounced firmly yet distantly, as if summoning an ancient wisdom. "A message urging one to hold their ground."

"Shoot them on sight," a voice demanded, sharp and urgent. "We can't risk our livelihoods and loved ones to these predators any longer!"

"But hunting them down isn't the answer," another voice countered, filled with conviction. "Wolves are vital for our ecosystem's balance; we must coexist peacefully."

"The only solution is to eliminate them all!" a third voice interjected fiercely. "They're vicious killers, a threat that must be eradicated without mercy."

Rike dismissed the idle chatter with a subtle shake of her head, her patience worn thin. *"Why can't people mind their own business?"* The transaction for the ski wax was swift and to the point, devoid of unnecessary pleasantries. Exiting the cozy co-op, she left behind both its warmth and the unwelcome advice that lingered in the air.

Her boots crunched rhythmically on the snow-covered path leading to Auberge Brew. The gusting wind played with her parka, carrying a foreboding message as it buffeted her weathered features. At the cafe's entrance, two shivering figures sought solace from the cold, their attire ill-suited for the harsh winter chill. One of them reached out a trembling hand, eyes filled with desperation pleading for assistance.

"Sorry," Rike spoke gently yet resolutely, evading the outstretched hand as she entered the coffee shop. Apologizing was a reflexive courtesy ingrained in her from Canadian customs. It did not she was sorry for not giving them money it meant she was sorry for the route their lives had taken.

Entering the quaint cafe, Rike was enveloped in a symphony of scents. The rich fragrance of freshly ground coffee beans mingled with the tempting aroma of warm pastries, creating a tantalizing atmosphere. The gentle murmur of conversations intermingled with the delicate clinks of cups meeting saucers, setting a serene backdrop for the bustling artisanal shop. A hint of cinnamon danced through the air, embracing customers like a comforting embrace. With each breath, Rike immersed herself in this sensory haven, finding solace in the inviting fragrances that wrapped around her like a soft, invisible shawl.

Rike's order for tea was promptly fulfilled, the steam rising from the cup as she settled at her preferred secluded table near the frosted window. The aroma of her favourite tea filled the air as she carefully placed a newly purchased tin of it beside her cup. As she let her tea steep, she indulged in the familiar feel of the newspaper's rustling pages beneath her fingers.

Suddenly, Autumn Evans burst into Auberge Brew with a gust of chilly wind that caused the bell above the door to protest loudly. The disturbance sent a shiver through Rike, causing the pages of her newspaper to flutter. Autumn's vibrant green eyes sought out Rike immediately. A radiant smile lit up her face, dispelling any lingering gloom that might have accompanied her entrance into the cozy establishment.

"Rike," Autumn's voice carried a soft melody that stood out against the hushed tones of the shop, momentarily breaking the tranquil ambiance. She waved and smiled. With a brief pause to place an order for two strong black coffees, she handed over a crumpled ten-dollar bill, letting the change and specks of clay from her fingers fall into the tip jar. Balancing the steaming cups in her hands, she made her way to Rike's table.

"Autumn," Rike acknowledged with a subtle nod, neatly folding her newspaper as she motioned towards the vacant chair opposite her.

"I figured you could use a caffeine boost," Autumn remarked as she settled into her seat, placing one cup gently in front of Rike. Wisps of steam danced upwards from the dark brew, mingling with the chilly air each time the door swung open.

"Thank you," Rike acknowledged, trading her tea for the steaming cup of coffee. The rich aroma of the dark roast enveloped her, a welcome departure from the usual. Having known Autumn for years, Rike understood that Autumn often got her way, even with as simple as coffee. Savouring the drink, Rike appreciated the gesture.

"Anytime," Autumn chimed in, a grin spreading across her face as she cradled her own cup, the sunlight filtering through the frosted window casting a gentle glow around them. Studying Rike, Autumn noticed the details of the older woman's features: strands of silver hair catching the light, deep lines marking her face like a map of experiences. Lost in contemplation, Rike's expression revealed a hint of concern.

Rike's attention lingered on Autumn, whose inquisitive gaze held a myriad of unspoken inquiries that rivaled the entire police force of Berna. A gentle smile graced her lips.

"How is your day going?"

Their dialogue meandered effortlessly, weaving through the fragrant steam rising from their coffee cups and punctuated by the comings and goings of other patrons. In these fleeting moments nestled in this haven of normalcy, Rike savoured a rare joy. It was within these simple yet profound interactions with Autumn, amidst the comforting warmth of their drinks, that Rike discovered a semblance of tranquillity.

Through the frosted glass of Auberge Brew's windows, Rike noticed the two figures she had encountered earlier on her way. Their breaths billowed out in wispy clouds in the icy air, their outstretched hands silently pleading for assistance. The addicts trembled, their faces a mixture of desperation and an unspoken yearning that transcended mere hunger.

Autumn, observing alongside Rike, whispered softly as she followed Rike's gaze, a hint of sadness shadowing her typically lively voice. "Look at them," she remarked, a crease forming on her brow. "It's as though they belong to a different realm."

Rike acknowledged with a silent nod, still captivated by the sight beyond the glass. The two individuals outside seemed to cast shadows that extended into the cozy interior of the coffee shop, dark tendrils weaving around the haven she had carefully constructed for herself in Berna Aux Étranger.

"The tranquillity of Berna used to be every day, a sanctuary from the big city," Rike remarked pensively, her eyes leaving the snow-laden landscape outside to meet Autumn's understanding gaze. "Now, it seems even here we are not spared from the encroaching troubles of the city."

Autumn, her coffee swirling in delicate patterns from the movement of her jeweled finger, pondered aloud with a touch of irony, "It's almost poetic, isn't it? Seeking solace and finding chaos following in our wake."

Rike reclined in her chair, its aged wood emitting a soft creak beneath her as she contemplated their conversation. "I sought refuge out here precisely to evade such disturbances," she explained with a sweep of her hand towards the window. "To distance myself from those urban plights that now seem determined to find me, even in this secluded haven."

Autumn sat across from Rike, the steam from her coffee swirling lazily in the cold air. Her eyes held a thoughtful glint as she raised the cup to her lips, savouring the rich aroma before speaking. "Troubles? They're like water finding its way through cracks in stone, aren't they? No barrier can truly contain them," she mused softly.

Rike's response was measured, her tone carrying a weight of experience. "No matter how fast or far we flee," she murmured, her grip on the coffee mug tightening imperceptibly. It was as if she sought solace not just from the warmth of the drink but from unseen shadows that lingered.

Feeling a shift in the conversation looming ahead, Rike steered their talk towards darker currents. With a rare hint of uncertainty in her voice, she broached the subject that had been weighing on her since morning. "There was something... unsettling that crossed my path today," she revealed, her words hanging heavy in the air between them.

Autumn's eyes widened with intrigue, her breath catching in anticipation. "What did you find out there?" she prodded, leaning in closer to Rike.

Rike's voice was steady but laced with unease as she disclosed, "Blood. A chilling amount of it, stark against the pristine snow." The words hung heavy in the air between them, thick with foreboding.

"Bloody hell," Autumn muttered under her breath, brows knitting together in worry. "Any clues what caused it? Signs of a struggle?"

"Only wolf tracks circling the scene," Rike recounted, her sharp detective instincts dissecting the details. "No human tracks to be found."

Just then, Paul Cantrell walked in, the door's abrupt clang against the bell echoing through Auberge Brew, heralding his arrival. With a nod to Autumn and Rike, and a friendly, "Ladies," he brushed past their table, leaving behind a trail of melted snow on the creaking floorboards.

Autumn greeted Paul with a warm smile, her eyes drifting to the window where the sky was taking on a dusky hue, signalling the imminent snowfall. A shiver traced down her spine as the first delicate flakes danced from the heavens.

Observing the wintry scene outside, Paul let out a soft chuckle. "Just another day in this winter wonderland," he remarked. "They say there's no such thing as bad weather, only bad timing."

Amused by his comment, Autumn chuckled softly, her gaze returning to Paul. "Indeed," she agreed, feeling the need to wrap her sweater snugly around herself for warmth. "Though I must confess, being snowed in with a captivating book and a steaming cup of cocoa sounds like pure bliss." With a playful wink directed at Rike, she savoured the cozy image that lingered in her mind's eye.

Paul's raised eyebrow hinted at a mischievous side as a playful glint danced in his eyes. "What about a cozy game of cards near the crackling fireplace? With the nicest couple in town?" he proposed, a playful smirk curling his lips.

Autumn couldn't help but roll her eyes, though a small smile betrayed her amusement. "You and your never-ending card games," she bantered, shaking her head in mock exasperation. "But I suppose that does sound like a rather pleasant way to while away the hours. Do you ever go easy on your wife during those games? Let her win?"

"Always, or I'll be banished to the couch," he quipped with a chuckle. "Speaking of which, I need to grab some coffee. I've got precisely... 43 minutes before I need to fetch her from the church social, or it's couch duty for me tonight."

Paul's voice cut through the quiet café as he placed his order for a medium double double with extra milk, the warmth of the steaming drink already enticing. With a quick nod to Rike and Autumn, he collected his cup and headed towards an empty table, his presence fading into the background.

One aspect of Canadian life Rike had never understood was ordering coffee. Tim Horton's is the ubiquitous coffee shop. The coffee tastes like the paper cup it comes in–if you're lucky. You tell them how much milk and sugar you'd like, but not in that order, and they put it into your coffee for you. You can order in "Timmie style" in any café in the country, and they know you mean. Paul's order of a double double extra milk, meant two sugars and three milk.

Autumn's eyes held a sense of urgency as she leaned in towards Rike, her question laced with concern. "Rike, did you notice anything else? Anything that felt off to you?" Her sincerity was palpable in the way she searched Rike's face for any hint of unease.

"About Paul?" Rike shook her head slightly, a furrow forming on her brow.

"Not about Paul," she replied softly, a flicker of uncertainty crossing her features before she clarified, "About the pool of blood, silly."

"Yes," Rike responded, her mind replaying the unsettling scene. "There was a cigarette butt, as if casually discarded by the poachers–I think it was from poaching–or perhaps just a passer."

Autumn's probing gaze encouraged more disclosure. "And a wolf," Rike revealed, her voice tinged with unease. She hoped no one would interrupt with their opinions of wolves. "Perched on the ridge, observing."

Autumn persisted, her intuition nudging her forward. "You must inform the authorities about the blood, Rike. Not the wolf."

Rike exhaled wearily. "The police likely have weightier matters to attend to than a possible poaching with such little proof. Besides, with an impending storm brewing, nature might just erase all evidence."

"Rike, if this was on your land, wouldn't you want to tell the police?" Autumn's voice sliced through the air, sharp and logical. "What if not an isolated incident? What if it's part of a pattern, and that cigarette butt holds the DNA key? What if someone is poaching wolves?"

"Perhaps," Rike conceded reluctantly. Her attention drifted back to the window just as the rich aroma of freshly brewed coffee was momentarily eclipsed by the wintry breeze coming through the door.

"Did you mention seeing a wolf?" Paul inquired, his sudden presence indicating he had been listening intently.

"Rike witnessed a significant amount of blood, isn't that right, Rike?" Rike acknowledged with a subtle nod, her reluctance to engage in the conversation proving futile.

"Where?" Paul asked as he drew nearer, his cup emitting wisps of steam. "It could simply be the aftermath of an animal hunt; it's common during this season. Blood in pristine snow isn't always a sign of tragedy," he began, his tone measured yet comforting.

A brief pause hung between them before he continued, his gaze drifting towards the distant horizon where untamed wilderness met civilization. "Since you saw a wolf," he remarked, inclining his head, "it's probably just a wolf's handiwork. Occam's razor." His explanation, though simple, carried the weight of experience and wisdom.

"True. The solution is probably the simplest answer," Rike agreed. Perhaps it was indeed just nature at work–brutal yet beautiful in its uncompromising cycle of life and death.

"Thank you, Paul," Rike acknowledged, her voice carrying a hint of hesitation that stemmed from a lifetime of scrutinizing the surface of things. Yet, amidst the serene expanse of Berna's wilderness, she found a glimmer of solace in its uncomplicated honesty.

"Anytime," Paul responded with a polite nod, his gaze lingering on Rike briefly before returning to his steaming cup of coffee. The cozy ambiance of the café wrapped around Rike like a comforting embrace, drowning out the chill outside and the lingering intensity of Paul's scrutiny. Perhaps he had a point; maybe she could allow herself to find peace here. After all, Berna was meant to be her refuge from the intricate webs and shadows of her past existence. But shedding those layers proved harder than she anticipated.

"Wolves don't smoke. That's all I'm saying," Autumn whispered.

Rike's coffee cup sat empty, its rich aroma a memory now replaced by Autumn's chatter. Her voice filled the room, alive with excitement as she gestured animatedly while discussing her latest pottery creation.

Rike's gaze followed the wisps of steam rising from Autumn's still hot cup of coffee, but her mind remained fixated on the haunting image of the wolf, the stark pool of blood in the snow, and Paul's words. Despite Autumn's well-meaning, one-sided conversation, a persistent unease clung to Rike.

"Autumn, I hate to cut this short, but the storm is coming and I have to get things home, her prepared. Sorry," Rike smoothly interjected, her gaze already drifting towards the looming clouds outside. Autumn reached out, placing a comforting hand on Rike's shoulder for a brief squeeze.

"You betcha. You're all alone out there. You need to be ready for anything. Take care of yourself," Autumn said softly.

Rike's response was laced with confidence as she replied, "Always vigilant." Her smile carried reassurance even as she rose from her seat. The cozy interior of Auberge Brew enveloped her like a familiar hug, but duty called her away. With a final nod to Autumn, she pivoted gracefully and strode towards the exit, the tea tin tucked under her arm. As she pushed open the door, a gust of icy air greeted her, signalling the harsh beauty of the winter landscape awaiting outside.

The chilling bite of the frosty air served as a stark contrast to the cozy warmth of the coffee shop she had just left. Rike wrapped her coat snugly around her, a comforting shield against the winter's icy grip. Each step she took on the sidewalk echoed with a satisfying crunch, the sound harmonizing with the gentle patter of snowflakes around her.

Time to go home.

Chapter 7

"Good afternoon, Rike!" A familiar voice pierced the crisp air, drawing Rike's attention. Fred Abbott approached with a confident stride, his coat adorned with delicate snowflakes that refused to melt on its dark fabric. The cold had painted his cheeks a rosy hue, contrasting sharply with his striking white hair that stood out like fresh snow against the winter landscape.

"Fred," Rike acknowledged with a subtle smile, her eyes scanning the horizon where ominous clouds loomed, hinting at an impending storm. "Have you heard about the approaching tempest?"

"Tempest? Ha, great word. Yup, the word is it'll be upon us before nightfall. Are you all set for it?" Fred inquired.

"I'm mostly prepared. Just a few errands left before I can seek shelter," Rike responded thoughtfully, observing how the sky above transformed into a tapestry of deepening grey hues, as if nature itself was preparing for the imminent showdown between light and dark. "Time to bunker down."

"You mean hunker down?" Fred echoed quizzically.

She meant what she'd said. Berlin was full of bunkers and their ruins. On more than one occasion, she'd sought refuge and comfort in a bunker. "Yes, of course. I meant hunker down." English is a beautiful monster.

"Good, good. Don't want to be caught unprepared. Berna is small, and she can get walloped sometimes. You never know which chocolate you're going to get," Fred chuckled, his breath misting in the air between them.

"Seems like Berna is full of surprises," Rike mused. She liked that Fred couldn't quite get the famous 'box of chocolates' quote, but he tried.

"Isn't that the truth," he agreed with a knowing look, then tipped his hat. "Well, don't let me keep you. Stay warm, Rike."

"You too," she murmured, her gaze lingering on his retreating figure as he strolled along the sidewalk. The simple exchange served as a brief interruption, a gentle nudge reminding her that she still had things to do.

Turning towards her weathered truck, Rike notices the howling wind carried subtle warnings, mirroring the unrest churning within her chest. With deliberate movements, she unlatched the door to her truck, greeted by soft snowflakes brushing against her cheek.

Nestling her tea tin among the groceries in the backseat, Rike got into the driver's seat.

Rike's pale hands on the worn leather of the steering wheel contrasted against the backdrop of the dark dashboard. Each exhale billowed out in a visible cloud, mingling with the frigid air that invaded the confines of her truck. The crossroads loomed ahead, a familiar junction where she typically turned right towards her remote cabin, but today, she turned left.

The memory of that sanguine pool stark against the pristine snowscape intruded upon her thoughts, an image refusing to be dismissed as mere happenstance. It stood out like a scar on untouched skin, demanding attention and stirring unease within her. With a quiet curse slipping past her lips, Rike had made a resolute choice.

As she navigated the winding road, her eyes narrowed with a mix of vigilance and anticipation, half-expecting shadows to reveal hidden secrets—a poacher lurking amidst the trees or the elusive figure of a solitary wolf blending seamlessly into nature's tapestry.

Delicate snowflakes pirouetted past the windshield, each one a fleeting performer in nature's wintry ballet. Despite the whimsical whirlwind that enveloped her vehicle, Rike's hands on the wheel navigated through the ethereal dance of wind and snow as twilight descended upon the icy landscape.

The Saint Berna Aux Étranger police station gradually emerged into sight, a humble structure that belied its significance within the close-knit community it served. Housed in a repurposed mobile home, it stood as a symbol of practicality rather than extravagance, its weathered siding exuding a welcoming aura as it sat snugly between two aged buildings. Soft light spilled from within, illuminating the delicate dance of fresh snowflakes and enveloping the building in a comforting glow amidst the wintry chill. This quaint setting exuded a unique charm, fostering an atmosphere of closeness that stark city precincts constructed of steel and glass could never replicate.

The truck eased into the parking lot, a patchwork of half-occupied spaces beneath a light dusting of snow. In the fading daylight, the lamppost cast a soft glow, illuminating

Rike's weathered vehicle as she parked it with precision. Stepping out onto the crisp snow, her boots created a symphony of crunching sounds that echoed in the quiet surroundings.

Approaching the entrance, Rike hesitated momentarily, steeling herself for what lay ahead. She'd only had one encounter with Officer Horton, and it had not gathered him any respect. Anticipating the rush of warm air that awaited her inside, she took a deep breath to steady her nerves. With deliberate movements, she reached for the door handle, preparing to enter the slightly claustrophobic realm of rural law enforcement.

The door groaned as it swung open, a testament to its years of faithful service. Rike entered the police station, her sharp eyes adjusting swiftly to the sterile glow of the fluorescent lights above. The room was snug, its walls adorned with a patchwork of local bulletins and weathered photographs capturing moments from community gatherings—a tapestry of small-town memories.

"Please, just give me a moment," a voice called out from the depths of the space. Rike acknowledged with a slight nod, her attention immediately drawn towards the origin of the sound. Officer Horton, a familiar face from his previous visit to her secluded abode, stood behind the desk, talking to someone else.

Craig Griffith slouched in a chair, leaning against the peeling paint of the police station wall, his hands buried in the faded denim pockets of his jeans. Officer Martin Horton, seated on the corner of his cluttered desk, exuded a relaxed demeanour that hinted at a familiar camaraderie. As Horton's gaze briefly flickered towards Rike Volk, an unspoken understanding passed between them before he refocused on Craig.

"Please, have a seat," Horton motioned towards a row of weathered chairs lining the wall, their cushions worn down by years of anxious visitors seeking guidance or reporting minor town incidents.

Rike settled into the chair nearest to the entrance, its faux leather surface gleaming subtly under the dim lighting. She perched upright, her attention keenly focused on the exchange unfolding within earshot. The timbre of Craig's voice carried a blend of genuine worry masked by a veneer of casualness as he voiced his concerns about Tammy's unexplained absence.

The storm outside lived its life, its gusts intensifying to a crescendo that matched the unease palpable in the air. What were once gentle snowflakes now transformed into frenzied projectiles, hurling themselves against the windowpanes with a relentless force that echoed the hidden turmoil simmering beneath Craig's composed facade.

"Is this a pattern of behaviour for her?" Horton inquired, his voice steady, almost concerned.

"She's had moments like this before, but never to this extent," Craig responded wearily, running a hand across his fatigued face in a gesture of frustration. "I'm sure she'll turn up safe, but I couldn't live with myself if I didn't say something."

Rike sat silently in the room, her keen detective instincts honed over years of experience picking up on Horton's too casual approach. There should be a checklist of questions: a recent photograph, physical and mental health, emotional state, cell phone numbers, the service providers, email addresses, social media accounts, banking information, credit card information, driver's licence, passport, significant friends and family, and places where she frequents.

As Officer Horton settled into his chair, the aged leather protested with a soft creak, underscoring the gravity of the conversation. "Craig," Horton began nonchalantly, brushing off the seriousness of the matter, "Tammy's been known to enjoy herself at the hotel bar. Those slot machines seem to be her favourite haunt. Maybe that's a good place for you to start looking." Rike felt a surge of disbelief at how casually Horton seemed to deflect responsibility back onto Craig, instead of taking charge as expected in such a crucial situation. Her personal opinion aside, Horton's actions were offensive.

The suggestion that Craig do the work hung in the air between them, and even as Rike felt her chest tighten with unvoiced objections. Craig's laugh, though lacking genuine mirth, echoed through the cramped space.

"Yes, there was that one time you were nice enough to bring her home after she had a bit too much. Thanks for that. I guess she'd be right at home there," he conceded, the corner of his mouth lifting in a sardonic half-smile.

"Give them a call, see if she's there."

Craig's tone turned sharp, his eyes flicking away from Horton's, suggesting, "Maybe she eloped with that trucker she's been meeting sporadically." The unexpected theory landed heavily in the room. Rike observed Horton's eyebrows shoot up, his forehead furrowing with concern.

"A trucker?" His reaction was authentic, a touch of empathy softening his words akin to sunlight piercing icy windows. "I had no idea, Craig. My condolences."

Rike rolled her eyes. *"Weren't condolences saved for death?"* she wondered.

Craig's voice carried a tinge of resignation as he spoke, his words heavy with insinuation. "Sometimes, women can be quite a handful," he muttered, his posture betraying a hint of discomfort.

"You said it," Officer Horton said.

Craig laughed. "Women. You can't live with them, and you can't–"

"Craig!" Horton hissed, throwing a side-eye at Rike.

Sitting amidst this unsettling exchange, Rike felt a wave of unease wash over her. She did not know what Craig was prevented from saying, but she was sure it wasn't polite. Outside, the storm raged on, its icy tendrils creeping into the confines of the space, chilling her to the core.

In that moment, within the cocoon of that room buffeted by both external tempests and internal discord, Rike found herself confronted once more by the intricate complexities that defined human connections.

Officer Horton's pen scratched across the paper, the sound filling the room. Rike's mind wandered back to the crimson-stained snow she had stumbled upon earlier that morning, a vivid memory that sharply contrasted with the apathetic air enveloping the police precinct. It struck her then, how storms—whether swirling outside or brewing within—paid no heed to the disarray they wrought in their wake. Amidst the palpable tension, a flicker of dread crept in; she silently prayed that the chilling pool of blood she had discovered was not linked to Tammy Griffith.

In a sudden shift of awareness, Officer Horton's gaze pierced through the veil of Rike's thoughts, drawing her attention back to the scene at hand. His voice, crisp and professional, sliced through the air as he inquired, "Could you provide a detailed description of this mysterious trucker?"

Craig's movements were uneasy as he nodded, his hand instinctively finding solace in rubbing the tension from the nape of his neck. "I never caught his name. Just glimpsed him once at the gas station, exchanging words with Tammy. He's got a good, strong build. Not a fat like most truckers."

Horton's pen hovered expectantly over his notepad, prompting Craig further with a subtle intrigue lacing his words, "Is there anything more distinctive you can recall about him?"

"Solid frame," Craig added, his brow furrowing as he recalled. "Athletic, you know? Looks after himself." Rike found his repetition curious.

"Hmm, specifics?" Horton probed, his approach systematic.

"Must be around six-foot-three," Craig estimated, gesturing with his hand as if sizing up an unseen figure. "His hair's dark and neatly parted on the side, and those eyes of his are a deep brown—".

Rike's gaze lingered on Officer Horton as Craig recounted the description. Strangely, the features described mirrored those of the officer himself: towering stature, neatly cropped hair with a side parting, and a trim physique. A faint smirk played at the corners of her lips briefly, amused by the fleeting notion that crossed her mind. The image of the steadfast officer engaged in a secret tryst by the gas pumps with this man's wife danced momentarily in her thoughts. However, any amusement evaporated swiftly, overshadowed by the seriousness of the matter at hand.

"Alright, this gives me a starting point," Horton remarked, his head inclining in acknowledgment as he carefully noted down the information provided by Craig. "Thank you for sharing this with me. I'll look around and inquire if anyone has spotted an individual matching this description in the vicinity."

Craig let out a heavy sigh, his brow furrowed with a blend of exasperation and acceptance. "I'm trying to stay positive here. Perhaps she just needed some time alone," he murmured, his voice tinged with hope amidst the uncertainty.

Horton nodded thoughtfully, the corners of his lips twitching slightly. With a gentle click, he shut his notebook, the sound muffled by the quiet surroundings. "Let's remain optimistic. Head over to the hotel bar first. If by chance she's there, don't hesitate to give me a call immediately," he instructed in a calm yet authoritative tone.

As the conversation concluded, the men straightened up, Craig extended his hand for a shake, met by Horton's strong grip. Their interaction was swift, polite words veiling the tension that tinged Craig's voice.

Before leaving, Craig hesitated and glanced back at Rike, offering a respectful nod. Rike reciprocated the gesture. In the quiet aftermath of Craig's departure, the weight of her gruesome discovery pressed down on her, hidden anxieties simmering beneath the surface of this seemingly ordinary exchange.

She hoped Tammy was safe.

Chapter 8

"Good day, Officer Horton," Rike greeted, her voice unwavering despite the storm of worry now swirling around Tammy's well-being. She stood tall, a pillar of resolve in the face of uncertainty. "I reside on Way Road, beyond Highway 27," she informed him. "This morning, near the north end of the old logging road, I stumbled upon a pool of blood in the snow."

Horton's brows lifted imperceptibly as he reclined in his seat, a mixture of professional intrigue and doubt colouring his expression. "Blood?" he inquired. "You're sure it was blood?"

"It certainly wasn't cranberry juice."

"That region is frequented by hunting wolves. It's likely just a deer they've felled."

Rike nodded thoughtfully, though the tension in her jaw betrayed her inner turmoil. "Possibly," she conceded hesitantly. "But it could be poachers. Which would indicate illegal activity."

Horton's eyebrows furrowed slightly, his interest piqued by the notion of an illegal hunt. "Any theories?" he mused aloud, his voice laced with mild curiosity as he mulled over the possibility.

Rike held his gaze steady, her eyes reflecting a mix of determination and uncertainty. "The Cumming twins come to mind," she offered thoughtfully, her words measured and deliberate. "Considering there was a cigarette butt at the site."

Leaning in slightly, Horton probed further, attempting to draw out more insights from Rike. "Someone threw a butt out the window, and you want me to ask the boys if they are poaching? Any other proof? Any other theories?"

Once again faced with Horton's subtle prodding for answers, Rike remained resolute in not shouldering the investigative burden. Her response was firm, yet tinged with a hint of reluctance. "I hadn't intended to bring it to your attention initially," she admitted candidly, a flicker of unease crossing her features. "Others convinced me otherwise. I can't say for certain if it holds any significance." Despite feeling uneasy about her admission, Rike stood her ground, unwilling to take on responsibilities that were not hers to bear. "And with Tammy now missing..."

"Someone is always missing from Berna. You know where I find them? Most times, down by the old railway tracks. Doing drugs or drinking."

Horton's posture shifted, leaning in with a sense of casual authority, his hands coming together on the desk with a subtle thud. "I'll make my way over there," he assured, his words carrying the weight of impending weather conditions. "Given the storm brewing, it might have to wait until tomorrow."

Rike acknowledged his response with a nod, though an unease settled within her like an old injury predicting rain. She had done her duty.

Horton's skepticism was palpable, evident in the nonchalant twirl of his pen between his fingers. It mirrored a familiar expression to Rike–one that sought comfort in simple explanations rather than facing the unsettling reality that lay beneath. The weight of doubt, a sensation she knew all too well, settled heavily within her.

"Officer Horton," Rike said, despite the internal turmoil she battled. "I have captured images of the scene." Retrieving her phone from her pocket, she deftly navigated to the gallery.

The officer's gaze swept over the images displayed before him, a hint of detachment colouring his expression. "I appreciate your concern, Rike, but it's likely just..." Rike interjected, her voice sharp as she finished his sentence, "...nothing?" His chuckle danced in the air, diminishing the seriousness of her discovery.

"Take another look," she urged.

Horton revisited the images, a brief moment of contemplation flickering across his features before he made his assessment. "You see this? A wolf track next to the blood. Clear print. It points to a wolf attack without a doubt."

Acknowledging the possibility, Rike's frustration tinged her words with subtle impatience. "Yes, that's one explanation. But poaching is also on the table."

"Sure, and maybe you think that could be Tammy Griffith's blood?" Officer Horton said casually, his hand waving dismissively. "Let's not blow this out of proportion. I have heard rumours that you once worked in homicides in Germany?" he inquired with a hint of curiosity.

Rike met his gaze steadily. "Yes, that was my life before I settled here in Berna. Retired now," she affirmed.

The seasoned officer nodded sagely. "Then you understand better than most that things are rarely what they seem," he remarked knowingly, a sentiment ingrained in every law enforcer.

Suppressing a flicker of impatience, Rike felt the echoes of her detective days stirring within her—a familiar yearning for investigation—but she reined it in. "Would you like me to forward these images to you?" she offered diplomatically.

Horton's response was swift and indifferent, his attention already shifting to the disarray of papers strewn across his desk. "No need," he stated crisply. "If you truly suspect something is amiss, you could wait until the storm subsides and gather more evidence if necessary."

Rike let out a quiet sigh, her eyes fixed on the officer's silhouette. In his demeanour, she detected a familiar sense of complacency, one she had once battled against fiercely—the very same that allowed too many secrets to lurk in the shadows. However, she had long abandoned that struggle—or at least that's what she tried to convince herself of.

"There is quite a storm brewing. I expect to be inundated with calls. You know how it goes in Berna when the flakes start falling. Suddenly, I'm not just a cop, I'm everyone's go-to guy for shoveling driveways, restarting generators, rescuing cats from trees, you name it! I'll be chasing shadows in the snow. Guess I'll be earning my keep this winter, hmm?"

Retirement suited Rike, or so she tried to convince herself as Officer Horton's banter danced around the weight of her past. His jovial tone barely masked the apathy that lingered in his gaze. The mention of chasing shadows in the snow struck a nerve within her, stirring up echoes of sleepless nights, brought on by the horrors she once faced.

With a forced composure, Rike met Horton's eyes, her posture rigid with unspoken truths. Despite her outward calmness, the reality was far from idyllic. She knew all too well the toll crime scenes took on one's peace of mind, how they could unravel even the most stoic facade.

"I've fulfilled my duty to this town," Rike stated evenly, though beneath her words lay a reservoir of buried emotions. "I trust you to handle things from here with your expertise."

"Thank you," Horton acknowledged, his gaze quickly turning to the glow of his computer screen. Rike smoothly extracted her smartphone from her pocket. With deliberate precision, she navigated through her device, crafting an email that encapsulated the chilling scene she had stumbled upon earlier that day. The photographs attached captured the raw intensity of crimson splattered on pristine white, a visual discord that pierced through the digital medium.

Her fingertip hesitated momentarily over the send icon before decisively pressing down, dispatching the haunting images into Horton's inbox. "I've forwarded those pictures for your reference," Rike declared with a touch more volume than intended, cutting through the monotonous drone of the station's aging heater.

Horton's response was a mere murmur, his attention glued to the screen in front of him, seemingly oblivious to the unsettling sight Rike had brought to his notice. "Thank you," Rike said, her tone carrying a hint of something akin to wistfulness or acceptance, a complex emotion swirling within her. Sensing the thick veil of disinterest that hung between them, as tangible as the biting chill outside, she realized there was no point in prolonging their interaction.

With purposeful strides, Rike pivoted and strode towards the exit, her movements deliberate and resolute. Each step she took seemed to echo with finality, signalling the end of the conversation, sealing off the room, and rejecting any unlikely action from a complacent officer. As she pushed the door closed, it groaned in protest against the howling winds that ravaged the surroundings. Stepping outside, Rike entered a world engulfed in an ever-expanding void, where snowflakes danced like chaotic spirits unleashed upon the earth. The biting gusts nipped at her cheeks like frosty needles, leaving a chilling imprint of the day's sombre occurrences.

Alone in the vast expanse of the now-deserted parking lot, Rike's truck stood as a solitary sanctuary amidst the rising storm. With determined steps, she approached it, her breath forming misty clouds in the frigid air. The biting cold nipped at her exposed fingers as she grappled with the keys, finally unlocking the door and seeking refuge inside. The heavy thud of the door closing echoed in the confined space, shutting out the relentless icy assault that raged outside.

As Rike ignited the engine, its growl filled the interior while the struggling heater fought against the persistent chill that had seeped into the cabin. Adjusting to the dim warmth slowly spreading around her, she activated the windshield wipers to combat the veil of snow obscuring her view. Their rhythmic motion was a feeble resistance against nature's onslaught, trying desperately to maintain a clear sight through the increasing snow.

Ahead, only a faint outline of the road was visible, a vague smudge of grey on a canvas dominated by swirling white snowflakes.

The truck's tires clawed at the icy road, each forward motion a battle against the unforgiving terrain. The journey home felt endless, the blizzard distorting the familiar landscape into an eerie and unfamiliar expanse. Despite the promise of her cabin nestled among the trees, the drive itself was a harrowing test of her courage.

Memories of past investigations tugged at her consciousness, their ghostly presence threatening to engulf her in a sea of darkness. The temptation to surrender to her former detective instincts, to pursue the phantom that lingered amidst the crimson-stained snow, whispered seductively in her mind. Yet she resisted, aware of the perilous path such recklessness would lead her down. This hesitance gripped her like the frost clinging stubbornly to her windshield, refusing to yield.

Cursing under her breath, she watched as her whispered words clouded the frosty glass. The relentless beat of the wipers did little to combat the intensifying storm outside, each gust of wind feeling like a direct challenge from nature itself. The road ahead appeared more like a faint memory, almost disappearing under layers of swirling snow whipped up by the howling blizzard.

Navigating through this perilous landscape felt like threading a needle in a hurricane. The narrow path snaked through the darkened woods, where skeletal trees groaned ominously in the raging winds. Feeble beams of light from the truck's headlights struggled to pierce through the chaos, their illumination swallowed by the darkness almost as quickly as it appeared.

In the unforgiving heart of the storm, hesitation and doubt found no refuge. Survival was the only language spoken here, each decision a step closer to safety or peril. The truck's tires bit into the snow with a determination matching Rike's own, drawing her towards the cabin like a beacon in the blizzard. She was glad the truck had a driver's side airbag.

Amidst the swirling snowflakes, the cabin's lights flickered like a distant promise of sanctuary, but Rike knew deep down that peace would elude her grasp. The mystery lurking in the shadows called out to her, its allure as dangerous as it was irresistible. Despite her inner resistance, she recognized the familiar pull of intrigue and danger.

It took Rike much longer than she anticipated to trudge back to her secluded cabin, the snow weighing heavily in her path. The journey home felt like an eternity, however, the struggle only heightened the sense of relief that flooded through her once she finally stepped inside the familiar warmth of her cozy cabin.

Within the comforting confines of her home, Rike meticulously stowed away the provisions she had purchased in town earlier that day. The rhythmic clinking of jars and rustling of bags filled the silence as she went about her cherished routine. Soon, the room was filled with the soothing aroma of freshly brewed tea, its steam curling upwards like wisps of smoke in the dimly lit space.

Nestling into a plush armchair by the crackling fireplace, Rike's gaze drifted to the howling storm outside, its fury muffled by the sturdy log walls that shielded her from nature's wrath. Seeking solace in distraction, she reached for a cherished volume resting on a nearby side table–a worn copy of Michelle McNamara's *I'll Be Gone in the Dark*.

As she flipped through its pages, each crease and dog-eared corner a testament to countless readings, Rike found herself drawn into McNamara's chilling narrative. The words painted a world as dark and ominous as the raging blizzard beyond her windows, yet there was a strange comfort in delving into a known mystery far removed from the events of her own day.

McNamara's fearless pursuit of truth despite its dangers resonated with Rike on some level. In those moments of quiet contemplation, lost in the gripping prose before her, she too embarked on a mental journey into shadows unknown, but strangely alluring.

The intricate sentences sprawled across the pages, weaving intricate and intimate connections that captivated her thoughts. Each self-reproach mirrored the depths of her own past struggles during her time as a detective. With the night progressing, the words on the page began to meld together, blurring before Rike's eyes. The tension that had gripped her since finding the blood in the snow slowly loosened its hold as the cozy ambiance of the room and the solace of the written tale beckoned her into slumber.

"My, my," she murmured softly, her breath mingling with the wisps of smoke swirling from the crackling fire. "If only I had held on a little longer." Her words drifted into the stillness of the cabin, embraced by the dancing shadows that the flickering flames painted on the wooden walls. As she lingered in that tranquil moment before sleep came, there existed a serene communion between her and the written word, where questions and urgency faded away, leaving behind only the quiet intimacy shared between reader and narrative. Eventually, as sleep enveloped her in its restless embrace, Rike succumbed to its insistent pull, sinking into its mysterious depths.

She dreamt. On her skis, Rike soared through the icy expanse, a world painted in twilight hues. The moon, a silver sentinel above, illuminated the snow like a field of diamonds. All was hushed, the only sound her skis whispering against the frozen ground.

Then, a jolt of primal dread shattered the peace. From the shadows behind her materialized a wolf, eyes aglow with an eerie light, its presence haunting yet palpable. Heart hammering, Rike surged ahead, each stride fraught with desperate speed as she raced to outrun the spectral predator at her back.

The wolf closed in, a relentless force propelling her forward. Its icy breath, tinged with hunger, brushed against her neck, sending shivers down her spine. With burning legs and gasping breaths, she pushed on, the line between reality and haunting recollections blurring dangerously. Devoid of any defence but speed, she urged herself onward through gritted teeth. "Don't stop," she wheezed, the words escaping in wisps into the frigid atmosphere. Yet, whether she was commanding herself or the ghostly predator at her heels remained as unclear as the snowy landscape around her.

The piercing sound of her alarm clock abruptly tore through the serene silence, yanking Rike from the depths of her slumber. Startled, she shot upright in bed, her heart pounding against her chest, a sheen of perspiration glistening on her skin despite the room's frigid air. Lying back, she struggled to shake off the remnants of a haunting dream that were intertwined with the eerie howls of the wind swirling outside. Yet an icy grip of unease lingered within her, refusing to dissipate.

Chapter 9

Grocery shopping is my solace, a ritual that fills me with contentment and purpose. As I stroll through the aisles, I carefully select the finest ingredients for my family's nourishment. The crispness of fresh vegetables, the marbling of choice cuts of meat, and the vibrant colours of ripe fruits all beckon to me, promising wholesome meals at our table. Canned and dry goods pale in comparison to the satisfaction of crafting my own pasta from scratch. In these moments among the bustling store, I find a tranquil connection with myself that transcends mere errands—it's a mindful act of love for those dearest to me.

I take great pleasure in hunting for bargains. While some may consider it insignificant, every saved dollar contributes to my family's well-being. As a traditional homemaker, this is my way of financially contributing to our household. The satisfaction I feel upon seeing the "you saved" message on my grocery receipt cannot be overstated.

Today proved a tad disappointing, as the store lacked the red grapes that my husband adores. Opting for the green variety instead, I chose the Hopkins Sweet Seedless grapes. They are delightfully crunchy and sweet. I hope he accepts them. Despite spending slightly over $150 on groceries, the cashier and I shared a moment of understanding about the elevated costs in this remote area. This reinforces the importance of making savvy purchases; investing in flour and yeast to bake a dozen loaves is far more economical than purchasing only two loaves of branded bread.

Living in this picturesque yet secluded area can be quite costly, both financially and socially, but there's a sense of divine tranquillity that blankets this land. Our community thrives on the unity within our four churches, where every soul is cared for and no one is left wanting. Personally, I make it a point to attend church daily, even if only for a moment of silent communion. It warms my heart to bake fresh loaves of bread for our elderly church members, a small gesture in the grand tapestry of our interconnected lives here.

On Sundays, the familiar faces fill the pews, sharing in the spiritual embrace that binds us together. However, I've noticed that it's often the transient visitors and newcomers who shy away from these gatherings, missing out on the profound sense of belonging we cherish. Some arrive seeking an escape from bustling city life yet struggle to integrate into our close-knit community. Whether carrying an air of urban superiority or maintaining a frosty demeanour towards the locals, they inadvertently distance themselves from the genuine connections that define our town's essence and our soul.

That German woman, Rike Volk, is a striking figure in the community. Her tall, lean frame moves gracefully as she skis through the snow in the mornings. I see her sometimes when I drive to town. Her silver hair glistens under the winter sun, framing her face like a halo. She's fluent in English and even speaks French, which comes in handy in our bilingual country but unfortunately not so much with German.

While I haven't had many conversations with her beyond polite exchanges, there's a sense of depth to her that intrigues me. Rumours once whispered about her orientation, suggesting she might be homosexual due to a flag spotted at her home. However, my own observations driving past her cabin have never revealed any such symbol fluttering in the cold breeze.

Gossip holds little interest for me; there are more important things to focus on in this small community nestled among snow-covered pines. So enough about rumours and hearsay; let's move on to more substantial matters.

After loading the groceries into my van, I meticulously checked everything before starting the engine. With just a quarter tank of gas left, I knew it was time for a refill. Living in this remote area meant always being prepared, especially during winter. A full tank could be a lifesaver if stranded in the snow. Practicality was key in these harsh conditions.

Driving to the gas station, I marvelled at the pristine beauty of the snowy landscape surrounding me. Each snowflake seemed like a gift from God. Skillfully filling up my tank—no damsel in distress here—I then made my way back home promptly to ensure the perishables stayed fresh. The cost of refueling nearly matched that of my entire grocery haul!

Arriving home, the groceries were swiftly brought inside in just two trips, leaving the door ajar as my hands brimmed with bags. Little did I anticipate the sinister intrusion that followed me in. Panic surged through me as a hand clamped over my mouth and an arm encircled my waist, lifting me off the ground. Despite my frantic kicks and attempts to scream, I was rendered powerless, flailing helplessly like a trapped insect.

Something constricted around my neck, a vice-like grip that sent searing pain through me. Gasping for air became a futile struggle, my voice stifled in my throat as tears streamed down my cheeks. In that harrowing moment, with the world fading to darkness, I found solace in prayers whispered amidst silent sobs. A bittersweet smile tugged at my lips, for in that agony, I embraced the certainty of ascending to heaven's embrace.

Chapter 10

The morning light filtered gently through the barren branches of the slumbering trees, painting the landscape with a peaceful radiance. A soft blanket of snow enveloped the world outside Rike's frosty window, its pristine expanse interrupted by billowing drifts resembling frozen waves frozen in time. The cold air, sharp and unforgiving, playfully nibbled at any exposed skin, leaving behind a crisp sensation that stung with a hint of playful malice. In her cozy kitchen, Rike Volk cradled a cup of tea brimming with steam between her palms, relishing in the comforting heat that seeped into her chilled fingers as she gazed outward.

"May fortune favour the bold," she murmured under her breath, observing a solitary cardinal darting towards the shelter of a snow-laden pine. Legends whispered that the cardinal symbolized good luck and unwavering loyalty. In Native American folklore, its sudden appearance heralded blessings, foretelling a positive turn within the upcoming twelve days.

Seated comfortably on the wooden floor of her quaint cabin, Rike assumed a cross-legged position. A modest iron stove crackled softly in the corner, casting a gentle warmth throughout the room. Atop the stove sat an ancient iron crafted from sturdy cast iron material; its surface radiated a near-red heat, imbuing the cozy space with a comforting glow.

Rike's weathered hands expertly lifted the iron from the crackling stove, its searing warmth penetrating the frosty air and thawing her numbed fingertips. Gently but with precision, she brought the hot iron to a solid block of wax, watching as it transformed from solid to liquid under the intense heat, forming rivulets that cascaded onto the ski beneath. As she worked, the fragrant scent of pine intertwined with the earthy notes of melting wax, creating a cozy ambiance that contrasted with the icy world beyond her secluded cabin walls.

The rhythmic swish of the wax brush against the skis carried Rike into a state of focused tranquillity. Each stroke was a deliberate homage to her expertise and unwavering commitment. As she worked, a profound connection to the untouched wilderness enveloped her, filling her with gratitude for the raw beauty and serene isolation of her surroundings.

Completing the task, Rike admired the ski's polished surface reflecting the warm glow of the crackling fire, a testament to her meticulous care. Rising from her knees, a wave of contentment washed over her, affirming her bond with this rugged terrain she called home.

Rike embarked on her morning ritual with practiced precision. First came the snug embrace of thermal leggings, followed by insulated trousers providing a shield against the biting cold. Layer by layer, she adorned herself in familiar armour: a fleece-lined top offering comfort, an insulating vest for added warmth, and finally a windproof jacket sealing in protection against the elements. Each garment was not just attire but a shield against nature's harsh embrace, preparing Rike for another day in this untamed paradise.

The moment Rike stepped outside, the frigid air enveloped her like a long-lost friend, its icy fingers tingling on her skin. She secured her feet into the bindings of her cross-country skis with a satisfying click that echoed in the silent landscape. As she glided forward, the pristine snow put up a resistance, challenging her with each stride. Yet, the wax coating on her skis allowed for effortless movement, turning every push into a dance of physical delight.

Gliding through the snow-covered expanse, Rike's skis whispered against the powdery surface, carrying her effortlessly forward. Each rhythmic push propelled her with a fluid grace that seemed to shed the world from her shoulders. The only interruptions in the serene symphony were the gentle swish of her skis and the distant melody of a bird's song, blending into a tranquil harmony that cocooned her in peace.

Alone in the tranquil expanse of the snowy landscape, Rike's skis carved through the pristine white, carrying her deeper into the solitude she craved. Memories of that case, the one that bore unyielding darkness, surfaced unbidden. It was that haunting investigation, the one that lingered like a ghost in her past, that eventually whispered the final push that led her away from the turbulent world of police work. As she glided on, the crisp chill of the winter air snapped her back to the present, the rhythmic swish of her skis a comforting cadence in the midst of her solitary retreat.

Immersed in this winter wonderland, Rike felt a deep connection to nature as she embraced the crisp air tinged with pine and snow. Approaching the edge of the forest, an eager thrill stirred within her, anticipating the familiar trails that awaited exploration beyond the frosted trees.

Rike's serene expression illuminated her features as she ventured deeper into the woods, the winding path unfurling like a tapestry of endless opportunities. Each bend and curve of the trail whispered tales of connection to her, weaving a profound bond with the pristine landscape that enveloped her in its tranquil embrace. Casting a fond glance over her shoulder at her cabin, it stood unwavering amidst the snowy vastness, like a stalwart guardian, its windows mirroring the soft hues of dawn. The weight of Rike's life experiences settled gently upon her, akin to the delicate descent of snowflakes from the heavens above, adding a layer of contemplative grace to her solitary journey.

Soon, a chilling sight halted Rike in her tracks. The tranquillity of the snow-laden forest shattered beneath her skis as she came upon a gruesome scene. Spread out in a grotesque display against the pristine white backdrop was a figure—what once might have been a woman, now reduced to an almost unrecognizable state, likely ravaged by scavenging creatures drawn to the aftermath of the death. Despite the brutality on show, there was an unsettling absence of blood, creating a haunting image that sent a shiver racing down Rike's spine, unrelated to the wintry chill that surrounded her. "Shit," she muttered under her breath, words dissipating into icy wisps in the frigid air. It was chaos personified, a scene she had encountered before but never failed to disturb her deeply.

She fumbled for her phone and cursed again when she found she has no service.

Beneath the weight of her winter gear, her detective instincts surged back to life. In a different time, this chilling discovery would have been hers to unravel, her expertise to wield. But now, it turned her stomach with dread. Keeping a cautious distance, she knelt down, peering intently at the lifeless form, the sun's glare piercing her eyes as she struggled to make sense of the brutality amidst the serene forest setting. Haunting recollections of past crime scenes flickered in her mind—ominous reminders of unsolved mysteries. These were memories she had hoped to escape by skiing this trail, yet they now clawed their way back with a vengeance.

Her fingers struggled to dial her phone. Pressing it to her ear, silence greeted her—no bars, no service. Isolation closed in around her like a vice, squeezing tighter than the icy chill.

"Damn it." Panic laced her words as she weighed the consequences. Reporting this could paint a damning picture. First the blood pool, now a body? The potential headlines loomed ominously in her mind, each word a sharp edge cutting into her already frayed nerves.

Her hands, encased in gloves that barely contained her trembling fingers, reached for the phone once more. The device emerged like a lifeline in the desolate landscape, its camera poised to capture the chilling tableau before her. Each click of the shutter echoed through the silent woods, a stark contrast to the eerie stillness surrounding her.

Every meticulous shot framed the scene with clinical precision, preserving the gruesome reality in cold digital clarity. As she stowed away the phone, a sense of unease settled over her like a shroud. The absence of any trace leading to this macabre discovery gnawed at her thoughts, amplifying her apprehension.

With a determined push from her ski poles, she propelled herself away from the haunting sight, urgency lacing each movement. Her retreat left behind a trail of disrupted snow, marking her passage through this pristine wilderness with an unsettling reminder of what lurked unseen in its depths.

Rike's fingers quivered as she cautiously nudged the cabin door ajar, the creak echoing through the silent room. A rush of warmth enveloped her as she crossed the threshold, dispelling the icy grip of the outside world. Shedding her gloves, she placed them on the worn countertop, her every exhale forming misty clouds in the frigid air until the crackling flames breathed life into the hearth. She snatched up her landline, her heart leaping with joy at the sound of the dial tone. She called the local police station.

"Officer Horton, Rike Volk here," Rike's voice remained steady, a stark contrast to her trembling hands as she clutched the phone against her ear. "I stumbled upon a body near my property. It's a gruesome scene."

Disbelief laced the voice on the other end. "A human body? Are you absolutely certain?"

"Absolutely. I have experience, Officer. I wouldn't make this call without being sure."

"Is there any sign of life?"

"The person is beyond help, Officer."

"Where exactly are you?"

"I'm at my cabin. There was no signal at the discovery site."

"Stay put. I'm en route." Despite Officer Horton's attempt at professionalism, his words offered little reassurance. She gave him her address again and ended the call, her heart pounding in her chest. A gnawing sense of dread lingered, twisting her insides. The gossip machine meant suspicion would inevitably turn towards her. Restlessly, she paced back and forth, each tick of the clock echoing loudly in the tense silence of her cabin. Unable to bear the waiting any longer, she grabbed the phone once more and dialled Autumn's familiar number.

"Autumn," Rike's voice trembled slightly over the line, "I stumbled upon something horrifying during my morning ski."

Autumn's voice crackled through the phone, filled with concern. "Rike, what's wrong? You sound awful."

Rike struggled to speak. Her throat constricted. "There's a body in the woods. It's... torn apart. Not much blood."

Autumn gasped, the shock evident in her voice. "Oh my God, Rike, that's chilling. Could it be connected to the blood from yesterday?"

"It has to be," Rike replied firmly, feeling the chill of the wall against her back. "There's no other explanation. I've called Horton. He's on his way."

"Should I come over?" Autumn offered, her worry palpable. "I can be there in a minute."

"I have to go with Officer Horton when he gets here. I won't be around. There he is. Thanks, Autumn," Rike's voice was firm, but her eyes remained fixed on the window.

The sharp crunch of tires slicing through the compacted snow as Officer Horton arrived. Rike peered out from the frosted window, observing his truck creep closer, the low growl of its engine piercing the eerie calmness of the post-storm morning. Without hesitation, she snatched her coat and marched outside, her every exhale forming a ghostly mist in the icy air.

Horton's gaze, sharp and calculating, raked over Rike as he addressed her. "Rike. Show me," he began, the weight of his words hanging heavy in the air. With a curt nod, she acknowledged him, her facade unyielding despite the storm raging within. She showed him the photographs she'd taken. "Yes. Yes, let's go."

Without a moment's pause, Rike strode towards her truck. The engine roared to life at her touch, its powerful hum filling the frosty air like a harbinger of events to come. As she pulled onto the road, Horton's patrol vehicle trailed closely behind, casting long shadows in the wake of their journey.

The journey crawled along, the icy roads treacherous and winding, leading them further into the heart of the dense forest, where an eerie stillness enveloped them. In a place where skis would have swiftly carried them, every bend in the road now stretched out ominously. Rike maneuvered her truck carefully along roads buried by the storm.

The truck's engine sputtered to a stop. "I can see my ski trail there through the woods. We have to go on foot." Rike and Horton had no choice. With determined strides, they trudged through the snow, the only sound their footsteps muffled by the icy blanket beneath them. Breaking the eerie silence, a branch snapped under their weight as they neared their destination.

Halting, Rike pointed to her own ski tracks etched in the snow like a haunting trail leading to the grim discovery ahead. Following her gaze, Horton's breath caught in his throat as they closed in on the chilling scene. Before them lay a woman, sprawled amidst the desolate landscape, her torn clothes fluttering in the cold wind. A sense of dread washed over them as they noticed the ghastly absence of both her hands and feet, painting a macabre picture of violence and horror.

"Sweet mother of...," Horton gasped, his palm shooting up to muffle the sudden retching that erupted from him. Rike maintained a cautious distance. Her gaze fixed on Horton's distress as he staggered away and emptied his stomach onto the snow, wisps of vapor rising from the sickening sight. She averted her eyes momentarily, torn between offering him space and confronting the chilling scene laid out in front of them—half-expecting it to vanish into thin air at any moment.

Horton's face twisted in a grimace, his hand hastily rising to cover his mouth, the metallic tang of bile lingering in the air. Frustration etched deep lines on his forehead as he grappled with his unresponsive phone, the screen mocking him with its lifeless blackness. With a heavy exhale, he shoved the useless device back into his pocket.

Meanwhile, Rike observed Horton's measured steps around the fallen figure, each movement deliberate despite the unease that had gripped him moments before. "Seems like predators found her first," he muttered under his breath before falling silent, his gaze capturing the brutal remnants of a once vibrant existence.

"How did she end up here?" Rike's voice trembled with a mix of dread and determination.

Officer Horton's eyes scanned the surroundings, his brow furrowed. "Possibly through the gully. If she was caught in the whiteout, she would have easily lost her way," he suggested, his tone laced with unease. A heavy silence lingered before Rike turned to look. The gully sprawled wide and untamed, its rugged terrain challenging yet passable for a determined individual. Doubt crept in, whispering accusations of fading expertise in her ear, intensifying the gripping fear clawing at her chest.

"Wolves likely got to her after she froze to death. Don't you think?"

Rike's response was just a nod. She stood back, her sharp gaze sweeping over the frozen canvas, capturing every nuance—the unblemished snow stretching beyond her footprints, the skeletal branches looming overhead like silent sentinels bearing witness to the grim scene below.

Horton's expression turned sombre as he cautiously navigated the mental boundaries he had set up around the scene. "I believe... it appears to be Kelsey McDaniel," he murmured, his words strained with emotion. "Warren will be shattered by this news." Rike's heart clenched at the mention of Warren, recalling their encounter just the day before.

"Does your police radio function properly? The one in your patrol car?" she inquired softly.

"Yes, it's working. I need to report this," Horton replied, shaken from his thoughts by her question. He trudged back towards his vehicle, bracing himself against the biting cold wind. Rike shadowed him to the road, observing as he lifted the radio handset with hands that betrayed a hint of tremor.

Officer Horton's voice crackled over the radio in urgent tones, breaking the stillness of Phillips County. "This is Officer Horton. Requesting immediate backup and the medical examiner at Old Mill Road. We've got a grim situation—a body that appears to be a victim of an animal attack." After a brief pause for confirmation, he added, "It's a gruesome sight."

By the police truck, Rike stood silently at the open door, her breath forming misty clouds in the cold air, as Horton gave his GPS information. She watched as Horton retrieved a worn blanket from the back seat, its fabric showing signs of past use with scattered dark blemishes. With care etched on his face, he approached Kelsey's lifeless form and tenderly covered her with the blanket, shielding her from further indignity as they awaited the arrival of the medical examiner. The makeshift shroud may have been imperfect, stained by previous encounters, but it was a gesture of respect amidst the tragedy unfolding before them.

"The idiot just contaminated the scene," Rike thought to herself. Something stirred deep within Rike, a long-forgotten sense of obligation that once defined her life as a detective. Yet, instead of the expected surge of emotions, she found herself oddly detached, her reaction more analytical than emotional. Suppressing the urge to speak out, she remained silent, knowing this was no longer her responsibility. It was possible probably that, in fact, she had died by misadventure.

Kelsey could not be seen from the road, but when the wind picked up the blanket and whipped it into the air, Horton sighed. "I guess she does not need it." A mournful crow's cry echoed in the distance, and the biting winter air enveloped them in an eerie stillness. It felt as though they were mere players on a meticulously crafted stage, where reality blurred with fiction in an unsettling harmony.

Officer Horton's breath billowed out in a frosty cloud, mingling with the icy air that enveloped them. "I'll need to tell her husband," he stated with a sense of duty.

"It should be done in person," Rike responded. "I just spoke with him. He will be devastated."

In this unforgiving wilderness, they were insignificant observers, confronted by the raw power and occasional cruelty of the natural world.

Turning towards Rike, Officer Horton's voice held a sombre note as he addressed her, a subtle undertone of suspicion colouring his words. "Rike," he began cautiously, his gaze searching hers, "did you have any connection to the victim?"

Rike's response was sharp, her eyes locking onto his without flinching. "I knew of Kelsey McDaniel, but not intimately," she stated firmly.

"Intimately?"

"Well. I did not know her well. Never as much as a single personal conversation. My English..." she trailed off.

"Can you stay here? Until others arrive?" Officer Horton fidgeted, his gaze flickering nervously towards the lifeless form under the sheet. In that moment, he appeared diminished, uncertainty clouding his features as the idea of solitude with the deceased in the quiet, snow-blanketed landscape sank in.

"Yes. I will need my hat from my truck." Rike went back to her truck, happy to be isolated from the man. It looked to her like he was about to cry.

"Alright," he relented, reluctance evident in his tone. "Thank you," Rike acknowledged, the gratitude laced with a hint of bitterness. With a deliberate turn away from Horton and the grim scene before her, Rike's boots crunched on the snow as she made her way to her weather-beaten truck, wisps of frosty breath escaping her lips into the icy air. She reached in and grabbed her balaclava. She pulled the black knit mask over her face, giving her a buffer between skin and wind.

Just as she turned to shut the door, a distant rumble heralded an approaching vehicle. "Hey there, what's happening?" Craig Griffith's concerned voice cut through the brisk air as he rolled down his window, his eyes scanning Rike and Officer Horton standing near the edge of the snowy trees.

"Body found," Officer Horton's voice sliced through the icy air, his demeanour oddly composed despite the grim discovery. "Not Tammy, in case you were worried. You should keep going."

Craig's curiosity got the best of him as he strained to catch a glimpse past the fluttering police tape. "Who is it? Do I know them?"

Horton's reply was clipped. "Can't say for sure. Just someone out for a walk in the storm. You know how it is."

A shadow of uncertainty clouded Craig's expression as he hesitated before bidding farewell. Casting a questioning glance at Rike, Craig maneuvered his truck around and vanished into the snowy landscape, leaving behind an unsettling aura of mystery and unease.

The wail of the sirens heralded the arrival of the fire truck, its red paint stark against the snowy environs. Despite the presence of the volunteer firefighters, it was evident that their skills were not necessary in this grim situation. Soon after, the ambulance pulled up with a sense of urgency, its flashing lights casting an eerie glow on the wintry landscape.

As Rike stood amidst the flurry of activity, she turned to Officer Horton with a mix of impatience and readiness etched on her face. "May I take my leave now, Officer Horton?" Her voice cut through the cold air like a sharp blade. With a nonchalant tilt of his head, Horton granted her permission to depart from the scene, allowing her to step away from the unfolding tragedy.

She eased her truck backwards, guiding it onto the snow-covered road. Her fingers gripped the wheel with a gentle touch. As she set off, she stole a quick glance in the rearview mirror, watching Officer Horton's figure diminish alongside the first responders—a poignant symbol of life's delicate nature. Fixing her gaze on the path ahead, each passing mile carried her away from the scene of tragedy, yet the unsettling feeling persisted, enveloping her like the icy tendrils of winter. Blood and an almost bloodless body. She hated the feeling of wanting answers.

Chapter 11

The soft, muted light of the winter sun seeped through the frosted panes of The Auberge Brew, painting a dreamlike aura over the gathered clientele swathed in cozy coats and speaking in subdued tones. Wisps of breath and tendrils of steam from hot drinks lingered in the air, creating an almost tangible veil around the room filled with murmured conjectures. Amidst the plush seats and comforting scents, Rike sat upright at her table, a stark silhouette amidst the warmth and chatter.

Autumn's voice reached Rike across the intimate space, laden with unease that mirrored the turbulent sea. "Rike," she whispered, her words carrying a sense of urgency. "The entire place is alive with chatter about your discovery out there."

Rike's gaze lingered on the wisps of steam dancing from the porcelain cup she cradled, a subtle tremor rippling through her jaw. "Yes," she answered, her voice steady but lacking its usual warmth.

Autumn inched nearer, her features etched with concern. "Tell me, Rike. Who was it that you stumbled on?" Her slender fingers wrapped around the handle of her own mug, seeking solace from the pervasive chill that seemed to seep beyond the wintry landscape outside.

"I can't say for certain," Rike hedged, her weathered hands skimming the ceramic edge of her cup, almost as though she was tracing the contours of a yet-unveiled crime scene map. Uncertainty lingered in her words as she withheld information about who Officer Horton identified, steadfast in her refusal to engage in idle gossip and guessing.

Autumn's voice lowered, carrying a weight of unease that mirrored the hushed tones around them. "Whispers in the town paint a sombre picture," she murmured, her eyes darting anxiously across the room where conversations swirled like eddies of apprehension. "Some speculate it might be Tammy Griffith. She vanished without a trace Tuesday."

Rike's keen gaze flickered at the mention of Tammy, a subtle hint of recognition crossing her features before she settled back into her usual composed demeanour. "I'm certain it wasn't her," she stated firmly, her voice betraying no emotion.

Autumn jumped in with a flurry of speculative scenarios. "Perhaps a visitor passing through?" she suggested eagerly, eager to unravel the mysteries swirling in her mind. "There's talk of a city slicker who fancied a bear as a selfie partner. Or..." Her voice trailed off briefly as she contemplated the grimmer rumours circulating in town, her brow furrowing. "Maybe someone tangled up in a dangerous drug affair gone awry. You know how volatile those situations can be."

Rike carefully placed her cup on the wooden table, the delicate clink of ceramic meeting wood emphasizing her next words. "Speculation is a dangerous game," she remarked, her voice steady yet laced with an underlying tension. The notion of a drug deal gone awry in this desolate landscape seemed preposterous.

Autumn acknowledged Rike's point, momentarily forgetting about her own drink. "People crave answers, even if they must fabricate them," she admitted. "Not everyone possesses your sharp investigative skills."

"I may have retired from solving crimes, but I can't ignore my instincts," Rike responded, her posture rigid as she absorbed the palpable unease permeating The Auberge Brew. A subtle incline of her head silently urged Autumn to elaborate.

Autumn edged nearer, her breath barely a whisper. "Rike, listen. Horton's spinning tales to calm the chaos. He's selling this as a lost-in-the-snow wolf strike. Does that sound right?"

Rike's gaze turned flinty, doubt seeping into her words. "Is that right? No, I don't think so."

"Unbelievable, right? A wolf attack," Autumn derided, her head shaking in disbelief as she scanned the swirling snow outside.

"Unlikely, but the chances of any particular scenario are never zero," Rike murmured, her eyes tracking Autumn's towards the wintry dance unfolding outside. The notion dissolved into the blank expanse of snow beyond the windowpane.

"Rike..." Autumn's voice, barely a whisper now, carried a gravity that lingered between them. "How are you holding up? That must have been horrific. I can swing by later, whip up some dinner if you're not feeling up to it."

"No need, thanks. What I stumbled upon was unsettling, but I've faced worse," Rike replied curtly.

A heavy silence settled over their table like a thick blanket of snow, the weight of unspoken fears and suspicions pressing down on them. Autumn hesitated before breaking the quiet, her voice barely above a whisper. "Some people are whispering about it being satanic."

Rike's gaze sharpened, her eyes glinting with a mix of disbelief and frustration. "Ridiculous," she retorted sharply, a faint quirk at the corner of her mouth betraying a hint of sarcasm. "Baseless rumours only serve to taint the investigation," she added firmly, her tone unwavering. "Ignorance breeds fear, no matter where you are. It complicates matters and clouds the truth."

Autumn's brow furrowed with genuine concern, her eyes searching Rike's for any sign of distress. "Does it bother you?" she asked softly, the tension palpable in the air between them.

Rike stood up, a picture of unwavering composure amidst Autumn's worry. Her voice, steady and resolute, cut through the room like a sharp blade. "No, it's not my investigation," she stated firmly, her gaze reflecting a history of facing much darker storms than mere town gossip.

As Rike smoothed the front of her jacket with meticulous precision, Autumn urged her to stay. "I know. Where are you going? Sit down, keep me company a little longer," she implored, reaching out her hand in a gesture reminiscent of coaxing a hesitant child.

Grasping Autumn's hand tightly, Rike eased back in her chair at the Auberge Brew. The café usually offered Rike solace, a haven where the rich aroma of freshly ground coffee intertwined with the soft hum of morning chatter. But not today.

"Did you hear?" Mary Townsend's voice pierced through the silence like a sharp blade, her sudden appearance at Rike and Autumn's table unwelcome yet unavoidable. "It's Kelsey McDaniel. They found her."

"Oh my gosh! Kelsey?"

"Is that official word from the medical examiner?" Rike asked, doubting the identification of such a disfigured body could be performed that quickly.

"It was Kelsey. An angel told me," Mary said firmly.

Autumn reached out, her voice tinged with urgency, "Mary, please." But Mary's fervour surged unrestrained, her words cascading forth with unwavering zeal.

"It's a sign," Mary insisted, her eyes ablaze with a fervent glow that hinted at unyielding faith. "The world is in chaos, and this is a divine message. A punishment from God for her sins."

Rike interjected firmly but calmly, anchoring the escalating debate, "If it is Kelsey and we do not know that, I understand she was kind-hearted, devoted to her community—attending church faithfully and volunteering selflessly. God wouldn't mete out punishment on such a soul."

"Sin touches us all. *You* know that," Mary insisted, her voice carrying a weight that seemed to settle heavily in the room, her long, light brown hair framing her face like a veil. "She faced the consequences of her actions."

"God doesn't deal in such brutality, Mary. That's not how He would operate. If he existed," Rike shot back, the atmosphere crackling with unspoken accusations, wrapping around them like a suffocating fog.

In her periphery, Rike caught sight of Craig Griffith and Warren McDaniel, Kelsey's husband, their expressions frozen masks of sorrow, silently observing the confrontation with haunted gazes.

"Mary, Warren is present. It's best to keep your thoughts to yourself."

"Who could commit such a heinous act, Rike? If not the Divine, then who? A malevolent being, perhaps, under the sway of darkness," Mary's accusation cut through the air, her tone escalating with each word. "You, you found her."

"I found someone and beyond that, I know nothing," Rike's words sliced through the air, her body tensing at the mere suggestion of her involvement.

"Then use those detective skills of yours!"

"Why do you think it was not misadventure? What do you know that none of us do?" Rike knew her words were accusatory, but did not care.

"It was murder!" Mary's accusation pierced the tense atmosphere, her voice dripping with condemnation. "You're only concerned about yourself while a killer lurks in our midst!"

"A moment ago, it was the Devil. And before that, God. Mary, you are a fool," Rike said as she calmly took a sip from her cup.

"An angel told me," Mary said. "An angel!"

The quaint cafe seemed to constrict around Rike, the warm ambiance now suffocating as she rose suddenly. Her chair screeched on the floor, a sharp noise mirroring the turmoil within her. The clash of opinions filled the air, creating a dissonant melody that trailed after her as she attempted to navigate around Mary's presence in her path.

"Angels? You dare talk about angels while a woman lies dead?" Rike's voice thundered, her anger palpable as she leaned forward, her fist crashed onto the wooden table with a resounding thud that reverberated through the room. The sudden impact was like a gunshot, cutting through the hushed atmosphere of Auberge Brew and freezing every onlooker in place. "I dedicated my life to looking death in the face, finding closure beyond 'prayers and thoughts' and now your macabre fascination and misplaced sense of righteousness is poisoning the pot? There are proper authorities equipped to deal with this! No God required." The tension in the air crackled like electricity, transforming the once serene café into a battlefield where unsuspecting bystanders found themselves unwilling participants in a war of words.

"You're a foolish little woman," Rike snapped back, her patience wearing thin. Without another word, she shot a chilling glare that sucked the warmth out of the room before storming out. The coffee shop door shut behind her, and she emerged into the biting cold, snowflakes stinging her face as if nature itself was trying to restrain her with its icy touch.

The drive home stretched on, the desolate road offering a canvas for her inner conflict to unravel, the snow swirling around her truck like a relentless dance. Amidst the flurry of feelings, a sense of purpose emerged, driving her forward. Navigating the roads became a cathartic experience, each twist and turn demanding her full attention and granting temporary reprieve from the burdens she carried from Auberge Brew.

As she distanced herself from the chaos behind her, each mile marker served as a tangible symbol of progress towards peace. The serene hush of the falling snow soothed her frayed nerves, offering a tranquil sanctuary amidst the wintry tempest.

The persistent buzz of her phone faded into the background as Rike swatted it away, shutting out Autumn's name flashing on the screen. The distraction was dangerous. Suddenly, a sharp turn loomed ahead, and Rike to it properly. The truck fishtailed and slipped, triggering a haunting memory from Rike's past. It was as if time had folded in on itself, merging the present danger with a chilling night in Berlin marked by twisted metal and shattered peace.

The visceral recollection hit Rike like a physical blow, her grip on the wheel tightening as sweat prickled her skin despite the biting cold. Each breath felt like shards of glass in her lungs, the car's heater roaring futilely against the frigid air.

Before her mind's eye materialized the twisted metal wreckage, echoing with anguished moans and cries of pain. A vivid memory flashed before her eyes: she was a raw recruit standing at the site of devastation, confronting the harrowing sight of metal melded with human flesh in an unforgiving dance of tragedy and fate.

Her first body was a terrible traffic accident. Though what remained bore little resemblance to anything human.

Rike's head swam with haunting images, her willpower battling to push them aside. "Not now," she muttered through clenched teeth. Gradually, her grip on the wheel loosened, the quivering in her fingers easing as she guided the truck through the hazardous terrain. As she finally steered into her driveway, a wave of relief washed over her. The internal storm had passed, leaving behind an eerie calmness. With a heavy sigh, she turned off the engine, the sudden quietness amplifying the exhaustion that weighed on her. Bone-tired, she trudged through the blanket of snow towards her front door, each step a labourious journey in itself.

The interior of the cabin enveloped Rike in a comforting darkness, the stillness like a gentle embrace. She reached out, searching for the light switch, and when she found it, her eyes blinked against the sudden flood of brightness. Shedding her coat and boots with practiced movements, she hung them meticulously to dry by the crackling fireplace.

In the kitchen, her hand instinctively found a vibrant red apple from the bowl on the counter. Each juicy bite was a burst of sweetness that seemed to reward not just her hunger, but something deeper within her soul as she settled in front of the dancing flames in the iron stove.

Moving towards the bedroom, a simple space dominated by a bed tucked into a corner, Rike allowed herself to collapse onto its welcoming surface without bothering to change. As exhaustion washed over her, pulling her into slumber's grasp like a heavy shroud, she succumbed to its soothing oblivion.

Chapter 12

Five years ago, a nor'easter held the world in its icy grip, commanding the winds to swirl snowflakes in a mesmerizing dance that cloaked everything in a white blanket. From her secluded cabin, Rike Volk emerged, standing resolute in the face of nature's fury. The biting cold nipped at her cheeks, evoking memories of childhood winters when the frost was a welcome companion rather than a foe.

Guided by a beam of light from her headlamp cutting through the blizzard's veil, Rike glided on her cross-country skis along the snow-covered road. A rifle slung over her back silently spoke of her readiness, a symbol of protection in the vast and untamed wilderness where nature held sway with unquestioned authority.

Rike's exhalations transformed into ethereal wisps in the icy atmosphere, vanishing like fleeting spectres amidst the swirling snowfall. The frosty air caressed her skin, sending a shiver down her spine, a sensation that electrified her senses with its crisp embrace. She found solace in the raw intensity of the cold, a familiar partner in this wintry ballet choreographed by seasons gone by. Every movement she made on the snow-covered terrain resonated with a poetic synchronicity to the unforgiving gusts that swept around her.

The beam of Rike's headlamp pierced through the thick darkness, illuminating the snow with a steadfast glow that painted eerie shapes around her. In the midst of near-zero visibility, she relied on more than her sight; every fibre of her being was finely tuned to the storm's chaotic melody, guiding her effortlessly forward. The wind howled like a primal beast, its symphony rising to a thunderous crescendo that harmonized with the rhythm of Rike's resolute steps. With an intimate connection to nature's whims, she glided on skis, etching a lone path across the white landscape.

From the swirling vortex of snow, a silhouette materialized—a white SUV, almost lost in the wintry expanse, stranded on the roadside like a wounded creature in the icy terrain. As Rike drew closer, her headlamp pierced through the darkness, illuminating the vehicle's frost-kissed windows. Through the glass, a faint figure stirred within, veiled by the storm's shadows.

Rike rapped on the window, prompting movement from within. The window hesitantly slid down a crack, releasing a rush of warmth that battled against the biting cold outside. A woman's voice quivered with fear as she implored for help, her plea cutting through the howl of the blizzard. "Please," she begged, "help me! My SUV stopped working."

"Open the passenger door," Rike's command pierced through the howling storm. She unclipped her skis with ease, entering the vehicle's shelter cautiously. The door shut with a heavy thud, enveloping them in a protective bubble amidst the raging tempest.

Inside, a woman on the brink of hysteria awaited, her wide eyes contrasting sharply with her flushed face. "I was sure I'd meet my end out here," she stammered, words rushing out in a jumble of relief and dread. "Thank heavens you found me."

"I'm Rike Volk," she stated firmly, her outstretched hand steady and unwavering, devoid of any hint of the stranger's tremor. "Autumn," came the response, the woman's hands accepting the handshake with a quiver not solely from the cold but also from a surge of adrenaline bordering on desperation. "Autumn Evans." As their eyes met, Autumn's gaze held a blend of gratitude and an undercurrent of something more—perhaps admiration or curiosity—barely registering with the retired detective whose focus remained fixed on the pressing situation before them.

Autumn's words flowed, weaving a tale of vehicular woe that Rike absorbed with the precision of a detective dissecting clues. "The SUV came to a sudden halt. No flashing warning lights, no beeps, no buzzers, nothing, just silence. I called 911, but all they did was transfer me to a tow truck company? I've been waiting for a while, but they're swamped due to the storm," Autumn explained, her voice laced with urgency.

Rike's investigative nature kicked in as she probed further, each question calculated and sharp. "Any unusual sounds before it shut down? Grinding, perhaps?" Her inquiries were delivered with a clinical edge that sliced through Autumn's distress.

Autumn shook her head. "Nothing out of the ordinary. It was purring like a kitten until it simply gave up," she sighed, frustration tainting her words with a hint of panic that lingered in the air between them.

Rike's gaze lingered on the scene, her eyes betraying nothing as she analyzed the predicament before them. While Autumn's admiration for her was palpable, Rike remained steadfastly focused, untouched by the subtle dance of affection attempting to entwine itself into their shared moment.

"Could you please open the hood for me?" Rike's voice was composed, a blend of authority and assurance cutting through the air.

Autumn hesitated, uncertainty colouring her words. "I'm not sure how…"

Without missing a beat, Rike leaned over Autumn with practiced ease, her hand moving with precision to locate and release the latch. "It's right here," she stated matter-of-factly, her touch fleeting yet purposeful against Autumn's leg.

"Oh, aren't you friendly?"

Rike frowned, shook her head, and shrugged. "Yes, friendly to help you out, you mean?"

"I meant…never mind. The hood is open." Autumn's attempt at humour fell flat in the biting cold air, her cheeks tinged with a deeper flush. Rike chose to brush off the awkward joke instead of delving into its meaning. The hood of the SUV had clicked open softly and Rike stepped out, immediately greeted by the blizzard's fierce embrace. Each snowflake felt like a tiny icy pinprick against her skin, a relentless assault from the wintry storm.

Examining the vehicle, she raised the hood, her headlamp casting a beam that sliced through the veil of darkness and swirling snowflakes, revealing the intricate machinery within. With precision, she studied the timing chain, meticulously inspected the alternator cap—every component seemed to be in its rightful place. Everything seemed attached and moveable if it were meant to move.

"Give it a try now," Rike directed as she stepped back into the cozy interior of the car, her gaze flickering to the dashboard to watch for any flicker of activity from the engine indicators.

Autumn's fingers twisted the key in the ignition, a hopeful anticipation filling the air. However, the SUV responded with nothing but a mocking click that echoed in the surrounding stillness. The dashboard lights flickered to life, and the radio crackled softly, but the engine remained stubbornly silent.

"Damn," Rike's voice was barely above a whisper as her eyes shifted to the gas gauge. The needle lay motionless against the barren "E," a simple yet crucial oversight in these unforgiving conditions—one that could easily spiral into disastrous consequences.

"Looks like you've run out of gas," Rike observed, her breath forming misty clouds in the frigid air, the hint of snowflakes swirling around them. Her words carried a subtle reminder of the importance of preparedness without overt criticism.

"Gas?" Autumn's voice held a blend of disbelief and relief, a soft gasp escaping her lips. "I... I didn't even think to check."

"Stay here. I'll take care of it," Rike reassured her, her features stoic and unreadable despite the underlying exasperation at the situation. With a determined set to her jaw, she readied herself to brave the biting cold once more.

As Rike geared up to confront the storm anew, Autumn watched with a newfound admiration blossoming in her eyes for this woman who seemed to emerge unscathed in the relentless tempest—a beacon of security amidst Autumn's oversight.

"You're my saviour, Rike Volk," Autumn whispered, a tremor in her voice betraying the depth of her appreciation for Rike's unwavering support.

Rike's response was curt, a faint grunt accompanying her dismissive remark before she briskly zipped up her thick jacket, preparing to face the biting cold once more. Assuring Autumn of her return with gas, she secured her skis.

Through the side-view mirror, she caught sight of Autumn's lingering gaze—a silent plea for more than just assistance in this harsh environment.

Rike's disapproving gaze lingered on Autumn, silently faulting her for overlooking the harsh realities of winter in this unforgiving northern terrain. The bitter cold held the power to turn even a momentary lapse in preparedness into a fight for survival. It baffled Rike that anyone would dare to venture unprepared into these wilds.

She smoothly glided away from the stranded SUV. In the midst of the blizzard's relentless assault, Rike navigated with practiced ease, the wind's mournful howl serving as a familiar backdrop to her senses.

Upon reaching her cabin, Rike didn't indulge in the comfort of shelter; instead, she headed straight to the storage shed where she stored essential supplies for emergencies. Among them, precious fuel awaited. With practiced precision born of experience, she selected one of the three jerry cans brimming with gasoline, wrapped it with carry straps and effortlessly hoisted it onto her back. Each movement was deliberate and efficient, a testament to her expertise honed over years of navigating treacherous landscapes. Despite the strain on her muscles from the added burden, Rike remained resolute in her purpose.

Returning to the frigid outdoors, Rike's every breath materialized into delicate frost, adorning her eyelashes with tiny, glistening icicles. The freezing air seemed to reach out with icy fingers, nipping at any exposed skin it could find. The sheer disbelief that anyone could end up stranded in such a harsh environment—running on empty amidst a snowstorm—clung to Rike like a persistent shadow, much like the snowflakes stubbornly clinging to her brows. This unforgiving landscape demanded reverence, a lesson that Autumn was painfully learning.

The blizzard raged on, a relentless symphony of wind that whipped around Rike, swirling snowflakes like a flurry of icy arrows. Her figure stood out starkly against the whiteout, determined as she made her way towards the SUV.

Rike's voice, a mere whisper against the howling wind, announced her return to Autumn. From the aging vehicle, Autumn emerged, shivering as she instinctively hugged herself against the biting cold. The pale light from Rike's headlamp cast an otherworldly glow on Autumn's face, revealing a mix of relief and gratitude painted across her features. Attempting to speak her gratitude, Autumn's words were swiftly devoured by the relentless storm that surrounded them.

"Get back inside!" Rike shouted, flummoxed that the woman had stepped out without as much as a coat. Autumn's response was a nod, her communication sparse, particularly in this unforgiving environment. With precise movements, Rike twisted open the jerry can, releasing a pungent gasoline scent that sliced through the biting cold before dissipating swiftly. The fuel cascaded into the tank with a rhythmic glug-glug sound that seemed to blend seamlessly with the howling storm. In the glow of Rike's lamp, Autumn observed intently, her eyes capturing and reflecting back the light, along with a glimmer of hope for their imminent rescue.

"Try starting it now," Rike directed once she had securely fastened the gas cap, her tone firm yet reassuring.

With a cautious twist of the key, the engine grumbled to life, its initial sputters fading into a comforting hum. Autumn couldn't contain her excitement, and burst from the SUV again as she cheered, "You're my gallant rescuer!" Her words carried a hint of playfulness, a touch of flirtation dancing in her tone.

Rike responded with a noncommittal grunt, brushing off any hint of Autumn's charm. Her mind was fixed on the stark practicalities of survival, uninterested in unraveling emotional nuances veiled in frosty layers.

"Put a coat on," Rike chastised, like she was talking to a child.

"Let me but you a coffee, please, as a thank you," Autumn shouted.

"No, thank you. I must go. It is getting late."

"Come into the SUV for a moment. To warm up before you head back," she pleaded. Autumn's insistence continued, her eagerness to show gratitude evident in her persistent offer of coffee. Rike, however, remained resolute in her solitary preferences, already envisioning the comforting warmth awaiting her in the seclusion of her home. Prolonged social interactions held no appeal for her, knowing well the complications they often entailed.

Reluctance tugged at Rike as she uttered, "I should head back now." Her voice carried a subtle impatience, though she treaded carefully to avoid causing any unintended hurt. Autumn, understanding the unspoken, nodded reluctantly before saying, "Another time, then," and driving off into the night. Left alone in the quiet darkness, Rike lingered for a moment, her gaze fixed on the dwindling taillights disappearing into the distance. With a deep breath, she pivoted towards her sanctuary—a welcoming refuge where steaming tea could be had, accompanied by the comforting crackle of the fire that masked the eerie whispers of the wind beyond.

Years had passed, yet the memory of that frigid rendezvous lingered vividly in Rike's mind. It was a moment born from the harsh demands of nature, where fate intertwined their paths. Amidst the relentless dance of snowflakes and the chilling howl of the wind, an extraordinary bond began to form between Rike and Autumn. Unbeknownst to her then, in the unforgiving heart of the blizzard, Rike discovered an unexpected companion in Autumn, their friendship blooming like a rare winter flower.

Chapter 13

The morning air nips at my cheeks as I make my way through the frost-kissed backyard towards the rabbit hutch. The routine of this daily task offers a semblance of normalcy, a distraction from the unsettling thoughts that linger in the corners of my mind. As I approach the hutch, a silent question lingers: why do I tend to these rabbits when they serve no clear purpose? They are neither cherished pets nor destined for our dinner table. Yet, here they are, multiplying under my care. What started as three has now ballooned to ten, though I suspect more have been born than remain within these wooden walls. Sorting them by gender becomes a puzzling task; I attempt to separate the males from the females with uncertain accuracy, lacking expertise in deciphering rabbit anatomy intricacies.

Their fluffy tails twitch with excitement, creating a flurry of anticipation as they sense my approach to their hutch. It's a heartwarming sight to see them all wiggly and joyful, their tiny noses quivering in delight at the promise of a meal. If someone pampered me with breakfast in bed, I'd surely be just as wiggly and delighted!

I've been contemplating the idea of adding rabbits to my diet in the near future. While it may not be a typical choice around here, I know it's a common practice in other parts of the world. Like China. That German lady, Rike Volk. My last conversation with her was unpleasant. She strikes me as someone who might enjoy rabbit meat. It's not meant as a criticism; rather, it's an observation. With her frequent skiing trips and ever-present rifle, she exudes a sense of self-reliance that aligns with such activities. I can almost envision her traversing the snowy landscape with a rabbit slung over her shoulder–a testament to her independence and resourcefulness. I find myself reminiscing about her unexpectedly. Why? Oh yes. It all started with the rabbits, peculiarly enough.

The other day, I came across a captivating dress adorned with rabbit fur. It wasn't the entire garment, just delicate trimmings that exuded elegance. This unique piece was showcased in Maple Sweets, a quaint tourist shop crafted by a talented Indigenous artisan.

The price tag read $899, quite steep, yet its allure was undeniable. Maple Sweets never fails to enchant me; from sugary delights to Sal's renowned homemade spaghetti sauce and Johnny D's intricately carved wooden ducks on display. I take pleasure in leisurely strolling through its aisles, simply indulging my eyes with the array of offerings. There's an innocent joy in these moments of quiet admiration.

The icy sting nips at my cheeks, painting them a rosy hue as I survey the snow-laden driveway. Despite my brother's promise to clear it, the pristine white blanket remains undisturbed. Determination sets in as I make my way to the garage. The familiar silhouette of the snow blower rises up, awaiting its task. As I pull the starter cord, a symphony of mechanical sounds fills the crisp air, harmonizing with the invigorating scent of gasoline and snowflakes. With a steady grip on the handles, I commandeer the roaring machine down the lengthy, winding path, effortlessly carving through the fluffy layers. Each pass reveals the dark asphalt beneath, contrasting sharply with nature's wintry veil. Here's hoping this noisy spectacle rouses my slumbering sibling from his cozy den!

Every time I guide the snow blower through the thick layers of snow, it unleashes billows of fine powder that dance and twirl in the frigid air. The mechanical hum fills my ears, overpowering the tranquil winter stillness that surrounds me. There's a rush of excitement that courses through me as I tackle nature's wintry chaos using the marvels of modern technology. As I push forward, each movement strains my muscles, the machine pressing down on me like a steadfast companion as I carve a determined trail through the snowy expanse.

As I engage in the rhythmic dance with the roaring engine and the soothing hum of the blower, my thoughts meander to sun-kissed memories of leisurely afternoons basking in warmth, yearning for the gentle embrace of spring. The whimsical nature of rabbits aligns with the essence of spring. Yet, amidst this reverie, I anchor myself to the present task at hand—the relentless snow blower's drone serving as a grounding force. Despite each gust of wind threatening to impede my progress, my resolve remains unwavering as I persist in my quest to overcome winter's unyielding grasp.

Hours slip away unnoticed, a hazy blend of sun rising higher above me as I wage war against the relentless winter. The biting cold creeps through my gloves, mingling with the acrid fumes that assault my senses. Yet, amidst these adversities, a deep contentment unfurls with every inch of cleared path. At last, the driveway emerges, a tangible victory over nature's icy grasp and a tribute to the modern marvels aiding my labour. As the engine hums its final tune and falls silent, I rest against the handles, drawing in sharp breaths to fill my lungs and relishing in the serene majesty of the snow-draped scenery. In this tranquil moment, surrounded by glistening white expanses under the sun's gentle caress, I find myself enveloped in a wordless awe at nature's quiet magnificence.

I returned the blower to the garage, the metallic clinks echoing in the quiet morning. As I pulled down and locked the door, a sudden impact sent me hurtling forward, crashing face-first into the unforgiving wooden post on the patio. Pain exploded through my skull, a white-hot burst of agony that stole my breath. Struggling to speak, my voice caught in my throat as shock paralyzed me. Before I could gather my senses, another force slammed me back into the post with bone-jarring intensity. The world spun around me, distorted and distant, as if seen through a veil of chaos. A feeble attempt at sound escaped my lips, drowned out by the deafening ringing that enveloped everything around me.

That sinewy arm coiled around my neck, squeezing like a vice. I struggled against it, my hands clawing desperately, but it held firm, cutting off my breath. A stifled cough escaped me as a chilling thought pierced through the fear—who would tend to the rabbits now?

Chapter 14

The early morning sky blushed with delicate shades of lavender and rose, casting a tranquil backdrop for the intricate lace-like patterns of the bare branches in the northern Ontario forest. Rike's exhalations materialized into fleeting clouds, dissipating like whispers as she gracefully maneuvered through the snow. The rhythmic hiss of her skis against the snow sang a melody of practiced expertise, each pole plant and weight shift executed with meticulous precision, transforming her cross-country skiing into a harmonious waltz with the winter landscape.

As Rike skied through the silent woods, a ghostly whisper of the past brushed against her thoughts. *Adlergestell* echoed in her mind, a street lined with secrets and shadows she wished she could forget. Along the edge of those woods, where the trees stood sentinel over chilling truths, five bodies had been found over two years. Women whose stories were etched into the very fabric of the landscape. The unresolved whispers of the dead cast a pall over her mind. Yet, as the wind murmured through the branches, carrying echoes of long-lost secrets, Rike pushed forward, the present reclaiming her focus with each glide through the snow.

A profound stillness blanketed the landscape, where the only sounds that dared to break through were the soft groans of frosty timber and the gentle rustle of pine needles caressing each other. Rike, a seasoned veteran of winter pursuits, where quietness often carried the weightiest messages, tuned in to the delicate dialect of nature. In these moments of unity with the untamed surroundings, she sought solace from the chaos of human transgressions.

In her periphery, a sudden motion snagged Rike's attention—a distinct wolf, its fur a mosaic of silvery greys and whites, gliding with fluid elegance amidst the foliage. Rather than quickening, her heart steadied its rhythm; she interpreted the animal's presence as a symbol of tranquillity reigning over this remote enclave. "Exquisite," she breathed out, watching as her breath billowed and dispersed in the icy atmosphere. The wolf paused, its amber gaze locking onto hers in an unspoken exchange before melding into the shadows like a fleeting apparition among the trees.

Skiing out of the sheltering arms of the dense forest, Rike's skis glided effortlessly along the snowy path that ran parallel to the road. Despite the biting cold that painted her cheeks with frosty kisses and nipped at the small strip of skin between her cap and scarf, she found solace in its sharp touch, a poignant reminder of vitality coursing through her veins. Each inhale felt like a rush of icy crystals filling her lungs, creating a symphony of crackling sensations that awakened every sinew in her body.

The peaceful morning shattered when the flashing blue and red lights of two police cruisers pierced through the dawn's gentle glow, casting an ominous shadow over Rike's driveway. She rolled her eyes, wondering whether it was Craig Griffith or the Cumming twins who had run a foul on her property. With sharp eyes scanning the vehicles, she sought answers in their silent yet imposing presence.

Rike's skis disengaged with a sharp click, echoing through the silent snow-covered landscape. As she trudged towards her driveway, each step created a loud crunch that seemed to reverberate in the frosty air. The two officers, Horton and a chubby second officer, unknown to her, stood rigid, their gazes locked on her advancing form. Wheezes escaped the unknown officer's lips, forming misty clouds that clung to his glasses like ghostly tendrils as he hugged his bulky frame for warmth.

"Morning, Rike," Officer Horton greeted, his tone striving for nonchalance but failing to conceal the palpable unease simmering beneath the surface. "Rike Volk, this is Officer Juno."

Rike acknowledged them with a brisk nod, her demeanour a blend of politeness and a seasoned vigilance honed by years spent amidst crime scenes and their aftermaths. The weight of their gazes bore into her, an unwelcome intrusion that set her nerves on edge. A silent exchange passed between the officers, their eyes darting between each other before flicking away, hinting at unspoken truths hanging heavily in the frigid atmosphere.

"Excuse me, why are you obstructing my driveway?" Rike's tone sliced through the air, accustomed to swift clarity. Without waiting for a response, her eyes locked onto it—a looming silhouette sprawled just beyond their parked cars. A jolt of fear gripped her, transporting her back to the shadowed alleys of Berlin, where death lurked around every corner. Brushing past Officers Horton and Juno, Rike advanced toward the looming figure, her detective instincts snapping into focus.

"Hold on there!" Officer Juno shouted, though he did not move to stop her.

As she drew closer, the shape came into focus—a chilling stillness that could only belong to a lifeless form. In her driveway, a mere twenty feet from the roadside, a woman lay crumpled on the icy gravel. Words froze in Rike's throat as she struggled to comprehend the grim scene before her.

"Good Lord," Rike finally choked, her sharp gaze dissecting the gruesome sight before her, a chilling dread coiling in her stomach. "Was it a hit-and-run?"

"No," Horton responded gravely, his attention fixed on the lifeless form. "Step back."

"How far?" Rike pressed.

"There, by the cars," Officer Horton directed tersely.

"What in God's name happened here?" Rike demanded, her initial shock morphing into a surge of frustration and fury. The tranquil seclusion she had craved in this remote corner of Ontario now shattered like fragile ice beneath her skis.

The officers shared a significant glance, hinting at unsettling revelations to come. Horton advanced, his expression etched with professional remorse.

"Rike, we need to talk." The voice cut through the crisp air, pulling Rike's attention away from the snowy landscape that surrounded her.

"Where are you coming from?" Officer Juno asked, his round face flushed with cold. His gloved hand reached out, a gesture of formality in the frosty morning. Glasses fogged and sliding down his nose emphasized his struggle with asthma as he spoke.

"Morning ski routine," she responded sharply, meeting his handshake firmly.

His breath visible in the icy air, Officer Juno pressed on, "Anything unusual on your ski today?"

Rike's gaze pierced through him, searching for comprehension in his eyes but finding none. "Just a wolf by the trees," she disclosed coolly. "Majestic creature. Nothing more."

Officer Juno's pen scratched hurriedly across the paper, his uneasy gaze darting towards the lifeless body. A sudden gust of wind howled through the trees, whipping up a flurry of snow that lashed against Rike's cheeks like icy needles. The crimson stain on the snow, the contorted figure sprawled before her—it all resonated too deeply, mirroring Kelsey McDaniel's body.

Officer Horton, a looming presence nearby, inched forward. "The victim... preliminary identification points to Mary Townsend," he disclosed.

"Mary?" The news struck Rike like a lightning bolt, disbelief crashing over her at the thought of someone like Mary becoming the focal point of such savagery. And savage it was. This was no death by misadventure. This was violence taking another soul. Mary may have had her flaws, but nothing she'd done warranted this level of brutality.

Rike's voice faltered, her gaze fixated on the harrowing scene before her. The woman's once delicate features were now distorted, grotesquely swollen, making it nearly impossible to identify her except for the familiar cascade of light brown hair that cruelly framed the brutality inflicted upon her face. "How can you be certain it's her?" Rike's words sliced through the chilling air, a mix of disbelief and horror gripping her as she struggled to connect this nightmarish sight with the memory of Mary Townsend she held in her mind.

Officer Horton pointed his finger honing in on the glint of a silver Medic Alert bracelet adorning the pale wrist, his tone devoid of emotion as he drew attention to it. Rike's reaction was immediate, a quiet curse slipping past her lips at the grim realization that once again, death had intruded upon her solitude. The icy tendrils of fate seemed to tighten around her as she grappled with the unnerving prospect of being entangled in yet another end to life. Despite her lack of any apparent ties to the unfolding tragedy, she found herself standing resolute in the face of the biting wind that carried whispers of secrets through the stark trees, each gust echoing the chilling touch of both nature's cold embrace and the ominous circumstances looming ahead.

Shaking her head vigorously, she fought to banish the haunting image, beads of sweat forming on her brow in defiance of the icy surroundings. With hands betraying a subtle tremble, she delved into her jacket pocket and extracted her phone. Each click of the camera intensified the urgency pulsing through her veins. This wasn't just about documentation; it was a lifeline to her past, a tether to a world she thought she had left behind.

Officer Juno's bark shattered the icy silence, his laboured breaths billowing out in white puffs as he lunged towards her. "Hands off that camera!" he roared, closing in to seize the device.

Rike danced aside, her senses on high alert, muscles responding to a long-forgotten rhythm of command and control.

In a swift and practiced motion, she secured her phone out of his reach, a glint of defiance in her eyes. The confrontation crackled with tension, each heartbeat marking a battle for power and autonomy in the face of authority.

"Give me the phone," Juno demanded.

"Give me a search warrant," she declared firmly, locking eyes with Juno, who appeared flustered. "You'll need one if you want to proceed with this."

"Fine," Juno retorted, adjusting his glasses in a rush of embarrassment. "You're coming with me to the station, Ms. Volk. We need to ask you some questions. And we don't need your phone; we have our own evidence."

"Did you take photos?" Rike inquired sharply.

"No. You did, didn't you Horton?" Juno asked.

"Not me. I, uh..." Officer Horton said.

Without wasting another breath on the incompetent exchange, Rike strode towards Horton's idling cruiser. The red and blue lights danced ominously on the snow as she settled into the backseat. In the distance, the arrival of the medical examiner signalled the grim reality of death invading her once peaceful abode. She waited impatiently as Officer Horton came over to let her into the back seat.

Horton settled into the driver's seat, his eyes briefly meeting Rike's in the reflection of the rearview mirror. "Looks like we're in for quite a storm," he observed as the wipers laboured tirelessly to clear the snowflakes cascading from the darkened sky. The words hung in the air, a feeble attempt at conversation that barely masked the tension enveloping them during their brisk journey to the station.

The snowy scenery raced past Rike's vision, the once pure white now tainted by the day's unsettling turn of events. Though her thoughts were a whirlwind, she maintained a calm exterior. The situation had escalated beyond just seeing a crime scene; it now involved safeguarding herself from the incompetent authorities meant to take control and find the truth.

Inside the cramped confines of Berna's makeshift police station, Officer Horton carefully poured coffee into two Styrofoam cups, his movements betraying an underlying tension. The bitter aroma of the coffee mingled with the faint scent of antiseptic and old paperwork that hung in the air. Seated at a metal table firmly anchored to the floor, Rike sat upright and tense, her breath visible in the poorly heated room.

"Would you like it black?" Horton inquired, without lifting his gaze from the steaming pot.

"Yes, thank you," Rike acknowledged, her voice crisp as she took the cup from him. The faint quiver in his hand didn't escape her notice. Outside, the storm raged, its fierce howls creating a chilling backdrop to their tense quiet. As Horton settled into the chair across from her, the harsh scrape of metal against linoleum sent a shiver down Rike's spine.

Horton's eyes bore into Rike, his voice cautious yet insistent as he broached the sensitive topic. "Kelsey McDaniel," he started, each word deliberate, "you stumbled upon her body. And now, Mary Townsend is discovered deceased in your front yard."

Rike's jaw clenched, her stare piercing and resolute. "I came across Kelsey while trekking," she retorted sharply, her breath visible in the frigid air. "And this morning... I was skiing. Are you suggesting something different?"

"Well," Horton murmured under his breath, almost as if thinking aloud. "Always solitary, always the one to chance upon such grim scenes."

"Are you implying I had a hand in this?" Rike's disbelief dripped with fury, her voice edged with indignation. "That notion is preposterous. How did you know to come to my and find Mary?"

Horton's voice remained steady as he explained, "Received an anonymous tip about a body on your property. You can't see it from the road. They knew it was there. But the caller hung up before providing more information."

Rike shot back, her tone sharp with disbelief, "I was out skiing this morning like any other day. Whoever phoned in isn't connected to me. Her death is not my doing."

Horton's gaze bore into Rike with a hint of doubt. "This does raise some questions," he remarked, his tone laced with skepticism.

"Sometimes things aren't what they seem," Rike shot back, her composure starting to fray. "You might benefit from a seasoned hand guiding you through this. After all, the medical examiner hasn't confirmed Kelsey or Mary as homicide victims yet, have they?"

Admitting grudgingly, Horton responded, "No, not officially. But the circumstances are troubling."

"They are troubling. So, focus on the facts," Rike interjected sharply, her impatience seeping through. "Save your implications for another time."

The mobile home creaked under the force of the wind outside, mirroring the unrest within. Across from Rike, Horton's gaze lingered on her, the forgotten coffee cooling between them. It was as though he was truly seeing her for the first time, his features drained of colour. "I'll find the truth," Horton admitted at last, his voice heavy with the weight of the situation. Despite years spent as a small-town officer content with minor infractions and simple cases, this new challenge demanded more than he had ever faced before.

"This situation is unfathomable. I've dealt with arresting Bob Garret for shooting his wife, but never have I encountered two deaths occurring in such proximity and seemingly without motive." Rike rose from her seat with a suddenness that caused her chair to grate loudly against the cold linoleum floor. Officer Horton involuntarily twitched at the abrupt motion, yet Rike's focus was elsewhere as she strode purposefully towards the exit.

"I refuse to be a pawn in your inadequacy." With two deceased women–one discovered by Rike's own hands and another within the confines of her property–the ominous link loomed, casting a shadow of unease.

Horton fidgeted, the worn chair protesting beneath his shifting weight as discomfort radiated from him. "Ms. Volk, sit back down" he started tentatively, seeking solid ground amidst the swirling uncertainties, "I've been exploring various hypotheses regarding these fatalities."

Rike's unwavering gaze bore into Horton, slowly returning to the table. "Wild animal predation," Horton cautiously suggested. "It's a theory we must consider. An aggressive or disturbed wild bear in these parts could have been behind the incidents."

Rike's brow furrowed, her skepticism palpable. "A wild bear?" she prodded, arms defensively folded across her chest.

"Or perhaps it was misadventure, like we thought with Kelsey," Horton offered hesitantly. "Both victims might have met their end due to some unfortunate accident. Like Mary taking a fall and suffering fatal injuries."

Rike leaned in slightly, her voice sharp with suspicion. "Was there any evidence of head trauma?"

"Yes. Multiple blows, I think. Okay, maybe not that. But," Horton hesitated slightly, his voice tinged with uncertainty, "there's the slim chance of ritualistic elements or a cult connection. The crime scenes... they're peculiar. It could suggest a sinister ceremony or a sequence of events masterminded by individuals with a hidden motive, possibly linked to supernatural or occult practices."

Rike's expression turned steely; worry etched deep lines on her face as she absorbed Horton's baseless theories. Leaning in, her gaze bore into Horton's eyes. "Officer Horton, that's not the case. You're veering off course."

"What's your theory then?" Horton's voice held a blend of defiance and desperation, his gaze locking onto Rike.

Rike knew she should not provide a theory of either case: if she was wrong, she would send the poor officer in the wrong direction. If she was right, she would look guilty. "My advice? Seek assistance. This situation surpasses your expertise," she asserted firmly.

Horton's face flickered between defensiveness and contemplation. A part of him grappled with the notion that Rike, the outsider with a haunting past in law enforcement, might be orchestrating a dark scheme amidst the chaos, just to humiliate him.

"Neither Kelsey nor Mary have been officially declared murdered," Rike reiterated, her words cutting through the crisp, icy air that seeped into the room. "The medical examiner will determine the cause and manner of their deaths. Until then, theories do more harm than good."

Horton, his authority wavering, struggled to hold his ground. "Your presence at both scenes can't be mere chance."

"Circumstance doesn't equate to guilt," Rike shot back, her gaze unwavering. "If I were you, I'd bring in reinforcements. But not just anyone—nit Officer Juno. The best you can find."

"Are you suggesting I'm incapable of handling this?" Horton's pride flared, his voice tinged with defensiveness.

"Truth can be a bitter pill to swallow, Officer," Rike's voice cut through the air, her expression an unreadable mask of determination. "But in this case–these cases–clarity is more crucial than preserving anyone's feelings."

Officer Horton reluctantly reached for the phone. His fingers moved deliberately across the dial pad, each number echoing in the heavy silence of the room. Seated across from him, Rike leaned back in her chair, her arms folded as she watched his every move with a piercing gaze.

"This is Officer Horton calling from Berna local police," his words were measured, yet beneath the surface lay a subtle tremor betraying his unease. "We have a pressing matter at hand—two bodies discovered under suspicious circumstances. We urgently require the expertise of a seasoned homicide detective to assist us."

Rike's focus sharpened, capturing the faint static of the reply at the other end. Horton's voice, precise and businesslike, relayed more information, each word measured. She detected a subtle change in his mannerism; the weight of their situation reflected in the tightness of his jaw and the crease between his brows.

Horton's hand lowered the phone, his gaze meeting Rike's with a blend of hesitation and a hint of admiration. "The RCMP is sending assistance," he informed her tersely.

"You are a smart man," Rike replied coolly, her tone stripped of any hint of satisfaction. "It takes courage to admit when you need help. Shows character."

Studying her intently for a beat, Horton eventually nodded in reluctant agreement. With a deliberate cough, he reclaimed his authoritative demeanour.

"While I wait for the detective to here, I need you to stay in Berna," he stated firmly, his eyes piercing into Rike's.

A bitter chuckle slipped past her lips, the sound echoing oddly in the stark, temporary police setup. "I'm not planning on fleeing, Officer Horton. But I don't live in Berna. Once the scene is cleared, I would like to go home." Horton's interest sparked, but he restrained himself from delving further.

Rike rose from her chair, a fluid motion that contrasted sharply with the tension in the room. "In Berlin, where I cut my teeth," she began, her voice sharp and cutting through the air, "your current methods would have landed you directing traffic quicker than a blink." Officer Horton's jaw clenched at the criticism.

"Can I leave now?" Rike's question hung in the air as she made her way purposefully towards the door.

"Stay away until Officer Juno clears the scene. But, yes," Horton replied sternly, his eyes fixed on Rike. "Just... make sure you're reachable for questioning."

"Absolutely," Rike responded with a nod, swiftly sliding into her coat, bracing herself for the chilling embrace of the storm outside. Her thoughts swirled with the morning's disturbing find and the unsettling exchange with Horton.

Chapter 15

A bitter gust swept through the desolate streets of Saint Berna Aux Étranger, carrying with it a sharp tang of pine and snow that clung to Rike Volk's skin like a chilling reminder of her solitude. Officer Horton's stern demands echoed hollowly against the backdrop of the looming mountains, but to Rike, the vast expanse of untouched snow whispered promises of escape as she pondered slipping away unnoticed into the unforgiving wilderness beyond.

The warmth of the police station faded behind her, replaced by the chilling uncertainty of her surroundings. Trudging through the swirling snow, Rike regretted not having her truck; now she had to rely on Autumn for a ride.

The Auberge Brew, a cozy refuge amidst the relentless cold, enveloped Rike in its embrace. Seated near the frosted window, she clutched a delicate porcelain cup filled with fragrant chamomile tea, relishing how its heat thawed her icy core. Amidst the murmured exchanges that filled the café, an unspoken unease lingered like static in the air. Every subtle movement around her felt amplified—heads swiveled discreetly in her direction before jerking away, and fleeting gazes locked with hers, only to flee like startled rabbits into the shadows.

Two elderly men, their weathered faces etched with deep lines from years of harsh winters, huddled together in thick, hand-knit scarves and cozy woolen hats at a nearby table. Their murmurs barely rose above the soft hum of the café, shrouded in an air of secrecy. Occasionally, they shot furtive glances towards Rike, their eyes brimming with a mix of apprehension and suspicion. As Rike raised the steaming cup of tea to her lips, the fragrant blend of herbs enveloped her senses like a shield against their unspoken accusations.

The snowy landscape outside painted a scene of relentless white, with snowflakes hurling themselves at the café windows like miniature projectiles. Amidst the storm's fury, Rike's eyes honed in on a lone figure bracing against the elements, unmistakably the meth addict she had seen just days before. His usual partner was conspicuously absent, stirring a twinge of concern within Rike. In such brutal conditions, the biting cold held the power to swiftly turn deadly.

The café fell silent for a second as the door swung open, unleashing a blast of icy wind and snow that twirled into the room. Autumn Evans entered, her cheeks tinged pink from the cold, a stark contrast against the wintry backdrop. Spotting Rike, her eyes lit up, breaking into a radiant smile.

"Rike!" Her voice cut through the chilled air, and she strode over, flicking off snowflakes from her coat. The patrons stole glances at their reunion. Rike got up to meet her, and they locked in a swift embrace, a fleeting moment.

Autumn chuckled softly, her breath visible in the chilly air as she settled into the chair opposite Rike. Ordering a steaming hot chocolate from the server, she fixed her gaze on Rike, her features transitioning to a more sombre expression.

"Rike, brace yourself," Autumn's voice dropped to a whisper, drawing closer. "The town's abuzz with rumours linking you to Mary Townsend's death. It's absurd, but in these close-knit communities, idle talk can quickly turn into damning accusations."

The biting words pierced Rike's tough exterior, much like the relentless wind outside that clawed at the windows. She sensed the room's collective gaze shift towards her, their hidden stares peering over newspapers and above steaming mugs. A fleeting vulnerability pricked at her, but she squashed it down swiftly, locking eyes with Autumn whose expression held a mix of worry and affection.

"Let them chatter," Rike retorted, her tone unwavering. "The truth always surfaces in the end."

Autumn's nod was hesitant, the creases around her eyes deepening with worry. "I believe in your innocence, Rike. But as long as doubts linger, tongues will wag..." Her voice trailed off, a sombre gesture towards the outside world.

"Let them gossip up a storm," Rike declared firmly, lifting her teacup to her lips. The warmth of the liquid offered a brief respite from the icy tendrils of loneliness clawing at her heart.

The coffee shop door creaked open, a blast of frigid air sneaking in to nip at Rike's exposed neck. She instinctively clutched her mug, the warmth seeping through her fingers. Autumn sat opposite her, delicately blowing on her tea as wisps of steam danced around her fogged-up glasses.

"Mary cornering you here at the Auberge was odd," Autumn remarked, casting a wary glance around the sparsely populated cafe. "Talking about Kelsey McDaniel's death, and then…"

Rike's muscles coiled with tension. "I'd prefer not to delve into it," she stated firmly.

Autumn fixed her gaze on Rike, her eyes magnified through the lenses of her spectacles. "She thought it was fate, Kelsey passing away so young," she probed. "And now Mary… do you see that as some kind of higher power at work too?"

Rike snorted dismissively. "Absolutely not."

"But what about your faith?" Autumn pressed. "Do you have any belief in God?"

The tension crackled in the air, heavy with the bitter aroma of coffee. Rike's sigh was a gust of frustration as she carefully placed her mug on the table, meeting her friend's intense stare head-on. "I'm an atheist," she stated firmly, her words cutting through the charged silence like a knife through butter. "My beliefs are rooted in reason, evidence, and critical thinking, not in gods or supernatural entities." Each word carried weight, echoing in the room where ears strained to catch every syllable. Regret gnawed at her insides; she knew she had just given them another reason to despise her.

Autumn's demeanour shifted, a fleeting shadow casting a veil over her features—was it disappointment, hurt? Rike struggled to decipher the emotions playing on Autumn's face. The air grew heavy with unspoken words. The only sounds punctuating the silence were the sharp hiss of the espresso machine and the clatter of mugs in the background. Rike clutched her cup tighter, seeking solace in its warmth against the biting cold seeping through the frosty windows, mirroring her own melancholy. It was evident that their exchange had created a chasm between them, one that even the steaming beverages couldn't bridge.

Autumn's posture slouched, her gaze fixated on the table before her. Concern etched lines on Rike's forehead as she observed her friend's palpable distress.

"What's troubling you, Autumn?" Rike's voice was soft, her concern evident in the furrow of her brow. Autumn remained silent, her lips forming a tight line as she stared down at the remnants of her latte. It was as though the faint patterns in the foam held all the answers she sought.

Rike leaned in, her hand gently resting on Autumn's arm, a silent reassurance. "Please," she urged, her tone gentle yet insistent. "You can talk to me. I'm here for you. If I've upset you in any way, I want to know."

With a heavy exhale, Autumn delved into her purse and retrieved a delicate velvet box typically reserved for precious jewellery. Placing it deliberately on the table between them, a surge of anticipation rippled through Rike, quickening her pulse.

Autumn opened the jewellery box, revealing a delicate gold chain intricately woven with a simple cross pendant that caught the dim light of the room, its luster untarnished and gleaming against the backdrop of deep shadows. "I got this for you," Autumn murmured softly. Her gaze darted up to meet Rike's, hazel eyes shimmering with a mix of uncertainty and hope. "I understand your beliefs, but... could you wear it? Just for me?"

Rike hesitated, her emotions in turmoil. The necklace exuded elegance, yet the weight of significance carried by the cross left her grappling with inner conflict. Her hand hovered over the box, suspended in indecision. "Why, Autumn? I don't understand." Rike's breath misted in the cold air, her eyes searching Autumn's face for answers.

"So I know you're safe," Autumn's voice was barely audible, a tremor betraying her usual composure. She fought to steady her voice, the words hanging between them like frost-laden branches. "Please, Rike."

Rike felt a pang in her chest at the raw vulnerability in Autumn's plea. It was a side of her friend she had never seen before, a crack in the facade that left Rike feeling exposed to emotions she wasn't ready to confront.

"Autumn, I..." Rike's voice faltered. She grappled with conflicting sentiments, gratitude warring with unease as silence settled around them.

Autumn's hand shot out before Rike could object further, her fingers deftly seizing the necklace. A pleased grin lit up Autumn's face as she drew near, her breath brushing warmly over Rike's cheek. "Allow me," she murmured, her tone gentle yet insistent. With surprising ease, she secured the clasp around Rike's neck, the fine chain draping softly against Rike's skin.

Rike's muscles tensed involuntarily as Autumn's fingers brushed against her skin, a subtle reaction that didn't escape her friend's notice. Ignoring Rike's discomfort, Autumn fixated on the necklace she had just placed around Rike's neck. "There!" Autumn declared with unwavering certainty, her eyes gleaming with a mix of determination and satisfaction as she leaned back to assess her gift. "This will protect you. It suits you perfectly, Rike."

Rike's forced smile strained against her unease, her fingers tracing the intricate design of the cross pendant. She knew she had to wear it now, a gesture to soothe Autumn's emotions. Yet, as the golden symbol lay cold against her skin, a shiver of discomfort ran through her.

She drank her tea quickly, letting Autumn fill the air with light and meaningless chatter. With little ado, she said her drink was gone, and it was time to leave.

The ride back was silent except for the crunching snow under Autumn's Jeep tires. The headlights pierced the dimming twilight, illuminating Rike's cabin in the secluded wilderness. With a soft hum, the engine halted, leaving only the ticking of cooling metal in the frosty air. Autumn turned to Rike, her eyes a mix of worry and solidarity.

"If you need anything," Autumn's voice cut through the tension, leaning in slightly towards Rike, "anything at all, just call me. Promise?"

Rike's nod was firm, her expression resolute as she ventured into the chilly evening air. She observed Autumn's departure before turning back to her abode–a bastion of seclusion she relished. Inside the cozy cabin, Rike dined on a simple meal, her actions mechanical, the taste of the food lost on her numb senses. Amidst the silence, the ticking of the clock filled the space, a constant reminder of time slipping away like snow melting outside her window. When night fell, she succumbed to slumber's grasp, her dreams turbulent and unsettling.

With the break of dawn casting a gentle glow of amber and rose across the sky, Rike expertly fastened her skis, the pristine snow beneath them responding effortlessly to her touch. The forest embraced her like a majestic sanctuary, towering pines standing guard with snow-laden branches that appeared to murmur hidden tales to any who stopped to heed their whispers.

As the day progressed, Rike smoothly glided through time, the sun casting long shadows that danced around her. With a sense of purpose, she grasped the axe in her weathered hands, each swing a symphony of power and precision. The logs succumbed to her expertise, releasing the rich aroma of pine that mingled with the cold air like a sweet offering. The woodpile grew steadily beside her, mirroring the growing sense of pride swelling in her chest; a primal joy stemming not just from her physical labour but from the reassurance that she was crafting comfort and safety for herself in this remote winter haven.

Nightfall draped the kitchen in a tapestry of scents, embracing Rike as she expertly worked dough, each fold and press a symphony of precision. The oven radiated warmth, painting her cheeks with a rosy hue as the loaf transformed inside, its surface turning into a perfect golden armour around the tender core. Dinner unfolded in tranquil solitude, the ritual of breaking bread a moment both ordinary and sacred.

As darkness claimed the sky outside, Rike yielded once more to the siren song of sleep, her body lulled by the day's endeavours into a peaceful surrender to dreams.

Chapter 16

After two days of relentless snowfall, the small airport designed for turboprop aircraft emerged from the storm's icy grip. The airfield, typically a hive of activity, now lay silent and haunting beneath a thick veil of snow. Ground crew members clad in vibrant orange vests toiled diligently to clear pathways, their exhalations crystallizing into wispy clouds in the biting cold. The planes, usually bustling with life, rested serenely against the canvas of the unforgiving winter sky, their metallic bodies casting a subtle sheen under the soft glow of the sun timidly peeking through dense grey clouds.

The elegant Beechcraft King emerged in the sky, its polished metal exterior catching the winter sunlight and casting a radiant glow. Drifting down with a gentle hum that resonated through the chilly atmosphere, the aircraft descended gracefully above the snow-covered terrain, its wings slicing effortlessly through the frosty air. Executing precise maneuvers, it appeared to pirouette before executing a flawless landing on the freshly plowed airstrip. Officer Horton stood on the cold tarmac, his exhalations forming ethereal wisps in his excitement, captivated by every nuance of the plane's descent with eager anticipation.

The Beechcraft glided effortlessly towards the terminal. As its engines hummed in descent, the once roaring noise gradually ebbed away, prompting a delicate flurry of snowflakes to fly around its sturdy landing gear. Amidst the wintry hush, a lone airport attendant, also swathed in a vibrant neon orange jacket, moved towards the aircraft. He pulled along a clattering set of metal stairs that chimed softly in harmony with his movements.

Officer Horton's gaze remained fixed on the unfolding scene before him, captivated by each deliberate motion as the door of the Beechcraft groaned open, unveiling a tantalizing peek into the cozy interior suffused with a gentle, inviting glow.

RCMP Detective Ada O'Neill descended from the aircraft, a vision of confidence amidst the snowscape. Her sleek, dark locks framed a face etched with sharp features and eyes that gleamed with unwavering focus. Clad in a parka, Ada's formidable aura radiated a captivating mix of power and grace as she set foot on the frosty airstrip. Officer Horton stood as a sturdy figure amidst the glistening expanse of white, offering a respectful nod of welcome. "Detective O'Neill," he greeted with crisp precision.

"Officer Horton," Ada's voice, laced with authority yet tinged with a touch of warmth, sliced through the tension. "Nice to meet you."

"Detective O'Neill, your presence is crucial," Horton acknowledged, his posture rigid, as if trying to assert dominance unconsciously.

"Please, call me Ada. Shall we get out of the weather?"

"Yes, of course," Officer Horton said as he motioned for her to follow him to his truck. "I appreciate you coming in."

Officer Horton led Ada towards the idling squad car, their steps creating a rhythmic crunch on the snow, each sound reverberating through the crisp, frigid air. Ada's keen eyes scanned their desolate surroundings, taking in the haunting tranquillity that draped over them like a weighty veil. In the vast silence of the wintry panorama, a solitary crow's caw pierced through, shattering the oppressive stillness that clung to the landscape like a ghostly presence.

Ada slipped into the passenger side of the truck as Horton brought the beast to life.

"Nothing new since the latest victim near Rike Volk's land," he informed, worry etching lines on his forehead.

Ada's eyes honed in sharply. "Have you established a link between deaths?"

Horton's expression darkened. "Not yet. But it's uncomfortably close. The RCMP had to be called in."

"You made the right call." Ada's voice cut through the crisp winter air, her words tinged with a hint of wryness. The vast expanse of the snow-clad landscape unfolded before them, a serene canvas of pure white that sparkled in the soft winter sunlight. Towering evergreen trees, their boughs heavy with snow, stood sentinel along the winding path, each branch adorned with shimmering frost that caught the light in a mesmerizing dance. En route to Berna, the occasional rumble of massive trucks passing by left behind intricate patterns etched into the icy road, adding a dynamic touch to the tranquil scenery.

As they drew closer to Berna, Ada's sharp gaze absorbed the charming town cradled within the snowy embrace. Each building wore a delicate veil of glistening snow, enhancing its cozy allure. Wisps of smoke meandered from chimneys, dancing with the icy air, creating an ethereal scene under the sombre clouds that draped the sky in a muted palette. Beyond its postcard-worthy visage, Ada detected a subtle tension lingering in the air, whispering of hidden mysteries veiled by Berna's tranquil exterior.

In the confines of the dimly lit police station, Ada and Horton found themselves seated at opposite ends of a weathered wooden table, its surface bearing the marks of time and countless investigations. The air was saturated with the lingering scent of burnt coffee, its bitter notes mingling with the silent tension that hung between them. Overhead, the harsh fluorescent lights flickered erratically, casting sharp shadows that played upon Ada's striking features and Horton's weathered countenance. Within this space, charged with unspoken inquiries and imminent truths, a palpable sense of disquiet settled like a shroud over the sterile walls, creating an atmosphere thick with anticipation and apprehension.

Horton's voice quivered, the cold winter air carrying his urgent words that depicted the grim scene of Kelsey McDaniel's death and Mary Townsend's tragic fate. "The sight of Kelsey's body sent shivers down my spine," he admitted, visibly shaken by the unfolding tragedies. Ada, her gaze sharp as a hawk's talon, locked eyes with Horton without a trace of uncertainty. "And Mary was callously discarded at the roadside. Like garbage."

"You were acquainted with both victims?" Ada inquired as they sat in silence at the station. Horton nodded solemnly. "I am familiar with most people around here."

"What about the woman who discovered them both? Rike Volk?" she probed. With a grave expression laden with meaning, Horton confirmed, "Rike stumbled upon Kelsey and reported it, while an anonymous tip came in about Mary on Rike's own land."

"How well-acquainted are you with her?" Ada pressed further.

"Not very well. I had only spoken to her once prior to all this commotion when she first arrived in town. She had some issues with her neighbours. She's a German lady who used to work homicides in the Berlin police force," Horton explained.

Ada was surprised Officer Horton hadn't done a basic internet search on Rike and wasted no time taking charge, her authoritative demeanour slicing through the tension like a knife through ice. "I will handle that. Bring Ms. Volk in promptly. I need to untangle this mysterious link she has to our dark enigma."

Horton swiftly dialled Rike Volk's number, his fingers tapping the keys with precision, urgency colouring his voice as he requested her presence at the station to discuss the Townsend case. After ending the call, a subtle yet charged glance was exchanged between him and Ada, brimming with unspoken inquiries and veiled intentions. "We must address Rike's blood pool discovery as well," Horton declared, his movements purposeful as he carefully poured them each a cup of freshly brewed coffee from a steaming carafe. The fragrant aroma enveloped the room, adding a layer of tension that hung thick in the air, creating an almost palpable atmosphere of anticipation.

Ada's expression shifted, a single eyebrow lifting in silent curiosity. "A pool of blood?" she prompted, her voice laced with intrigue. She cautiously sipped scalding coffee, the heat searing her throat like a foreboding warning. Officer Horton proceeded to recount Rike's unsettling discovery during her morning ski—a vivid crimson stain starkly contrasting the pure white expanse of snow. Each detail unfurled with an ominous weight, casting a shadow of suspicion that lingered palpably in the air between them, hinting at even darker secrets waiting to be unveiled.

Chapter 17

The phone call abruptly ended with a sharp click, jolting Rike as she swiftly pocketed the device. Slipping into her heavy, weather-worn parka, its insulated layers whispering with each of her movements, she braced herself for the bone-chilling cold awaiting outside. Stepping into the icy air, her exhaled breath materialized in a haunting swirl before dissipating into the wintry stillness. With a reluctant growl, the truck's engine reluctantly rumbled to life, protesting against the frost that had invaded every nook and cranny during the night. As she navigated the vehicle out of her driveway, the tires grated over the hardened snow with a menacing crunch, echoing through the desolate landscape like an ominous prelude to what awaited beyond.

Lost in the rhythm of the tires on snow, Rike's thoughts drifted to a name that haunted her dreams—*Der Adlergestell Würger*, the serial killer who prowled the shadowy forests that lined the edges of the Adlergestell, leaving a trail of terror in his wake. His true identity remained a mystery, a spectre that eluded capture, mocking her efforts and shrouding her in a cloak of failure and shame. The memories of his victims, their voices silenced by his ruthless hand, echoed in the trees that zipped past, a reminder of the darkness she had faced and the darkness that still lurked beyond her grasp. Yet, as the land along the side of the road transformer, Rike's focus sharpened, the present reclaiming her attention.

Driving through the desolate rural roads, Rike expertly maneuvered her way towards town. The world around her was a canvas of white, where skeletal trees reached out like frozen claws towards the bleak sky. Nature's icy embrace had silenced the once lively landscape, casting an eerie stillness over everything. Passing by lonely farmhouses, tendrils of smoke spiralled from chimneys, painting ghostly patterns against the winter backdrop.

She approached the police station, parked her truck, and stepped inside. The contrast between the biting cold outside and the welcoming warmth within sent a shiver down her spine. Pausing to let her eyes adjust to the harsh transition to artificial light, a figure caught her attention...Detective Ada O'Neill.

The air crackled with tension as Rike's gaze locked onto Ada's form in the room, a sense of unease creeping into her mind. Time seemed to slow as their eyes met, each woman holding secrets and suspicions beneath their composed exteriors. This unexpected encounter set off a chain of events that would challenge everything Rike thought she knew about the case at hand, propelling her deeper into a web of mystery and danger.

Ada commanded the room with her presence, standing like a beacon of authority in the dull police station. Her athletic frame was outlined by the impeccably fitted suit she wore, a seamless blend of professionalism and personal flair. It wasn't just her sharp brown eyes, smooth dark skin and stunning smile that captivated Rike's attention; there was an undeniable aura of confidence around her that seemed to pull Rike in.

However, Rike quickly reined in any fleeting thoughts as the grim reality of their situation settled back in. Amidst the weight of two recent deaths, Rike scolded herself internally for allowing a momentary distraction by this captivating newcomer.

"Rike Volk, this is Ada." Officer Horton's voice sliced through the air, snapping Rike out of her reverie. She pivoted to meet his gaze.

"Detective Ada O'Neill, allow me to introduce Rike Volk," Horton announced formally.

"Just Rike is fine," she interjected, proffering her hand, which Ada grasped with a firm shake.

"Detective O'Neill. Ada," Ada responded coolly. "Unfortunate circumstances bring us together."

Seated across from Ada, Rike eased into the chair, her demeanour poised yet vigilant. "I have a history with the Berlin police, specialized in homicide," she disclosed, studying Ada's every reaction intently.

Ada's sharp gaze honed in on Rike, a flicker of intrigue dancing in her eyes. "So I read," she remarked, her interest spiking as she assessed Rike with a newfound curiosity.

Drumming her fingers rhythmically on the tabletop, Ada leaned forward, commanding attention with her authoritative presence. "Tell me, Rike," she demanded, her voice cutting through the quiet room like a blade, "what do you make of these deaths? Natural, accidental, suicide, or homicide?"

Rike's voice was unwavering as she spoke, her eyes piercing. "Until the medical examiner rules, they are undetermined. In this uncertainty, we're left chasing elusive shadows. It could be a tragic mishap or the doing of the wilderness. These woods hold more than meets the eye."

Officer Horton snapped his attention from the file with her words. "The examiner's findings are inconclusive at this point. No definitive answers yet."

Ada reclined slightly in her seat, her gaze narrowing in contemplation. "We can't discount the possibility of foul play, with nature lending a hand to hide the truth. The ambiguity surrounding this doesn't promise an easy resolution."

"True," Rike acknowledged, her breath forming mist in the cold air. "And with Kelsey and Mary, our suppositions are mere surface ripples. I couldn't have foreseen any lurking shadows in their lives."

Officer Horton's stare bore into Rike, his words sharp as ice. "Weren't you and Mary Townsend engaged in a fiery debate about faith not long before her demise?"

Rike locked eyes with him, unwavering. "It was a clash of beliefs, a clash of wills. Mary was resolute, as am I. That doesn't paint me as a perpetrator." Her fingers drifted to the intricate gold cross hanging against her chest, a silent talisman against accusations.

Officer Horton's features tightened. "Craig Griffith spilled the beans. Mentioned the heated exchange between you and Mary—right before she met her end. He claims it was more than just a disagreement."

Rike stiffened in her seat, her jaw clenching with determination. "Mary was convinced Kelsey's demise was some kind of divine payback. She insisted Kelsey got what was coming to her for her sins," she disclosed, her tone laced with a defensive edge. "I couldn't stand by and let that vile notion slide. It's repugnant to even suggest such a thing."

Ada's features contorted in disbelief, her sharp eyebrows shooting up like startled birds as the words hit her. A flicker of shock crossed her face, freezing her expression for a heartbeat before the mask of professionalism settled back in place. "Divine retribution? What could justify such a brutal act?" Ada's voice sliced through the air, laced with incredulity and a hint of underlying tension. "So Mary insinuated that Kelsey deserved this fate?" Her words cut through the tense silence, each syllable heavy with accusation and disbelief.

"Exactly. Preposterous."

Officer Horton pondered aloud, the rhythmic tap of his pen echoing in the room. "It does raise questions, doesn't it?" he remarked thoughtfully. "Perhaps Kelsey was entangled in actions deemed sinful by some, yet not punishable by law." His scrutinizing gaze then returned to Rike, as though trying to measure her against an intangible standard.

As their exchange unfolded, a palpable chill settled in the room, almost like a spectral presence bearing witness to the escalating tension between them. Despite the shadow of suspicion looming over her, Rike remained stoic, her countenance a veil of inscrutability that concealed her true emotions.

"What kind of action is a sin unpunished but law, Officer Horton?" Rike asked, though she knew he was hinting at sexuality.

"Let's steer clear of religious texts," Ada interjected, her voice cutting through the tension. "At this point, we're grasping in the dark on how Kelsey and Mary met their end. Suspicious circumstances aside, we lack solid proof."

"Absolutely," Rike responded firmly. "No evidence, no definitive cause of death—just a maze of troubling uncertainties. Was there another purpose for summoning me here, Officer Horton?" Rike's gaze bore into Horton after a pause, her question sharp and unwavering.

Closing the investigative file with a decisive snap, Officer Horton met Rike's eyes and shook his head. "That'll be all for now. You're free to leave, Rike."

"These are questions well-suited to a phone call, Officer Horton. I do not appreciate having to travel here, in these driving conditions, for what could have been a simple call," Rike said, her voice conveying her annoyance.

"That was me," Ada said, raising her hand as if confessing to a classroom prank. "I needed to meet you. As a person of interest. You understand, n'est pas?"

"Of course. Thank you. Nice to meet you, Ada," Rike replied coolly, her gaze unwavering as she rose from her seat. The police station's harsh fluorescent lights seemed to intensify, casting ominous shadows that danced like spectres across the linoleum floor, hinting at the dark secrets lurking within its walls. With a brisk nod, Rike left the station, the heavy door groaning in protest against the frigid night air.

Outside, a fierce wind howled through the deserted parking lot, swirling snowflakes in a frenzied dance around her. Each step towards her truck felt like a battle against the biting cold, her breath forming frosty clouds in the air. The truck loomed before her like a silent guardian amidst the wintry chaos, a stark contrast to the eerie stillness that enveloped the town as it huddled under nature's icy grip.

"Ms. Volk!" Ada's urgent voice sliced through the biting wind, her silhouette materializing from the station's dimly lit interior, each exhale crystallizing in the icy atmosphere. Rike halted, and made a fraction of a turn to register Ada's approach. She stood still as Ada closed the distance, enveloping herself in the protective layers of her coat.

"Call me Rike."

"Rike," Ada panted, her tone edged with an undercurrent of urgency. "What do you make of all this, Rike?" Ada inquired, her sharp eyes probing Rike's expression for any hidden truths.

"Local hunters are tossing around theories about wolves being behind Kelsey's death," Rike responded, squinting as the frigid wind whipped against her face like icy claws. "Officer Horton thinks it is misadventure. And as for Mary... finding her in my driveway without a trace of how she got there? It just doesn't add up."

Listening intently, Ada mulled over Rike's words. They shared an unspoken understanding that the unforgiving wilderness held countless dangers, yet these mysteries defied simple explanations.

"No signs of dragging a body down my driveway? No footsteps? Tire tracks? Officers Horton and Juno are not properly trained, and it showed." Rike's voice carried a tinge of exasperation, a hint of being unjustly targeted. "My truck was up by the cabin. Did you notice any tracks leading from there to where she was found?"

Ada's response was swift, her head shaking in denial. "No trace of that in the photos I've seen so far. Officer Horton hasn't brought me out to the site yet, especially with this relentless weather."

"No traces of Mary coming from my cabin. But it is possible she came v from the road. But they destroyed evidence with their own vehicles, Detective O'Neill," Rike asserted firmly, her words cutting through the icy air with each visible exhale. "Had I hauled Mary from my vehicle to the end of the drive, there'd be evidence. Yet, there's nothing. So, I didn't relocate her."

The tension in the air was palpable, mirroring the frost that encased the nearby trees. Rike's eyes blazed with unwavering determination, a silent oath to her integrity. "Noted," Ada murmured softly, her breath forming wisps in the frigid atmosphere as she studied Rike intently. "You seem strong enough to have carried Mary instead of dragging her," she observed sharply.

Rike locked eyes with Ada, her expression resolute. "But I didn't," she asserted bluntly. Sensing the chill seeping into their bones, Rike broke the silence, her voice slicing through the biting cold. "Let's move from this icy grip," she proposed, taking charge as she strode towards her rugged truck, a beast designed to tackle the harsh Canadian wilderness.

Nestled inside the cab, Rike and Ada found solace from the biting wind that cut through their winter attire. With a twist of the key, the engine roared to life, sending a wave of comforting heat to thaw their chilled bones. As Ada intertwined her fingers, coaxing the warmth back into her icy fingertips, she couldn't help but marvel at the relentless cold of Berna. "I've heard tales of frosty lands before, but experiencing this frigidity firsthand is something else," Ada remarked softly, a faint smile playing on her lips. "I am stationed in Victoria. It seems like no amount of preparation can truly brace you for the true Canadian chill."

"It does have a certain allure for me," Rike responded, a subtle grin playing on her lips as she reached to adjust the heater vents, the warmth spreading through the car. Casting a quick, inquisitive glance at Ada, a spark of interest lit up her eyes. "What were your initial impressions of the crime scene visuals?"

There was a brief pause as Ada deliberated before confessing, "I haven't had the chance to visit the actual site yet or closely examine the images. I prefer to view them digitally; I find zooming in and highlighting details aids my analysis. I have not had sufficient time. As you know, it can take hours of scrutiny to find the smallest but most important of clues."

"I have photographs, though I did not review them," Rike said.

"Photographs of what?"

"Every scene. Take a look," Rike's voice was steady as she retrieved her phone from her pocket. With precision, she unlocked the device and navigated to the photo gallery before passing it to Ada. The screen displayed a series of chilling images, each capturing the stark reality of the scene. Ada's composed demeanour faltered for a moment as she absorbed the gruesome contents with unwavering focus.

"Dear God," Ada's breath hitched, her gaze locked on the haunting pictures. "Her hands and feet..."

"Gone," Rike interjected gravely. "No sign of them anywhere close. And see this," she indicated a specific photo, "no traces of dragging marks."

Ada's expression froze in a mask of astonishment, the grim truth of the murder stark in her widened eyes. "This... it's methodical. Savage," she murmured, her voice edged with disbelief.

Rike interjected quietly, "Deliberate. Human." She observed Ada intently, catching the slight clench of her jaw and the subtle narrowing of her gaze. It was evident—the detective was unraveling the mystery piece by resistant piece. "Indeed," Ada concurred sharply. As they pored over the images, each frame not only depicted death but also unraveled a haunting riddle that lingered in the air like an unspoken accusation.

Rike couldn't tear her eyes away from Ada, watching as her fingers delicately danced over the gruesome images, almost as if seeking hidden truths within the chilling scene of blood and snow. Inside the confines of the truck, with only the constant thrum of the engine breaking the silence, their shared scrutiny created an atmosphere heavy with unspoken dread.

"It's...calculated," Ada's voice sliced through the tense air, her tone as icy and unyielding as the wintry landscape around them. "This is methodical. It's maniacal—a skilled hand at work. A cruelty thoroughly human."

"True, and this hints at someone with hunting skills," Rike responded, a bitter taste lingering in her mouth. Death was no stranger to her, yet the scene in the images was chillingly different.

Returning the phone with measured poise, Ada's gaze pierced through Rike's, each glance a calculated move in their deadly game of unraveling the truth. "We must uncover the motive behind this. If indeed there is one," Ada's voice held an edge, her eyes sharp and probing for hidden truths beneath the surface.

Ada pressed on, her gaze unwavering as she probed, "So, tell me, how did she end up here, in your driveway?" Each word carried weight, emphasizing the significance of even the smallest detail.

"Thrown from a truck that pulled into my driveway," Rike affirmed, cutting the engine. The abrupt halt plunged them into a chilling silence that seemed to thicken around them like a cloak. Outside, the icy air seeped through the vehicle's thin metal shell, a stark reminder of the unforgiving harshness lurking in the shadows.

"Let's reconvene at the station first thing tomorrow," Ada suggested, her hand hovering over the door handle, a sense of urgency in her tone. "A fresh look might unveil what we've missed. Save my number. If anything clicks in your memory before then, don't hesitate to reach out."

"Will it be worth my drive?" Rike asked.

"I promise," Ada said, flashing a beautiful smile.

She was disarmed. "Tomorrow," Rike affirmed, her nod sharp as she swiftly entered Ada's contact details into her phone. "With a promise that it will be worth it."

Chapter 18

The winter's breath kisses my cheeks gently as I venture into the snowy woods, camera poised to capture the serene magic of this untouched world. Each footfall creates a symphony of soft crunches in the snow, marking my path through the pristine landscape. My photography has garnered a dedicated online following, providing a welcome source of income through sales on my digital storefront.

The forest embraces me with its majestic presence; trees towering overhead, adorned with thick coats of glistening snow. I envision the perfect shot in my mind, already considering the ideal keywords to accompany it in my online gallery.

Navigating through the labyrinth of tree trunks and tangled branches, my eyes catch a sudden pop of crimson against the blanket of snow—a cardinal gracefully resting on a frost-kissed bough. Fingers steady, I lift my camera, carefully composing the bird against the pure canvas of winter. Each snap of the shutter freezes in time the vivid hues of the cardinal's feathers, a radiant splash amidst the frozen expanse that surrounds us.

Continuing my trek through the serene, snow-covered landscape, I stumble upon a series of intricate tracks imprinted in the fresh powder—a mesmerizing trail left behind by a majestic wolf passing through. Excitement pulses through me as I carefully track the footprints, my camera at the ready to capture the elusive beauty of this wild creature's journey through the winter wonderland. Each step I take deepens my bond with nature, filling me with a profound sense of awe for the intricate dance of life and death that plays out in these frost-kissed woods. As long as I keep a respectful distance, that is.

As I walk around a bend, a cluster of evergreen trees emerges, their boughs weighed down by thick blankets of snow. The air hangs heavy with stillness, broken only by the gentle crunch of my skis over the frozen terrain. Filled with awe, I lift my camera once more, capturing the intricate beauty of the snow-laden branches set against the backdrop of the wintry heavens. Each click immortalizes nature's enduring spirit, a silent tribute to the unyielding fortitude that resides beneath the tranquil surface of our world.

Navigating the snowy woods, my senses come alive with the crispness of the winter air. Each press of the camera's shutter captures not just images but fragments of serenity and tranquillity that envelop me. The snow-laden branches whisper tales of ancient secrets, and the soft crunch beneath my boots creates a rhythm in harmony with nature's symphony.

Heading homeward, my camera holds snapshots of this ethereal world, preserving moments that imprint themselves on my soul. Gratitude swells within me, a profound appreciation for being a part of this untouched wilderness. These stolen moments among the snow-covered trees etch themselves into my memory, promising to remain as timeless treasures that remind me of nature's ability to soothe and uplift even the weariest heart.

My steps labour through the pristine snow, each footfall sinking into the soft powder, sending tiny flurries dancing around me. The winter's icy grip creeps through my bundled layers, nipping at any exposed skin. The camera slung around my neck tugs gently at my shoulders, a constant reminder of its presence. As I breathe out, my warm breath mingles with the frigid air, creating delicate tendrils of mist that dissipate into the wintry landscape around me.

Ahead, the road emerges like a lifeline in the sea of snow, a promise of safety amid the unforgiving wilderness. Each step I take feels like a battle against the biting cold, my breath forming misty clouds in the frigid air. The idea of sanctuary beckons me forward, a flicker of hope that fuels my weary limbs as I press on towards the distant haven. The urgency to outrun the encroaching chill drives me, a relentless force pushing me to reach shelter before the icy grip of winter claims me completely.

As I emerge onto the desolate road, my breath hangs in the frigid air, a visible testament to the biting cold that gnaws at my skin. I where I am. This is the back of the land owned by Rike Volk. I recognize the area that was ravaged by fire a few years ago. Town gossip was the Cumming twins set it on fire to burn her out of her land. A silly reason, as she did not work the land. A few burned acres would mean nothing to her. I heard she was a police officer. I suspect she can handle her own. But it is weird that she found Kelsey plus Mary was practically at her front door.

Then I suddenly wondered, am I alone? I feel like I am being watched. I didn't see anyone, or any animal. But something feels off. I don't want to be here.

The eerie silence of the wintry wilderness envelops me like a sinister shroud, intensifying the sense of isolation that grips my heart. My eyes dart frantically, searching for any flicker of movement, any hint of life in this barren expanse.

A faint glimmer of hope flares within me as I see a truck coming toward me, a fleeting chance to escape this frozen purgatory and find solace in the familiar embrace of humanity. Each step I take is laden with anticipation, every footfall echoing loudly in the oppressive stillness around me. The yearning for warmth and safety propels me forward, driving me relentlessly towards an uncertain fate lurking beyond the icy horizon.

The growl of the approaching truck rips through the serene winter air, sending a shiver down my spine. Before I can comprehend its intent, it crashes into me with bone-jarring force, launching me into a terrifying flight through the icy sky. In that heart-stopping moment, suspended in mid-air, time itself seems to stretch infinitely as I hurtle towards an uncertain landing that may never come.

Chapter 19

Soft tendrils of mist clung to the frost-kissed pines, shrouding the sleepy town in a hushed embrace. Through the frosted windowpanes of the cafe, a dim light filtered in, painting the worn wooden tables with a muted glow. Nestled in a corner, where the aroma of freshly brewed tea mingled with the crackling fire's warmth, Rike lingered, her presence a stoic anchor amidst the whispered conversations and clinking cups.

Rike sat at the rustic wooden table, her weathered fingers gently caressing the intricate patterns etched into the ceramic surface of her cup. Lost in thought, she was transported back to a crisp winter day from years ago when she had come to Autumn's rescue after her SUV ran out of gas. The memory of that fateful day lingered vividly in Rike's mind, where fate had woven their paths together once more in a serendipitous moment that would forever be etched into her soul.

Rike sat with a book spread out before her. Despite the open pages, her gaze didn't linger on the text but instead wandered to the snowy world outside. She saw Autumn Evans, who in turn watched Rike's solitude. Autumn waved and came inside. A subtle smile played on Autumn's lips as she weaved through the tables and chairs with a graceful step that resembled a leaf dancing on an autumn breeze—effortless yet purposeful in its movement.

Autumn had settled at Rike's table without invitation, but Rike found comfort in her presence and embraced the unexpected companionship.

Autumn's voice cut through the ambient sounds of clinking cups and hushed conversations, carrying with it the weight of a shared past. Her eyes met Rike's gaze with a quiet intensity that spoke volumes about their bond.

Rike lifted her eyes, her expression transforming like a landscape under shifting light, a flicker of understanding crossing her features. Grounded in pragmatism, she remained a steady presence, but a flicker of something more danced in her gaze, revealing a fondness for the unexpected twists that had brought them together.

As they chatted, Autumn found herself unconsciously mimicking Rike's every movement. When Rike furrowed her brow in deep thought, Autumn's own expression mirrored the contemplation, creating a silent dance of synchronized actions between them. Each time Rike raised her cup to her lips, savouring the hot liquid within, Autumn would reflexively do the same, feeling the cozy warmth spread through her like an old friend. Though Rike noticed Autumn's subtle mirroring, the unspoken connection between them added an intriguing layer of intimacy to their interaction.

"Ever climbed up to the old fire tower on Ridgeline Path?" Autumn asked, her tone casual yet loaded with intent. The suggestion lingered in the air, a subtle offer disguised as a shared passion. "The view up there this season is truly breathtaking."

Rike's gaze sparked with interest, the promise of untouched beauty and seclusion resonating with her unspoken desires. "No, I haven't," she confessed, slipping a bookmark into her novel as a sign of openness to the idea.

"Maybe we could head out together," Autumn proposed, her words drifting like fallen snow on a moonlit night. "Imagine the crunch of fresh snow under our boots, the icy air biting at our cheeks." Her tone lowered, evoking scenes of winter enchantment—a portrait painted with the glistening frost of the season. "And later, a snug evening by the hearth, just letting go of the day's chill?"

A subtle smile played on Rike's lips as she tried unraveling the nuances hidden in Autumn's suggestion. Rike and Autumn immersed themselves in a rich tapestry of conversations that ebbed and flowed like a river, reflecting their deepening connection. They delved into the depths of literature, dissected the intricacies of politics, and shared fragments of their own histories. Laughter intertwined with contemplative pauses, creating a harmonious cadence in their dialogue that resonated like a finely tuned orchestra—every word a delicate note, every sentence a captivating melody.

"Another chamomile tea for you?" the barista inquired, her voice cutting through the cozy ambiance of the shop.

"Yes, please. And for Autumn?" Rike turned to her friend.

Autumn's grin widened. "I'll indulge in a pumpkin spice latte," she chimed in.

"Coming right up," the barista responded with a warm smile that clashed pleasantly with the café's earthy decor. With that, she glided off, leaving Rike and Autumn cocooned in their world of lightness in the dark. Although Autumn wanted to talk about Kelsey and Mary, "and that new Black woman who just flew in to help Officer Horton," Rike refused.

"I do not want to be involved," Rike protested.

"Pumpkin spice latte for you, tea for you," said the barista as she put the cups down. As Rike's fingers reached for the freshly brewed tea, a melodic tune filled the air, only to be abruptly interrupted by a sudden jostle. The scalding liquid spilled over her hand, causing a momentary sting. Without hesitation, Autumn sprang into action, her chair grating against the floor in her haste to assist Rike. With deft movements, she grabbed napkins from a nearby dispenser and gently blotted Rike's damp skin, all the while angrily chastising the flustered barista. Fortunately, the tea hadn't been hot enough to cause any real harm.

"I am so sorry! I..." said the barista, almost on the verge of years.

"No need for apologies," Rike reassured them both, flexing her fingers to alleviate the slight discomfort. She couldn't help but feel touched by Autumn's swift and caring response, recognizing the protective instinct that had spurred her friend into action.

The barista began to walk away, but Autumn raised a finger and said, "Wait." Instead of the anticipated light aroma of chamomile, a sharp hazelnut fragrance wafted up.

Autumn's pleasant expression hardened into a mask of disapproval. "I'm sorry," she interjected firmly, her voice cutting through the ambient chatter. Rising gracefully from her seat, she assumed a protective stance beside Rike, her slender figure exuding determination. "This isn't what was ordered," she declared with unwavering resolve. "Rike requested a chamomile tea, not this... hazelnut monstrosity."

A soft rose hue bloomed on Rike's cheeks, betraying her unease. She was taken aback by Autumn's fierce defence of her, momentarily struck speechless. Seeking to calm the rising tension, Rike gently placed a hand on Autumn's arm. "It's fine, really," she whispered, but once provoked, Autumn was a force to be reckoned with.

"No way," Autumn retorted firmly, turning to the barista. "Get her order and make sure it's done right. Don't scald her either." As the barista hurried off, Rike lowered her gaze to the table, her fingers tracing the embossed design on the cover of her book—a grounding gesture amidst the sudden whirlwind of emotions.

"Thanks, Autumn," Rike murmured, her voice laced with gratitude and a touch of vulnerability.

Autumn settled back into her chair, the protective glint in her eyes fading to a simmering intensity. "I want what's best for you, especially given the spill," she admitted, a flicker of fragility piercing through her usual confident facade.

"Rike, I have the most amazing idea for my pottery studio," she began, her voice filled with enthusiasm. "Imagine a collection called 'Nature's Embrace,' where I capture the essence of the wild in my pottery. And the centrepiece? A magnificent wolf bowl."

Her words flowed with passion as she painted a vivid picture for Rike, describing the intricacies of the design and the symbolism behind it. "The bowl would embody the strength and beauty of the wolf, with earthy tones mimicking its fur and a touch of colour to represent its piercing gaze. It's a piece that speaks of nature's power and grace, a true embodiment of my theme." She went on to describe the tabletop deer planter, owl mug, and moose vase. Rike only half-listened to Autumn's ideas.

Rike's thoughts were interrupted by a chilling memory that sliced through the banality like a jagged blade. Der Adlergestell Würger, the phantom of her past, emerged from the shadows of her thoughts, a spectre that refused to be banished. Tuning out Autumn, she remembered the letters that arrived at the police station addressed to her. Each hateful word was a poison-tipped arrow aimed at her heart. The killer's twisted messages taunted her, promising an unfinished reckoning that cast a long shadow over her past. And then, as the echoes of his threats faded and Autumn's words came to the fore, Rike knew that was a mystery she would never solve, a darkness she could not dispel. With a heavy sigh, she let go of the burden of the unresolved, allowing the present to reclaim her focus.

As the conversation gradually faded into a comfortable silence, Rike got up from her seat, a sense of purpose guiding her movements. A much-needed escape from Autumn's overwhelming presence was required. "Thank you for sharing this with me, Autumn. I look forward to seeing your vision come to life," she smiled warmly.

With a parting nod, Rike left the café, the door chiming softly behind her. Autumn watched her go, a sense of fulfilment and anticipation lingering in the air.

Stepping out into the crisp air, Rike felt an immediate sense of relief washing over her. As she briskly crossed the street, she caught Autumn's gaze through the glass. Autumn waved.

Seated in the driver's seat of her sturdy SUV, Rike savoured the tranquillity that enveloped her. The quiet solitude of the vehicle stood in sharp contrast to Autumn's lively chatter. A sense of calm washed over her. Letting out a contented sigh, Rike pushed away the lingering concerns that had plagued her earlier.

The sun had dipped below the horizon, casting a soft glow through the windows of the small town's bustling grocery store. Rike navigated the aisles with practiced ease, her steps falling in rhythm with the hushed buzz of shoppers around her. Suddenly, a familiar silhouette caught her attention amidst the shelves of neatly stacked canned goods. Autumn, engrossed in her search, seemed to blend into the store's warm lighting.

Their gazes intertwined, sparking a silent exchange that spoke volumes. A ghost of a smile tugged at Rike's lips, reflecting a mix of recognition and surprise. The moment lingered between them, enveloped in an unspoken curiosity that danced in the air like snowflakes on a winter night. This encounter felt oddly out of place, yet strangely comforting in its unexpectedness.

"Imagine meeting you here," Autumn mused, closing the distance between them. Her tone was nonchalant, yet an underlying tension hummed palpably in the frigid air.

"A curious twist of fate," Rike responded, her fingers briefly clenching around the handle of the cart.

"It's almost as if destiny enjoys playing games, reuniting us twice in a single day." Autumn's grin widened, and she rested against the metal shelving, her head cocked inquisitively. "Tell me, how do you do it? Living alone with no one around to help you? If you needed it, I mean."

"It suits me," Rike responded, her tone measured as she observed Autumn's probing gaze. The subtle intensity in Autumn's eyes didn't escape her notice.

"Must get lonely sometimes, doesn't it?" Autumn probed softly, the gentle cadence of her voice revealing her curiosity.

"Sometimes," Rike admitted, a hint of vulnerability creeping into her words. She felt the weight of solitude settle between them, a silent but potent presence in their exchange.

Autumn's voice carried a hint of mischief as she posed her question, her eyes betraying a depth that Rike always found intriguing. "But what happens when the soul craves more than just the quiet of solitude?"

Rike considered her response carefully, her words measured. "In those moments," she began, pausing briefly for emphasis, "Berna is a quick drive away. Comfort is always close."

A spark of understanding lit up Autumn's face, her features animated with newfound insight. With a mischievous twinkle in her eye, she chimed in, "Precisely! Sometimes, the very thing we need is right before us, hidden in plain sight."

She responded with a soft chuckle, trying to mask the whirlwind of thoughts racing through her mind. "Surprises seem to find us when we least expect them," Rike remarked, her voice unwavering even as uncertainty gnawed at her insides. There have been too many surprises recently.

Autumn's eyes drifted from the intense conversation, seeking solace in the vibrant array of fresh produce. Her gaze settled on a cornucopia of fruits before lingering on the meticulously arranged apples. The hues blended like a masterpiece; rich reds, crisp greens, and sunny yellows competing for attention.

"Rike," Autumn's voice carried a lighter tone that seemed to dance through the air, "among all of these orchard treasures, which apple speaks to you?"

The question caught Rike off guard, yet it brought a welcomed diversion after their uncomfortable discussion. She paused briefly, then replied, "Granny Smith," noting how its tartness resonated with her own unadorned view of life.

Autumn's laughter danced through the crisp winter air, wrapping Rike in a cocoon of warmth. "Really?" she chuckled, her eyes sparkling with genuine delight. "Grannies are my absolute favourite as well! The way they crunch, the perfect blend of sweetness and tartness—it's just divine."

Rike frowned slightly at this revelation, the unexpected finding of common ground with Autumn fostering a sense of unease in her body. She was not used to simpatico. Autumn plucked a fragrant green apple from the pile and offered it to Rike, who reached to take it.

Autumn's touch was a gentle revelation, her fingertips grazing Rike's forearm like a delicate secret shared between them. "It appears we share more similarities than I realized," Autumn reflected softly, her hand deftly selecting more Granny Smith apples and putting them into her own bag. Rike nodded in agreement, her tone carrying a hint of amusement mingled with an elusive emotion that danced just beyond her grasp.

"Until we meet again, Rike," Autumn's parting words carried a hint of wistfulness. She glided elegantly, almost reluctantly, towards the cash register, while Rike stood still, watching her graceful departure into the bustling crowd. The sensation of Autumn's touch lingered in Rike's mind like a fading melody. A whirlwind of sentiments swirled within her, each as intricate and layered as the unique taste of the apples they both favoured. Taking a deep breath, she allowed the encounter to drift into the vast expanse of her thoughts, where it settled amidst the reflective solitude that enveloped her world.

As she continued to shop for a few more essentials, Rike thought of Autumn and the mysterious forces that had intertwined their paths once again.

Chapter 20

In the hushed stillness of the early morning, Rike Volk glided through the snow-draped landscape, her skis whispering against the natural canvas outside Saint Berna Aux Étranger. The air carried a biting chill that nipped at her exposed skin. Each push forward left a trail of imprints in the powdery snow, marking her solitary journey through the icy wilderness.

Rike's heart raced as she skied through the snow, each rhythmic swish of her skis creating a harmonious melody with the pounding of her pulse. The crisp air chilled as she breathed in deeply, savouring the icy freshness that filled her lungs. With every stride, she felt a surge of warmth spreading through her muscles, a stark contrast to the frosty surroundings. Her breath formed small clouds in the frigid air, punctuating each graceful glide and powerful push across the glistening terrain.

Skiing wasn't just a habit for Rike; it was a treasured ceremony. It served as her anchor to the realm beyond the confines of her convoluted life, where each sight whispered a secret and every word hinted at a new direction in an investigation she was no longer part of. Amidst the serene and unyielding allure of the landscape, she discovered solace from the complexities of human deceit.

Arriving back at her cozy wooden cabin, Rike smoothly unclicked her skis, the snow crunching beneath her boots as she made her way to the porch. With a practiced motion, she brushed off the snow before stepping inside, welcomed by the comforting shift in temperature that enveloped her like a familiar embrace. The ritual of starting a fire was second nature to her, each movement deliberate and efficient. As the kindling ignited and flames eagerly consumed the logs, a symphony of crackling sounds filled the room, casting out any lingering chill from outdoors. Gradually, warmth seeped into every nook and cranny, creating a haven of tranquillity within the walls of her secluded retreat.

Water trickled from the faucet into the stainless-steel kettle, its metallic surface gleaming under the dim kitchen lights. Rike's slender fingers carefully selected a tea bag from the colourful assortment in the box, opting for the bold peppermint variety that promised a crisp flavour. She aligned the ceramic mug, turning it so the handle was at a 45-degree angel from her as she anticipated the familiar whistle of boiling water.

In the tranquillity of her secluded cabin, a sudden jarring sound shattered the peace. Her cell phone vibrated insistently on the wooden countertop, casting a soft glow as Ada O'Neill's name flashed across the screen. Intrigue sparked in Rike's eyes as she swiftly picked up the device, holding it to her ear to answer the unexpected call.

"Ada," Rike's breathless voice carried the crisp tang of cold air, laced with a hint of amusement. "What thrilling adventure do you have in store for me today?"

There was a sense of urgency threading through Ada's response. "Rike, where exactly are you at this moment?" Chuckling lightly, Rike replied, unaware of the seriousness in Ada's tone. "Just at home, thawing out by the crackling fire. Why the sudden interest? Checking in on me or something more personal?"

"Rike, this is strictly business," Ada interjected firmly, her tone laced with authority. The smile on Rike's face faded, her fingers tensing around the phone. "What's the issue?"

Ada paused briefly, as if bracing herself before breaking the news over the crackling connection. "We've made another discovery. A body."

A chill unrelated to the wintry surroundings gripped Rike. She inhaled sharply, feeling her heartbeat race against her chest like a trapped bird yearning for freedom. "Another one?" she murmured, shock and sorrow mingling in her words.

"Yes," Ada's voice rang out with a solemn confirmation.

"A woman?" Rike's breath caught in her throat, her pulse quickening at Ada's terse response.

"Yes."

She hung up.

Alone in her cabin, the phone call had shattered Rike's composure. Ada delivered news that sent a jolt of dread through Rike's core. Another woman's body had been discovered, casting a pall over the peace she had sought in the quiet of this country. Der Adlergestell Würger, the name she had given the strangler who hunted the long stretch of the Adlergestell, was best whispered in the recesses of her mind. The serial killer was a chilling reminder of vile promises unfulfilled and shadows unvanquished. He was never arrested, never identified. Could he have followed her, his presence a malevolent spectre in her new refuge? Was he killing more women and dragging Rike into his trap? Despite the web of fear that coiled around her thoughts, Rike kept this unsettling possibility to herself, recognizing that the idea of this serial killer–her serial killer–tracking her from Berlin was pure speculation, and raising it with Ada would only muddy the waters. All she desired was to be left alone, away from the haunting shadows of her past.

In this whirlwind of chaos and disbelief, Rike's thoughts spiraled uncontrollably, a tempest of emotions raging within her. The desperate desire to prove her innocence clashed violently with the chilling realization that she was entangled in darkness, spun by a new, unknown adversary.

Her hands trembled as she clutched at the edges of sanity, teetering on the brink of despair. All she had ever wanted was peace—a respite from the haunting memories of past horrors that now threatened to consume her once more. But now, peace eluded her like a fleeting dream, replaced by a stark reality where danger lurked in every corner.

Before Rike could steady her racing pulse, a sharp rap echoed through the cozy cabin, matching the frantic beat in her chest. With determined steps, she traversed the room, a symphony of pine and crackling firewood lingering in her wake. Upon swinging open the door, Ada O'Neill and Officer Horton materialized against the snowy backdrop. Ada deftly stowed away her phone, prompting Rike's gaze to flick towards the device and register the abrupt end of their call.

Ada's voice sliced through the morning stillness, her words sharp and direct. "Rike, they found Skylar Mitchell's body in the woods behind your place."

Rike's thoughts scrambled to identify the name amidst the faces of the town. "Skylar Mitchell?" she repeated, searching her memory. Officer Horton interjected with a cold efficiency, detailing Skylar as the town librarian—black hair, piercing green eyes, and lacking in charm.

"Librarian?" Rike's brow furrowed, her gaze fixed on Ada, the howling wind outside mirroring the turmoil in her mind. "I... I don't recall her." Disbelief thickened the air, frosting over the cozy cabin's ambiance.

"May we come inside," Ada proposed, casting a quick glance past Rike into the welcoming glow of the cabin. Numbly acquiescing, Rike shifted aside, ushering in not just her unanticipated visitors but also the icy touch of reality into her once-sacred space.

The crackling fire in the hearth barely took the edge off the chill that pervaded the room. Ada's eyes roamed over the pile of books on the floor, absorbing their titles as Officer Horton's words shattered the quiet.

"Rike, any idea why Ms. Mitchell was on your land?" Horton's question sliced through the air, his tone laced with suspicion that pricked at Rike's pride.

"None whatsoever," Rike snapped back, her posture rigid and defensive. "I let people traverse my land. It's in Germany."

"But you posted your property," Officer Horton countered.

"To stop hunters and poachers. Plus, I do not patrol my property, hoping to catch trespassers. I lead a solitary life. Skylar Mitchell means nothing to me." An undercurrent of irritation tinged her words. "And I've never set foot in that library. Not once."

Ada's eyes drifted over the spines of meticulously arranged books, each one a testament to a life enshrouded in mystery and scrutiny. "Quite the collection for someone who avoids the library," Ada remarked, her eyebrow arching curiously.

"They are mine," Rike countered sharply, her tone terse. "They're intimate. I don't borrow; I possess. Ownership matters."

Rike's voice softened slightly as she continued, "If I were still in that world of investigations, these deaths would consume me. But…" She cut herself off with a decisive shake of her head, refusing to be labelled. "Any word from the medical examiner? Has a manner and cause been announced for any of the women?"

Officer Horton's doubt hung thick in the air as he remarked, "These deaths are suspicious, no doubt. If you're truly innocent, why not lend a hand? Show us those detective skills you claim you honed in Berlin."

Rike's response cut through the tension like a blade, her voice mirroring the biting chill outside. "I didn't just claim to be a homicide detective; I was one—a damn good one at that."

Ada stepped in with unwavering authority, fixing her intense gaze on Rike. "Enough, Officer Horton. Rike Volk's expertise is well-documented in news articles and commendations. Her career speaks for itself."

"My gratitude," Rike murmured, the chill of her words matching the icy disdain she held for Horton. She clung to Ada's defence like a lifeline amidst the accusations, a faint ember of solace in the wintry storm of suspicion.

"To be clear," Ada's voice sliced through the tense silence, authoritative yet laced with a hint of compassion. Leaning in, her gaze bore into Rike's soul, as if seeking answers in the intricate lines etched on her weathered face. "Were you acquainted with Skylar Mitchell?"

Rike's voice remained eerily calm, a stark contrast to the furrowed brow that betrayed her genuine confusion. "I've never come across anyone by that name," she stated firmly.

Ada's pen scratched across the notepad, capturing Rike's response before she lifted her gaze once more. The interrogation unfolded like a carefully choreographed dance, each question a precise step, each answer a calculated counterbalance.

"And when was the last time you ventured into the depths of your property?" Ada inquired, her eyes fixed on Rike.

Rike's focus shifted to the window, where the looming forest stood ominously silent and observant. "It must have been... around a week ago, perhaps two," she replied, her words hanging in the tense air between them. "The skiing is too rough."

"Where were you this morning?" Ada's voice cut sharply through the quiet of the room.

"Skiing," Rike motioned towards the door, indicating her skis leaning against the wall. "It's my routine."

"How is your truck? Have you ever hit a deer or moose?" Officer Horton asked.

His sad attempt to question Rike almost made her laugh. "No. I've hit nothing. Look for yourself, it's just outside," Rike responded as she toward the door.

Ada hesitated, her pen tapping a quick rhythm on the notepad. "Any enemies in these parts?"

A flicker of darkness passed over Rike's features, her expression hardening. "Craig and Tammy next door. They don't approve of my choices." She paused, tension thick in the air. "They've torn down my rainbow flag more than once. I caught them poaching on my land, and Craig tried to kill me. Officer Horton knows the details."

"It was not like that Rike. That's not–"

"I would like all police reports on activities between the Griffiths and Rike, please," Ada said as she glared at Horton.

Ada's next question cut through the air, her tone casual yet her eyes sharp, scanning Rike's every move. "Any weapons on the premises?" Rike didn't flinch, meeting Ada's gaze head-on. "Of course. My rifle, there by the door. Unloaded and it has a trigger lock. And a hunting knife in the kitchen drawer," she replied promptly, nodding subtly towards the kitchen. It was a subtle dare, a challenge to doubt her innocence that hung unsaid between them.

"Intriguing," Ada murmured, her piercing gaze lingering on Rike for an extra beat before shifting away. "Thank you, Rike. We'll be in touch."

As Ada rose from her seat, a sudden chill seemed to seep into the room, wrapping around Rike like an invisible shroud of suspicion. The warmth from the crackling fire in the stove no longer sufficed to dispel the icy tendrils of doubt that lingered in the air, casting a shadow over the truth.

The following day, as Rike ventured into town, she noticed a tangible drop in temperature that surpassed even the biting frost of January. Once-welcoming faces at the grocery store now shielded themselves behind a barrier of speculation, distancing themselves from Rike. As she reached for a loaf of bread, a hand swiftly beat her to it; the ensuing frigid glare pierced through her like a blade, colder than the wintry gusts outside.

Mrs. Langley, stationed at the register, greeted Rike with a half-hearted "Morning," her lips drawn tight as though tasting something bitter. Despite the frosty reception, Rike maintained a façade of calm, though inside, turmoil brewed. The gas station attendant mirrored this coldness, avoiding her gaze and handling the fuel nozzle roughly against her truck, his disdain palpable in the air. With a sinking feeling, Rike realized that the once comforting shield of isolation within the community had shattered, leaving her vulnerable to the icy whispers of supposition and doubt that now swirled around her like a biting winter wind.

Entering the cozy haven of the Auberge Café, Rike gently pushed the door, greeted by a wave of warmth that enveloped her from the harsh cold outside. The rich aroma wafted through the air, offering solace in its familiar embrace. In a quiet corner, Ada O'Neill was seated, exuding a sense of ease blended with unwavering vigilance. Her poised form cradled a steaming mug, emanating comfort and assurance in the midst of uncertainty.

"May I join you?" Rike asked, her tone warm despite the chill that lingered.

"Of course, take a seat," Ada's eyes held a depth that hinted at unspoken thoughts.

"I am not here to talk of work," Rike said as she sipped her chamomile tea.

"Me neither. What brought you to Canada?" Ada asked, settling in to her chair.

"It is more a matter of what drove me out," Rike said with a lightness in her voice that hid the bitterness of her move to a new country. "I wanted my future to bring me peace. What about you? I hear an accent. Africa, somewhere?"

"I was raised in Cote d'Ivoire," Ada revealed, a wistful gleam softening her gaze. "Moved to Canada two decades back."

"Côte d'Ivoire," Rike's voice lilted with a touch of nostalgia as she effortlessly switched to French. "It's been ages since I've conversed in French. Real French. Not what they speak here."

"The dialect is different. But is it really that bad?" Ada teased, a genuine smile breaking through the lingering seriousness, forging an unexpected connection between them.

"I don't mean native French speakers. But what the English think passes for French? C'est une situation épouvantable."

Their shared laughter danced through the air, a delicate melody cutting through the shop's tense ambiance. With each sip of their respective drinks, the comforting heat spread leisurely within them, thawing the chill of the room as they delved deeper into the intricate tapestry that connected their lives—discussing the languages they spoke, the distant lands they hailed from, and the relentless grip of law enforcement that had intricately woven their fates together.

"I must admit," Ada remarked with a mischievous glint in her eye, her gaze lingering on the array of pastries in a nearby display case, "scones have never quite won me over."

Rike nodded in agreement, her gaze meeting Ada's with a hint of intrigue. The air inside the Auberge felt charged with unspoken potential, swirling like the steam from their mugs. It was as if a delicate dance of attraction was unfolding between them, each word and gesture carrying a hidden layer of meaning. Yet, amidst this subtle flirtation, unspoken desires mingled together, creating a tantalizing tension that neither dared to fully acknowledge.

"I have to run some errands," Rike announced, placing her empty cup on the table. Giving Ada a nod, she left the cozy coffee shop and re-entered the biting cold outside. Despite both being foreigners in the land for quite some time, conversing with Ada had been a pleasant change. The frosty air nipped at her cheeks as she made her way to where her truck was parked, nestled under a blanket of fresh snow resembling powdered sugar. With swift movements, she cleared the windshield of the fluffy white coating before starting the engine and driving off towards Warren McDaniel's residence.

Chapter 21

Navigating the snow-laden streets, Rike felt the penetrating stares of the townspeople. Their eyes, like icy blades, sliced through the frigid air, carrying with them a mixture of suspicion and apprehension that weighed heavily on her. Her truck was distinct, and every glare at the truck was a glare at her. Her fingers clenched around the steering wheel, seeking solace in its solid familiarity as she pressed on.

Despite wanting nothing to do with dead women, Rike could not allow the intimations from both the public and the police to go unchallenged. She needed to speak with the men left behind.

Pulling up to the McDaniels' home, a humble abode cloaked in grief, Rike observed its sombre facade against the stark winter backdrop. The drawn curtains acted as a barrier, shielding raw emotions from the prying curiosity of outsiders. Gathering her resolve with a slow inhale, Rike approached the door and rapped softly, mindful of intruding upon their sorrowful sanctuary.

Warren McDaniel slowly swung the door open, his features drained of colour, deep hollows beneath his tired eyes.

"My name is Rike."

"Rike," he acknowledged with a slight nod, his voice barely above a whisper.

Rike hesitated for a moment before speaking, her gaze fixed on him. "Mr. McDaniel, I—" Her words hung in the air as she struggled to find the right sentiment. "I'm deeply sorry for your loss." His response was quiet, yet heavy with emotion as he gestured for her to step inside.

In the solemn living room, the walls adorned with joyful photographs of Kelsey, a stark reminder of what was lost. Warren's grief hung heavy in the air, casting a pall over their conversation. Rike again expressed her condolences before broaching the real subject of her visit carefully. Her voice laced with unease, she asked, "Any updates from the medical examiner?"

Warren's hands clenched together, his expression pained as he shook his head slowly. "Nothing new," he murmured. "It's like she vanished into the cold abyss, and then...was..." His voice trailed off, swallowed by the oppressive silence that engulfed them.

"Did Kelsey ever venture into the forest for walks? Was it a place she loved?" Rike's voice was a gentle breeze, yet it carried an undeniable weight.

Warren's eyes furrowed, a storm of bewilderment and anguish brewing on his face. "No," he replied, his fists clenched in silent frustration. "She avoided the woods, especially in winter. This doesn't make any sense to me."

Rike hesitated, her hand poised mid-air above Warren's tense knuckles before retreating swiftly. "Sometimes tragedies defy logic," she murmured softly. "If you require anything—"

Warren cut her off with a heavy exhale, weariness seeping into his posture. "Thank you for stopping by," he conceded, gratitude tinged with sorrow in his weary voice.

Rike expressed her sympathy again, a sombre acknowledgment of loss, before departing the residence. The lingering uncertainty weighed on her like a frosty shroud, leaving a trail of unanswered queries in her wake. As she embarked on the journey towards Mary Townsend's house, the treacherous path unfolded before her; the roads glistened with a deceptive sheen of ice concealed beneath a blanket of snow. Each twist and rise demanded her utmost vigilance as Rike skillfully maneuvered through the rugged countryside. Upon reaching her destination, she silenced the engine, casting a discerning gaze over the expanse of the property. A solitary beacon of light pierced through the darkness from the window of the living room, offering a glimpse into the quietude within.

Approaching the weather-beaten house, Rike's gaze swept through the frost-covered windows, spotting Paul Cantrell slumped on a threadbare sofa. His hands clumsily maneuvered a lighter and glass pipe, his movements sluggish yet purposeful. With unwavering determination, Rike knocked crisply on the door.

Startled, Paul jerked upright, his eyes widening in alarm as he swiftly concealed the incriminating items beneath a cushion. He strode to the door and swung it open, his expression shifting to one of displeasure upon encountering Rike's presence. "What do you want?" he grumbled.

"May I step inside?" Rike inquired, her voice steady but laced with an underlying firmness that hinted at her resolve.

"Who are you?"

"A friend of Mary's. I wanted to come by and tell you how sorry I am." Rike sounded very convincing.

"Fine," Paul grumbled, his heavy boots scraping as he reluctantly stepped aside. The air inside hung stagnant, a suffocating blend of despair and acrid chemicals that clung to the walls. Sinking back onto the worn sofa, Paul's defensive posture spoke volumes.

"Mary wouldn't want this for you, Paul," Rike's voice was a mere whisper, her gaze flickering towards an almost concealed pipe in the corner. She had no idea what Mary wanted for her brother.

"Mind your own damn business," Paul snapped back, a volatile mix of aggression and raw vulnerability colouring his words. "This is my damn house."

Rike released a slow exhale, her breath materializing in wisps in the frigid atmosphere. "I get it. Your pain is real, but tearing yourself apart won't bring her back."

"Fuck you!" Paul's outburst shattered the tense silence, his trembling hands betraying the storm raging within him.

"Did you and Mary have a good relationship?" Rike inquired, her back against the door frame leading to a room cloaked in memories and neglect.

"We did," Paul replied, his words barely audible. "She was everything to me."

"Can you think of any reason why she would have been outside in this freezing weather?"

"No. Mary hardly ever ventured out," Paul stated firmly.

"When did you last see her?"

"Two days b...before." His eyes darted away, as if grappling with his thoughts or seeking refuge from the harsh reality.

Before Rike could continue, Paul interjected sharply, "Just go! Get out!" Anger twisted his face, a pulsing vein betraying his inner turmoil.

She held her hands out to show she intended no harm. Rike's acknowledgment was subtle yet profound, recognizing the delicate line she had crossed into Paul's world consumed by grief. With a single nod, she conveyed her understanding before gracefully stepping out of the house, the door closing softly in her wake. Each snowflake that drifted down seemed to carry the sorrow that permeated the atmosphere.

Inside, through the frosted windowpane, Paul's hand trembled as he reached for the telephone, his eyes fixed on Rike's departure. The intensity of his gaze followed her every move as she made her way to her truck and drove off into the snowy landscape.

The drive back to her secluded cabin was a hazy blur, the relentless snowfall swept away by the rhythmic beat of the windshield wipers. As Rike's truck rolled to a stop in front of her refuge, the unexpected sight of Ada O'Neill's sleek vehicle parked outside sent a jolt of unease mingled with fleeting relief through her veins.

"Detective O'Neill," Rike acknowledged briskly as she exited the car, each step imprinting a crisp crunch on the freshly fallen snow beneath her boots. She doubted this was a friendly visit.

"We need to talk," Ada stated firmly as she emerged from her own vehicle, her expression grave and purposeful.

"Alright." Rike motioned towards the cabin door. "Let's do this inside."

Rike ushered Ada into the cozy cabin, the crackling fire pushing back the biting cold that seeped through the walls. With a purposeful air, Rike placed the kettle on the stove before settling across from Ada at the worn kitchen table. Their gazes locked in a silent exchange of unspoken tension.

"I was tempted to walk in. You do not lock your door. But, protocols. What are you doing?" Ada broke the silence, her eyes probing Rike's for hidden truths.

"Nothing," Rike's voice was steady, her hands gesturing around her. "I just arrived, as you saw. Other than that, you will have to be more specific."

Ada stood tall in her impeccably pressed suit, the rigid lines contrasting sharply with the cozy cabin setting. "Paul Cantrell contacted me," she stated, a hint of unease lacing her words. "He wasn't too thrilled about your unexpected visit."

Rike inhaled slowly, mindful of the fragile balance between truth and necessity. "I simply wanted to express my condolences," she clarified, her voice steady. "Given the recent events... it felt appropriate."

"Condolences?" Ada's eyebrow raised skeptically, her gaze piercing. "Or was there another motive behind your presence? You're well aware you shouldn't be meddling in an ongoing investigation, Rike. Despite what Horton may or may not want."

"I'm not interfering," Rike's voice barely rose above a whisper, the words hanging in the cold air like a fragile promise.

Ada's gaze bore into her, relentless and probing. "And what do you think you're doing, then?" The question cut through the tension like a knife.

"Showing concern," Rike shot back, her eyes locked on Ada's, daring her to challenge that. Her past as a detective lingered in every word she spoke. "And asking questions. I can't stand by when someone is trying to set me up."

"Set you up?" Ada's intense gaze locked onto Rike, her fingers pressing into the table's surface. "Accusations need more than just suspicion. Right now, we're facing three mysterious deaths."

"All linked to my land or close by," Rike countered sharply. "The connections are clear as day."

"Connections don't equate to evidence," Ada's tone remained unwavering. "Without the M.E.'s confirmation of homicide, we're dealing with unfortunate events, not murders."

"Coincidences seem to be aligning against me, painting a target on my back. And let's not overlook the fact that Officer Horton encouraged my involvement. Unofficially, of course." Rike's interruption hung heavy in the air, thickening the tension between them.

Ada's gaze narrowed imperceptibly, unable to dispute Rike's point. "Stop," she relented. "But if you do proceed, do so cautiously. If you're being set up, you might just be playing right into the killer's hands."

"Got it." Rike's response was solemn, her thoughts already racing ahead with the weight of their discussion. The atmosphere inside the cabin grew dense with unspoken fears. Despite Ada's guarded demeanour, a glint of sympathy shimmered in her eyes—a subtle admission that, beyond their professional facades, they were both mere pieces of a larger, unknown game.

"Whoever it is, they're orchestrating a twisted game," Rike asserted, her tone slicing through the frosty air with unwavering certainty. "Turning me into the scapegoat while I'm stumbling in the dark like everyone else."

Ada's features eased slightly, a fleeting moment of respite amidst the storm. "Walking this tightrope of suspicion isn't for the faint-hearted," she remarked, a veteran's gravitas underscoring her words.

The silence enveloped the room, broken only by the gentle crackle of the fire and the synchronized rhythm of their breaths, creating a tense atmosphere. In that moment, Rike tilted her head slightly in inquiry, her expression firm yet contemplative. As she met Ada's eyes, she noticed a lingering intensity in Ada's gaze, a silent exchange that hinted at a connection beyond mere professional courtesy.

They both sat down in the quiet space as time elongated like a pulled rubber band, creating a palpable tension in the air. Rike could almost hear the thud of her own heartbeats reverberating against the backdrop of crackling flames and the gentle illumination that painted Ada's resolute features with shifting shadows. She was beautiful. Ada interrupted the silence with a deliberate throat clearing, shattering the moment as she rose abruptly from her seat. "We will unravel this mystery," she declared, her voice unwavering yet tinged with a subtle hint of doubt that had stealthily crept into her tone. "And 'we' does not include you."

Rike's agreement was accompanied by a keen observation of Ada's graceful movements as she stood up. With purposeful steps, Rike trailed behind her, closing the physical distance between them with a gentle reach. Her fingertips lightly grazed Ada's arm in a silent gesture of connection. "I appreciate your concern," she expressed sincerely. Ada halted briefly at the touch, locking eyes with Rike once more. In that shared gaze lingered an unspoken inquiry, akin to the frosty mist that clung to the windowpanes, enveloping them in a moment filled with unspoken emotions.

"Be careful, Rike," Ada's voice, a soft murmur, lingered in the air as she reluctantly withdrew, her silhouette framed against the frosty backdrop of the Northern Ontario winter. The door whispered shut with a gentle finality, enveloping Rike in solitude amidst the fading warmth of the too-brief exchange.

Chapter 22

In the hushed expanse of the Co-Op, where the smell of the old refrigeration engines mingled with the earthy scent of fresh produce, Rike Volk navigated the aisles like a seasoned sleuth on a new case. Each selection she made—a dozen eggs, a rustic loaf of bread—was scrutinized for quality, her keen eye mirroring the precision she once wielded at crime scenes.

The bustling hum of the grocery store aisles enveloped her as Rike reached for a jar of pasta sauce, the rustle of her movements blending with the soft background music. Suddenly, a sharp trill shattered the tranquil atmosphere, cutting through the familiar sounds of shopping. Pausing, she extracted her phone from the deep pocket of her sturdy parka. The screen lit up with Autumn Evans' name, and without hesitation, Rike swiped to accept the call.

Bringing the phone to her ear, she braced herself for whatever news Autumn had to share, knowing it could be another knot in the intricate web of recent events that had gripped their small town. "Rike! You won't believe this—Craig Griffith just took down a bear near your property," Autumn's voice crackled with a mix of astonishment and exhilaration across the line. "And guess what he found inside it—a human foot!"

The jar of sauce almost slipped from Rike's fingers as shock coursed through her, causing an uncharacteristic fumble. With a steadying breath, she regained control and carefully returned the jar to its place on the shelf. Her mind whirred into action as she processed Autumn's words. "A bear?" she echoed softly, mulling over the implications before voicing her concern. "But isn't it against the law to kill them at this time of year?"

"Not in this case!" Autumn's words spilled out hurriedly, painting a picture of self-defence against a persistent bear that had made itself too comfortable near Craig's property. As the explanation sank in, Rike felt a revelation wash over her, each detail falling into place like the decisive strike of a gavel in court. The possibility that this bear wasn't just a mere nuisance but potentially a threat to humans loomed ominously in her mind, sending shivers down her spine unrelated to the chilly air surrounding her.

"Can we meet at the police station? I want to hear from Ada. And Horton." Rike's inquiry held both authority and urgency, her long-dormant detective instincts awakening with razor-sharp clarity despite years removed from active duty.

"Absolutely. I'll be there in ten." Autumn's voice clicked off, leaving Rike enveloped in the serene normalcy of the Co-Op, now a stark contrast against the unsettling news. Without hesitation, Rike abandoned her half-filled shopping basket, her thoughts already racing ahead to the police station, mentally assembling the grim pieces of this new mystery.

As Rike pushed open the heavy door of the police station, her gaze swept over the familiar surroundings until it settled on Ada O'Neill. The RCMP detective stood near the front desk, exuding a poised yet vigilant air. When their eyes met, genuine smiles lit up their faces—a bond that had transcended mere professionalism to blossom into a genuine friendship.

"Ada," Rike's voice cut through the room, her steps deliberate as she approached. "Tell me, is it confirmed about Craig and the bear? A human foot, was it?" Before Ada could answer, Autumn burst in, cheeks rosy either from the cold or the shocking revelation.

"So, Craig took down a bear with a human foot inside?" Rike echoed for Autumn's benefit. Her eyes locked on Ada.

"We're waiting for confirmation," Ada's voice remained steady. "Officer Horton's heading to Craig's now." A coffee machine sputtered its final protest in the corner, punctuating Ada's words. She poured herself a cup first, then extended the offer to Rike and Autumn. The steam curled upwards from the mugs like ghostly tendrils, filling the air with a comforting warmth that mingled with the rich scent of freshly brewed coffee. In that small kitchenette at the station, a collective sigh of relief whispered through them as they sought solace in this simple ritual, their eyes meeting over the steaming cups, tension palpable in the air.

"Let's take a seat over there," Ada proposed, gesturing towards the row of chairs by the crowded notice board filled with not-very-urgent community alerts. Rike grasped her mug tightly, relishing the comforting heat seeping into her chilled hands. Autumn exhaled softly, easing into the plush chair, while Ada exuded a poised sense of readiness.

"Maybe this is it, the breakthrough we've been waiting for," Rike pondered aloud, a glimmer of optimism lacing her words amidst the palpable tension in the air.

"Wouldn't that just neatly wrap everything up?" Autumn's voice quivered slightly, a fragile smile flickering on her lips. Ada's gaze sharpened, her features etched with concentration. "Though the delay in the autopsy results is intriguing," she mused, a subtle furrow forming between her brows. A tinge of impatience—or was it distrust—tinged her words.

The room fell into a spoken monologue by Autumn telling and retelling her feelings of relief. The faint echo of the radio dispatch in the background. Rike and Ada, enveloped in their individual contemplations, sat on edge, anxiously anticipating any update from Officer Horton. Eventually, as Autumn yielded the floor, their dialogue meandered towards light topics concerning the quaint offerings of Berna instead of delving into the pressing case at hand.

Two hours slipped away unnoticed before the door of the small-town police station creaked open, revealing Officer Horton's imposing figure. His confident grin matched the determined sway in his gait as he approached the cluster of women. With an aura of anticipation, he delivered his news, each word laced with a hint of satisfaction.

"Craig Griffith took down a rogue grizzly bear earlier today," he announced, his expression unwaveringly cheerful. "The beast had been loitering around his property, rummaging through his refuse—a true nuisance."

Rike's coffee cup hit the table with a sharp clatter, her brows furrowing in surprise. "Truly? But I'm his neighbour, and I haven't spotted any bears lurking nearby." Her doubt laced her words, while Autumn leaned in, eyes widening with curiosity.

"I saw it myself," Officer Horton insisted, his excitement palpable. "I was right there at the scene. We've secured the human foot and sent it for examination."

Ada interjected, her professional demeanour adding an edge to her voice. "Mary Townsend was missing both hands and feet. This detail might be crucial."

The weight of Ada's words lingered heavily in the room, dragging their brief moment of respite down to reality. A silent exchange passed between them, speaking volumes in a mere glance, each mind racing with the implications of what Ada had just said. "Let's hope this leads us closer to the truth," Officer Horton remarked, his eyes revealing a flicker of apprehension, a mirror of the burden they all carried.

A mixture of relief and disbelief filled the air, a shared exhale cutting through the tension that had gripped them for so long. Rike surveyed her colleagues in the station, noticing a subtle lift in their demeanour.

"Seems like that grizzly was more than just a troublemaker," Autumn pondered aloud, her voice carrying a mix of doubt and newfound optimism. "I wouldn't be surprised if it's been responsible for these attacks from the start."

Rike's brows furrowed, a flicker of doubt crossing her features as she contemplated the grim possibilities. "Perhaps Kelsey and Mary were merely caught in the crosshairs of fate," she murmured, her voice tinged with uncertainty.

Ada, her posture rigid against the desk, exhaled heavily, the unresolved cases pressing down on them. "If it turns out nature is to blame after all our fruitless pursuits..." she remarked, her tone edged with frustration. "I think I will be very relieved."

Officer Horton straightened his stance, a glimmer of hope cutting through the tension in the room. "Maybe tonight Saint Berna Aux Étranger can finally rest easy," he interjected resolutely. "It's time for closure, a moment to breathe free from this shadow. The whole town should be celebrating!"

"Town-wide celebration?" Rike's voice held a hint of skepticism, her arched eyebrows betraying her amusement while a faint smile played on her lips.

"Absolutely," Horton confirmed with a firm nod, his demeanour exuding certainty. "A fitting farewell for our unexpected culprit."

As Officer Horton strode away, brimming with purpose, Autumn pivoted towards Rike, her eyes alight with a sudden notion. "We should tag along, witness the communal relief firsthand. It's not often we witness such collective peace of mind."

"You go on ahead," Rike replied softly, giving her friend an encouraging grin as she gently shook her head. "I have a few loose ends to tie up here."

Autumn's expression flickered with a fleeting hint of letdown, swiftly masked by understanding. "Okay, your loss," she remarked before falling into step behind Officer Horton, who led the way eagerly. Pausing outside the police station, Autumn stole a quick glance back through the glass. Within, Rike and Ada shared a genuine moment of mirth, their laughter echoing in the room—a precious instance of connection that felt like a shared secret between them.

Autumn's eyes held a bittersweet expression, a faint curve of a smile gracing her lips as she observed Rike and Ada in their moment of camaraderie. With a wistful sigh, she turned away, the scene of their laughter and connection lingering in her mind like a gentle echo. Inside the station, Rike and Ada sat casually at the table. Each sip of coffee from their cups released wisps of steam that intertwined between them, carrying an unspoken bond akin to shared confidences.

"Looks like I'll be flying out soon," Ada remarked, a fleeting sense of sadness mingling with her relief. "Back to my regular beat."

"Saint Berna Aux Étranger will seem dull without your sharp wit to keep us on our toes," Rike responded, a subtle warmth in her gaze.

Before more words could flow between them, Officer Horton barged into the room, arms laden with a vibrant assortment of flyers. The paper crackled like dry leaves as he scattered them across the desk. Each flyer boldly proclaimed: "The Great Grizzly Riddance Revelry."

"Notice anything about the title?" Horton inquired, his grin barely contained.

Rike's eyes flicked from the flyers to Horton and back, a silent question hanging in the air.

"GGRR," he articulated with amusement, drawing out each letter. "Just like our late grizzly's growl."

Ada's eyes sparkled with amusement, a subtle smirk playing on her lips. "Clever," she remarked, a hint of sarcasm lacing her words.

"They better appreciate it," Officer Horton chimed in confidently, his smile unwavering.

Rike grasped the flyers, the rough paper scraping against her fingertips, grounding her in the moment. "I'll make sure these get out," she stated firmly, a newfound determination colouring her voice.

"Good luck," Ada's voice trailed after Rike as she left, fully engrossed in drafting her report.

Out in the chilly streets, Rike strode purposefully, pressing flyers into the hands of the curious townspeople who huddled together. The news had spread like wildfire, creating a sense of unity that had been absent for weeks.

"It seems the Cumming are off the hook," quipped a local, taking a flyer with a sigh of relief.

"And definitely not the Wendigo," chimed in another, sparking laughter from the gathering crowd.

Caught up in the moment, Rike felt an unfamiliar warmth seep through her usual reserve. As she continued to hand out flyers, each grateful smile and light-hearted jest lightened her heart amidst the tense atmosphere.

"Tonight's revelry awaits your presence!" her voice echoed through the air, carrying with it a sense of eager anticipation that lingered behind her like a trail of whispers. She spent two hours handing out flyers and gossiping with townsfolk.

The town square of Saint Berna Aux Étranger was aglow as the sun dipped below the horizon, painting the sky in hues of gold. Rike made her way towards the heart of the celebration, where a bustling crowd of approximately two hundred people had gathered.

The atmosphere was electric, filled with the lively chatter of united townsfolk and the tantalizing aroma of steaming beverages drifting from nearby stalls. Each exhale created delicate puffs in the crisp night air, adding to the festive ambiance. Amidst the throng stood Officer Horton, his usually rigid demeanour softened by an unfamiliar ease. A triumphant smile played on his lips, creasing the corners of his eyes and lending him a youthful air.

Taking centre stage atop a makeshift platform, Officer Horton commanded attention effortlessly. The hushed murmurs of the crowd subsided as all eyes turned towards their esteemed officer, ready to hear his words that promised to unite them further in this moment of unexpected closure.

"Listen up, residents of Saint Berna Aux Étranger!" Officer Horton's voice sliced through the crisp night air, commanding attention. "Tonight marks the end of our town's tormenting worry." His gaze swept over faces etched with relief, holding them captive. "Thanks to Craig Griffith's precise shot," he announced, his arms sweeping grandly, "the elusive 'culprit' stands revealed. The bear has been bested!" A surge of jubilation erupted from the crowd, hands clapping and boots thudding in unison. The square buzzed with a tangible release of tension, a wave of reassurance enveloping every soul present. "Let us banish our anxieties and toast to tranquillity restored!" Horton proclaimed, raising his plastic red cup high as the throng mirrored his gesture with fervour.

Rike stood on the fringes, her lips curving into a genuine smile. Ada glided to her side, her expression illuminated with the vibrancy of the celebration. "Rike," she murmured, drawing near to be heard above the clamour, "why don't we steal a moment at the Whispered Scandal pub? A quieter setting to raise a glass to our... unexpected resolution."

"Absolutely, though I doubt it will be quieter," Rike replied, appreciating the idea. Amidst the cheerful crowd, they weaved through, receiving nods and well-wishes as they navigated their way out of the bustling town square. As they neared the Whispered Scandal, Rike absorbed every detail of the pub's exterior with a nostalgic fondness. The brick front exuded a gentle warmth against the backdrop of the darkening sky, while the charming leaded windows hinted at a snug retreat from the encroaching cold. Overhead, the wooden sign bearing the pub's name swayed softly in harmony with the evening breeze.

"Shall we?" Ada's gesture towards the entrance was accompanied by a subtle yet playful arch of her brow, inviting Rike to join her. Without hesitation, Rike affirmed, sensing a unique camaraderie blossoming between them—a connection that felt like a beacon of hope in the midst of darkness. With a shared glance filled with unspoken understanding, they stepped into a new relationship.

Chapter 23

As the wind howled outside, rattling the windows of Whispered Scandal, Rike's gaze swept over the frosted glass, capturing the delicate ballet of snowflakes swirling in the stormy night. Inside, the cozy pub exuded a welcoming glow, a tapestry of flickering candlelight and murmured conversations. The scent of aged oak mingled with laughter, and plush crimson armchairs cradled patrons in intimate conversations. Amidst the soft clinks of glasses and distant echoes of camaraderie, secrets seemed to linger in the air like whispers waiting to be heard.

"The celebration seems to be drawing everyone out tonight," Ada observed, her gaze sweeping over the lively crowd in the town square as she savoured a sip of her pint.

"Even bad weather has a way of spiking spirits instead of dampening them, especially today," Rike replied, her voice cutting through the bar's cacophony with a deep, melodic tone. Leaning casually against the bar, she exuded a sense of relaxed vigilance reminiscent of her detective days.

A laugh escaped Ada, weaving through the ambient buzz around them. "Or perhaps it's the allure of being snowed in with great company."

Their eyes locked, a charged silence hanging between them. Rike's lips curled into a knowing smile. "Great company does offer its own set of advantages." Her words held a playful air, yet beneath lay an undercurrent of unspoken fascination.

"Advantages?" Ada quirked an eyebrow, mirroring Rike's lean with a hint of mischief. "And what might those entail?"

"Intelligent conversation, for one," Rike replied, her voice laced with a hint of amusement, the corner of her mouth quirking upwards as she delicately traced the intricate patterns on her glass with a fingertip. "A true gem to find in these parts."

"Well, I do try my best," Ada responded smoothly, a playful glint in her eyes matching the subtle dimple that appeared on her cheek. Her gaze held Rike's for a moment before dropping to her lips and then back up, a silent exchange passing between them.

"Ah, 'best' is my middle name," Rike teased with a smirk, the air around them thick with unspoken tension. "In your case, my dear Ada, you've already proven yourself." Rike spoke warmly, her words carrying a genuine admiration that mirrored the rich amber hues swirling in her glass.

"Smooth talker," Ada playfully accused, a hint of amusement dancing in her eyes as she tilted her head slightly towards Rike. "But you're not wrong," she added, clearly enjoying the banter.

Rike met Ada's gaze, a subtle smile playing on her lips as she appreciated the strength in Ada's jawline and the sharpness of her piercing eyes. "Just calling it like I see it," Rike replied, savouring the moment to openly admire Ada's striking features.

A mischievous glint sparkled in Ada's eyes as she suggested, "What do you say we turn this into a little competition? A battle of best detection, perhaps?" Her challenge carried a lightness that hinted at the hidden depths beneath.

Rike chuckled softly, her tone dipping into a more intimate register. "That does sound intriguingly risky," she pondered with a hint of allure. "I must warn you though—I don't take losing lightly."

"Absolutely." Ada's voice carried a hint of mischief, her eyes sparking with excitement. The crackling fire provided the perfect backdrop to their shared laughter, drowning out the storm raging outside. Amidst the clinking glasses and murmurs of other patrons at Whispered Scandal, Rike and Ada found themselves enveloped in an intimate bubble of connection.

"Berlin seems like a distant dream now," Rike reflected pensively, her gaze momentarily drifting past the assortment of gleaming liquor bottles behind the bar. She savoured the rich warmth of her whisky, relishing its familiar bite that anchored her to the present moment. "I miss the thrill of it all, you know? The unraveling mysteries, chasing down leads, seeking out the truth."

Ada's response was swift yet tender, a playful glint in her eye. "Ah, but isn't that what makes it all so exhilarating? The chase, the puzzle—it's not just a profession for you; it's woven into your very being."

"Absolutely," Rike affirmed, a sly grin playing on her lips. "Sometimes I contemplate delving into a new hobby... perhaps something to hone that instinct for the chase."

"Archery?" Ada proposed, a mischievous glint dancing in her eyes.

"Maybe," Rike chuckled, genuinely intrigued by the notion. "It would definitely spice things up from just skiing. Imagine combining the two; a unique biathlon of sorts. The thrill of pursuit and being pursued."

"Speaking of pursuits," Ada smoothly transitioned, leaning in closer with an elbow propped on the table. "My life with the RCMP takes me all over, untangling mysteries from one end of the country to the other." Her words carried a touch of self-assurance, rightfully so given her dedicated and courageous career path. "I've set my sights on joining the Integrated Homicide Investigation Team—the pinnacle unit in Canada."

"Quite the ambitious endeavour," Rike remarked, her admiration for Ada's determination evident in her gaze. "I do appreciate a woman with such fierce determination."

"Likewise, Rike," Ada responded, a subtle flush gracing her cheeks. "This case in Berna has been unlike any other. No motive. No typical suspects to track down. And now, no murders. Once this storm clears, it's back to British Columbia for me."

"The call of duty beckons," Rike acknowledged, raising her glass in a wordless salute to Ada's unwavering resolve.

"Always," Ada confirmed, locking eyes with Rike in a silent exchange that spoke volumes—the shared pursuit of justice creating an unspoken connection between them.

The crackling warmth of the hearth battled against the relentless cold seeping through the log walls, enveloping the two women. They shared stories of crimes and resolutions. The exchanges further cemented their bond, illuminated by the soft, golden radiance cast by the vintage lamps of Whispered Scandal. A sudden gust of frigid air swept in as Warren McDaniel entered, his presence heavy with grief that mirrored the icy draft trailing behind him. His haunted eyes conveyed a tale of recent anguish as he gravely acknowledged Rike and Ada, settling into a chair at their secluded table.

"Ada, Rike," he murmured, his voice laden with sorrow. "I'm grateful for your presence during these trying times."

"Warren," Rike's voice carried genuine sympathy, her words heavy with shared sorrow, "we can't imagine the pain of losing Kelsey." Ada's hand extended gracefully across the worn table, a silent gesture of solace resting gently on Warren's trembling hand. "Our hearts ache for you in this unimaginable loss," she spoke softly, her eyes reflecting a mix of compassion and unresolved curiosity.

"Thank you," Warren responded quietly, weariness etched into every line on his face as he absentmindedly traced his fingers over his stubbled jaw. "Who would have thought...

a grizzly bear," his voice trailed off, swallowed by the lively hum of the pub around them, blending with laughter and clinking glasses.

Ada's tone was soothing yet contemplative as she remarked, "Nature's ways are indeed unpredictable," her mind already spinning with unspoken inquiries that lingered in the wake of the wild mystery. Warren nodded in agreement, a shadow of bewilderment tainting his usual composure. "Unpredictable and unforgiving," he added sombrely, an undertone of disbelief colouring his words. "With the bear gone, I'm left waiting on the medical examiner for Kelsey's final closure... for all the practicalities to fall into place before I can truly begin to mourn her properly."

"Paperwork can wait," Rike's voice, gentle yet unwavering, advised Warren. "Allow yourself the space to mourn."

Warren, lost in a haze of disbelief, shook his head slowly. "It's all so surreal," he murmured, his eyes darting between the detectives in search of reason amidst the chaos. "The odds of a fatal grizzly attack are low, only around 14 percent. To have everyone perish in this manner?"

Reflecting on her training, Ada spoke thoughtfully, her words coloured by statistics. "Most bear encounters are chance occurrences. Dusk is when they're most active, often resulting in mutual surprise. One bear, hungry or mad, can cause such irreparable harm."

"Indeed," Warren interjected with a touch of intensity creeping into his voice. "Predatory attacks are uncommon. Typically, it's a matter of conflicting paths—humans fleeing one way and bears another—a natural ballet. But what happened to Kelsey..." His voice faltered briefly, emotions threatening to overwhelm him before he steadied himself once more.

"I'm sorry. I've intruded." Warren's voice wavered.

"Don't worry, Warren. You can stay," Ada's tone was firm.

"No. I..."

A burst of laughter erupted from another table, shattering the solemn atmosphere. Warren's gaze flickered towards the source of merriment, a fleeting grin crossing his face.

"Go on," Ada urged with a subtle gesture towards the jovial group. "Sit with your friends."

"Take care, Warren," Rike bid him farewell as he departed for the fireplace-lit gathering, their laughter echoing starkly in his wake.

Leaning in closer, Rike's elbows found support on the polished dark wooden table, her eyes intense and focused. "The whole thing doesn't sit right with me," she confessed softly over the pub's clamour and the haunting wind outside. "I live near where that grizzly was shot, Ada. And in all my time there, I've never seen a sign of one—only wolves."

Ada's nod was accompanied by a contemplative shift in her expression. The soft glow of the chandeliers above flickered in her eyes, emphasizing the gravity of Rike's words. "It's unsettling," she mused, her slender fingers delicately skimming the glass stem. "Especially that horrible discovery of the human foot in the bear's gut pile. While it's compelling evidence, I share your skepticism about not seeing the bear itself, only its remains."

"So, there was no intact bear?" Rike inquired sharply, fixing her gaze on Ada.

"Apparently not," Ada confirmed with a tight-lipped frown. "And to make matters worse, Officer Horton failed to document it properly, at least in terms of the scant evidence I have seen. Sloppy work at best. But Head Office has called me back and back I will go."

"Absolutely," Rike agreed firmly, her eyes locked onto Ada's with intensity. "Ultimately, it will be up to the medical examiner to draw conclusions. But I can't shake off my concern that Officer Horton might have overlooked crucial details."

"Let's hope not," Ada remarked, her voice carrying a hint of that trademark professional skepticism that had always steered her right. "In our line of work, nuances are everything. They're the fine thread that can either stitch a case together or unravel it completely."

The conversation tapered off momentarily as a sudden gust of wind whipped against the windows, causing a collective shudder to ripple through the pub. The patrons instinctively huddled deeper into their coats, finding solace in the cozy haven amidst the encroaching winter tempest. In the pause that followed, Rike and Ada shared a glance laden with unspoken understanding, a silent language known only to those entrenched in the pursuit of truth.

"You know what? I think it's time for me to head back to my hotel," Ada suggested with a playful glint in her eye. "Care to be my escort? I've had a drink."

"Absolutely," Rike replied with an undertone of delight at Ada's company. She was glad she had opted for a seltzer water. Rike and Ada ventured out through the groaning door of Whispered Scandal, stepping into the icy night's embrace. A symphony of howling winds engulfed them, stealing their words as they bantered back and forth in playful defiance against the biting chill.

Rike shivered, her breath forming misty clouds in the frigid air. "Geez, it's like the North Pole out here!" she exclaimed, her words almost lost in the howling wind.

Ada chuckled, the sound harmonizing with the storm's fury. "You weren't kidding about this icy blast!"

Shoulder to shoulder, they hurried towards Rike's truck, nestled under a flickering streetlight. The vehicle beckoned like a cozy haven amidst the snowstorm. With a click of a button, Rike unlocked the doors, and they both clambered inside, seeking refuge from the biting cold.

"Let's defrost this place," Rike suggested playfully as she ignited the engine. The truck sputtered to life, releasing a wave of warmth that thawed their frozen exteriors. "I'll be your chauffeur through this winter wonderland; no need for you to brave this blizzard just to get your truck from the police station parking lot."

"Thanks for the ride, Rike. It's chilly out there. I will pick up the truck tomorrow, when it isn't so cold," Ada said appreciatively, her breath forming little clouds in the cold air. The truck crept along the snow-covered streets, the tires creating a rhythmic crunch with each rotation. In the cozy cabin, the only sounds were the gentle hum of the heater and the swish of the wipers clearing snowflakes.

"Your hotel's just up ahead, right?" Rike inquired, her gaze fixed on the snowy path ahead.

"Yeah, that's it. The only one in town," Ada confirmed with a nod, gesturing towards the hotel's glowing sign battling against the swirling snowflakes.

Pulling into the hotel's entrance lane, Rike parked and turned to look at Ada. Having been alone for some time now, Ada seemed to bring a warmth that was both inviting and unfamiliar.

Rike's voice, soft yet filled with sincerity, broke the quiet air between them. "Ada, I must share something with you... your beauty is truly captivating." The words lingered, creating a delicate tension in the surrounding space. A rush of emotions flooded Ada as she felt her own longing mirrored in Rike's confession.

Meeting Rike's gaze, she challenged playfully, "Then why the hesitation to come in for a drink?" Her heart raced in anticipation.

"I must get home. But..." Rike closed the gap between them, moving closer until their breaths mingled. In that intimate moment inside the cozy cabin of the truck, their lips met in a kiss that spoke volumes. It was a blend of tenderness and urgency, a fusion of two souls drawn together by an undeniable attraction. The kiss carried a warmth that contrasted with the frosty exterior world surrounding them, igniting a fire that had smoldered beneath the surface for far too long.

After a lingering kiss, Ada's eyes fluttered open to meet Rike's unwavering gaze, filled with a soft yet profound intensity. Her face illuminated by a radiant smile, she murmured, "I'll give you a call before I catch my 3 p.m. flight tomorrow."

"I'll be waiting eagerly," Rike responded in a husky, subdued tone.

Exiting the truck, Ada encountered the biting winter air that sharply contrasted with the warmth they had shared moments ago. Glancing back, she found Rike fixed on her, an unspoken pact hanging delicately between them. With a final wave, Ada vanished into the hotel's inviting luminance, leaving Rike alone in the purring solitude of the truck.

The soft thud of the hotel doors closing echoed in the stillness as Rike lingered, her gaze fixed until Ada disappeared from view. With a gentle sigh, she eased onto the empty street, the snowflakes twirling down like delicate dancers erasing any hint of their fleeting connection. The hushed crunch of tires on fresh snow serenaded her departure into the wintry night, carrying with it the lingering essence of Ada's tender kiss, a whispered vow hanging in the icy air.

Chapter 24

As the first light of dawn painted the snow-covered landscape in hues of pink and gold, Rike Volk stepped into her skis, the crisp air biting at her cheeks. With each glide, the snow whispered beneath her, a serene melody that mingled with the distant echoes of awakening wildlife. Skiing was more than just a routine for Rike; it was a communion with nature, a sacred dance she performed with reverence and grace.

Pine boughs, burdened by the weight of snow, swayed ominously in the brisk breeze, casting eerie shadows that danced menacingly on the ground. Each snowflake fell like a chilling omen from the overcast sky, adorning Rike's practical hair before vanishing into oblivion. Despite the winter beauty surrounding her, a sense of foreboding clouded her features. In this frozen landscape that once brought solace, Rike felt a creeping unease clawing at her peace. The grizzly bear troubled her mind.

As she followed the trail back towards her secluded cabin, it emerged from its camouflage among the trees like a haunting revelation. The sight of the slightly open front door loomed before her like a sinister invitation into darkness. Her heart raced with a primal fear as her instincts screamed warnings in her mind.

She released herself from her skis. Every step closer to the cabin heightened the tension in the air. Rike's movements were deliberate yet urgent as she closed in on the entrance, abandoning her skis without a second thought. With practiced precision born from experience, she swiftly armed herself with a rifle, its weight offering both reassurance and an unsettling reminder of potential danger lurking within her own sanctuary.

The snow surrounding Rike's secluded home, once untouched except by her skis, now held the chilling evidence of an intruder's presence—boot prints defiling the purity of the landscape. They marred the snowy canvas, leading ominously to and from her haven, culminating in tire tracks etched into the ground.

With a steely resolve, Rike grasped her cell phone as she meticulously captured each intrusive mark with a sense of urgency. The mechanical sound of the camera shutter shattered the serene quiet, amplifying her sense of unease. She stayed away from the tracks lest they be important.

Stealthily moving towards the side of the cabin, she navigated through the snowdrifts to reach the kitchen window. Her breath materialized in fleeting clouds against the glass, obscuring her view of the once-familiar interior now cloaked in shadows that seemed to pulse with hidden threats.

Her heart raced erratically within her chest, a thunderous rhythm of apprehension as she strained to peer past her own reflection. The tension wound tighter within her like a coiled spring ready to snap as she pressed closer to the window, feeling the frigid air nipping at her cheeks with a menacing chill.

In the dim light, Rike's eyes strained to make sense of the shadowy figure sprawled on the kitchen floor. As her vision adjusted, the gruesome reality unfolded before her—a woman, motionless and savagely disfigured, laid out on the wooden boards. A primal scream ripped through Rike's throat, reverberating with a chilling echo in the stillness of the cabin. The sight triggered a relentless onslaught of memories from her years as a detective—each crime scene she had witnessed. Every grisly detail flooded back with merciless clarity.

Overwhelmed, Rike's legs gave way beneath her, sending her crashing into the snow outside. Clutching her head in a desperate attempt to block out the haunting images assaulting her mind, she was consumed by a whirlwind of past horrors. The tranquil winter landscape morphed into a nightmarish panorama of twisted limbs and blood-red stains that existed solely within the confines of her fractured psyche.

In the silence of the winter landscape, dread coiled around Rike like icy tendrils. The realization struck her with a force that stole her breath—the danger was inside, lurking in the shadows of familiarity. "Move, Rike," she willed herself, but her voice remained trapped within. Her body quaked uncontrollably, sprawled on the snow's frozen grasp.

Time blurred in the haze of fear, minutes slipping through her fingers unnoticed. Then a surge of primal instinct surged through her veins, eclipsing the grip of terror. With sheer determination, Rike forced her trembling form upright and began to crawl, each inch an agonizing battle against both numbing cold and paralyzing dread.

Away from the horror encased within her home, she dragged herself labouriously. Every strained motion resonated with a symphony of protest from her protesting muscles, a testament to the unyielding fear that clutched at her heart. The truth hidden within those tracks whispered deceit—the bear was but a façade, masking something far more sinister.

Her truck stood like a fortress of refuge amidst the swirling chaos. With desperation lending her unexpected strength, Rike clutched the door handle, her fingers slipping momentarily before finally finding a firm grip. A surge of bile surged in her throat, and she swiftly turned away just in time for her stomach's contents to spill onto the snow beside the vehicle, the acrid stench mingling with the biting cold air.

Using the back of her hand to wipe her mouth, Rike summoned every ounce of resolve left within her and heaved herself into the cab of the truck. The door slammed shut behind her, creating a barrier between herself and the outside world. Though meager, the interior provided a temporary sanctuary from the nightmare awaiting within her home—shielding her from the gruesome scene that had shattered the tranquillity of her life.

In a frantic flurry, Rike reached for her cell phone, her fingers numbed by both cold and shock. With hands trembling uncontrollably, she dialled 911, pressing the phone to her ear as if clinging to a lifeline, the icy plastic almost melding with her skin in its chilling touch.

The operator's voice pierced through the icy silence, jolting Rike into action. Her fingers trembled as she clutched the phone, the cold plastic almost slipping from her grasp. Each breath she took felt sharp, her chest tightening with fear as she forced the urgent words out. 'There's a body... in my cabin, on Way Road, 27 Way Road,' Rike managed to say, her voice quivering. "I need police and medical assistance."

"Stay on the line, ma'am. Help is already on its way. Do you know if the person is okay?"

"No. Dead. Very dead. There are footprints leading to my door. My door was open. I..." Rike's sense of duty clashed with her growing anxiety. With a deep breath, she hesitated for a moment, torn between the instinct to keep the line open and the pressing need to involve Ada.

With a tense pause, she made a difficult decision, ending the call with a reluctant, "I'm hanging up. I'll await help on the scene." As the line went silent, Rike wasted no time in dialling the hotel in Berna where Ada O'Neill, the formidable RCMP detective, was lodging.

"Connect me to Ada O'Neill's room," Rike demanded from the hotel receptionist, her voice barely audible above a whisper now.

Rike's phone buzzed insistently as the 911 operator tried to reestablish contact, a shrill sound cutting through the inane 'on-hold' music. With a deep breath, she ignored it. The call connected after two rings, and a voice filled with authority spoke, "Ada O'Neill speaking."

"It's Rike. There's been a murder in my cabin. A body!" Rike's voice quivered, the words tumbling out like an avalanche crashing down a mountainside. Panic clawed at her throat, making it hard to breathe as she struggled to articulate the horror she had stumbled upon. "Body, face, floor, door," she gasped out in disjointed fragments.

"I'm on my way," Ada's response sliced through the chaos with chilling calmness, her tone a stark juxtaposition of Rike's frantic utterances. Each word from Ada felt like cold ice settling over the tense air, promising a calculated approach to the grim situation unfolding. "I'll inform Officer Horton. We'll be there soon. Preserve the scene."

"Thank you," Rike whispered hoarsely before abruptly ending the call, her heart pounding in sync with the ticking seconds that separated her from the impending arrival of help. The metallic tang of fear lingered in her mouth, mingling with the acrid scent of adrenaline that saturated the very walls around her, painting everything in shades of dread and uncertainty.

Collapsing back into her seat, she felt her strength drain away. Wrapping her arms around herself, she shuddered violently from the unrelenting grip of fear that refused to release its hold on her. Her phone rang-it was Emergency Services still trying to contact her. She could not stand the thought of answering it.

Outside, a heavy blanket of snow muffled all sound, creating an eerie stillness broken only by the occasional groan of snow-laden branches. Suddenly, the shrill wail of a police siren shattered the quiet, sending a jolt of fear through Rike. She raised her head, eyes locking onto the road that now seemed like a path to impending doom.

A police car emerged, its flashing blue and red lights cutting through the isolation like blades. As it made its way towards her sanctuary turned sinister, each crunch of its tires over the frozen ground felt like an ominous drumbeat in Rike's ears. The vehicle pulled up near her truck with a menacing finality that made Rike's heart race.

Fury flared within Rike as she watched the unwanted interloper encroach on her sanctuary. The audacity of being so near her cabin ignited a seething rage within her. Why hadn't they considered tire marks or footprints left behind? Doubts clawed at her thoughts—had this reckless intrusion irreversibly contaminated vital evidence?

Officer Horton emerged from the patrol car, his features etched with a stern resolve beneath the shadow of his hat. Ada trailed behind in her own vehicle, parking at a distance as a real professional should, her demeanour a shield of impenetrable professionalism. Together, they advanced towards Rike's truck, careful only now not to disturb the snow.

With Officer Horton's support, the door of the truck creaked open, and Rike emerged unsteadily, her legs trembling beneath her weight. Leaning against the vehicle's frame for support, she met their gazes with a desperate plea for reassurance amidst the chilling air that carried whispers of death.

"There's a body inside," Rike managed to articulate, her voice strained by shock and frost. Pointing the way towards her cabin, she looked at her skis on the ground—a terrible reminder of the abrupt tragedy that had shattered the tranquillity of the morning.

Creating a path through the thick snow, Ada declared to Officer Horton to follow in her snowy footprints as she approached the cabin. By establishing a single path of ingress and egress for police, Ada did her best to preserve the outdoor scene. Stepping up to the door, Ada entered the shadowy room, her breath catching in her throat, muffled by the scarf covering her face. Inside, at the centre of Rike's cabin, lay a woman's lifeless body stiffly motionless on the floor. The contrast between the brutalized form and the tranquil snow outside shattered the peaceful atmosphere within Rike's home with a chilling finality.

Chapter 25

As the tranquil snow outside painted the world in a serene blanket of white, the restless atmosphere within Rike Volk's mind found no peace. The stark contrast between the beauty outside and the brutalized form she saw sent a shiver down her spine, a cold reminder of the darkness that could lurk beneath even the most pristine surfaces.

A flurry of conflicting emotions swirled within Rike as she stood, recalling the haunting sight, her usually unflinching demeanour faltering in the face of such raw and personal brutality. The tension in the air was palpable, a silent symphony of unease that seemed to echo the turmoil in her own heart.

And then, like a shadow creeping over her solitude, Officer Horton's grim presence intruded upon her mind. His hushed tone carried grim recognition as he leaned through the doorway, his words hanging heavy in the frigid air.

"It appears to be Tammy Griffith," Officer Horton murmured grimly, his hushed tone heavy with grim recognition as he leaned through the doorway to see.

"Tammy," Rike whispered, her breath catching in her throat. Her mind raced with a mix of shock and confusion. It was Tammy Griffith, the last person she expected to find in her cabin. The woman she openly despised, her absence causing whispers to ripple through the town for two weeks. Yet here she was, lying on the floor, a chilling puzzle that defied explanation. Despite their rocky history, the sight of Tammy sent a wave of unease through Rike, her usual confidence shaken by the sudden appearance of her neighbour. What could have possibly led Tammy to this unexpected and grim destination? The air in the cabin seemed to thicken with unanswered questions, leaving Rike standing frozen in a moment of uncertainty.

Officer Horton's voice shattered the suffocating quiet, slicing through the tension like a knife. "Where were you this morning, Rike?"

"Skiing," Rike responded firmly, fighting to mask the tremor in her words. "It's what I do. Every morning." She locked eyes with Officer Horton, her glance a challenge.

Horton's eyebrows knitted closer, the lines on his forehead deepening as he scrutinized her, trying to unearth signs of duplicity that weren't there. Rike's stance was solid, her jaw set in defiance; she would not acquiesce to baseless suspicion. The air between them crackled, the silence filled with confrontation.

"You go out every morning," Horton echoed skeptically, "and today someone ends up dead in your cabin?"

"I don't make appointments with death," Rike snapped back, her patience fraying at its edges.

Ada stepped inside, sparing them both a curious glance before her attention shifted to the grim tableau before her. She knelt beside Tammy's body with measured grace, her fingers tentatively probing for clues that might reveal the narrative of Tammy's final moments. A seasoned investigator, Ada's movements were both methodical and reverent. The dead bestowed their secrets upon her in silent whispers.

Rike watched Officer Horton carefully pivot his stance to track Ada's examination. He was out of his element here. Horton's usual beat involved calming domestic disputes and chasing off wildlife that strayed too close to town. But now, under Ada's watchful eye, he appeared keen to assert his authority.

"Rike," Horton pressed again, unwilling to let silence claim the moment. "What's your relationship with Craig Griffith?"

Rike's eyes flitted from Tammy's body to Officer Horton. Each word from her mouth was precise and clipped. "The same as with Tammy. You have absolutely everything on file. Don't you?"

Ada rose and stood stoically between them, a silent observer and a silent supporter. Her gaze held an unspoken understanding, torn between duty and compassion. Though bound by professionalism, her eyes lingered on Rike with a hint of longing to offer comfort amidst the storm of suspicion and sorrow.

In the crisp winter air that stole its way inside, Officer Horton's breath escaped in a doubtful whisper that hung like a ghostly spectre. "Skiing alone in the woods, no one to vouch for your story? Who saw you? Did you speak with anyone at all?"

Rike's sharp inhale shattered the icy stillness. "Are you pointing fingers at me, Officer Horton?" Her words pierced through the frozen morning, a mix of disbelief and indignation colouring her voice. "Go outside and you can follow my ski trail. You jackass!"

"Hey, now, let's not name call," Ada said as she moved now, her hand held up as if to hold back the torrent that threatened to spill forth.

"You seem to find trouble often," Horton retorted, his accusation hanging between them like a bitter frost. "Some play innocent better than others."

Ada's voice sliced through the escalating confrontation with unwavering authority. "Stop this. Not here, not now. Let's stick to protocol. Out. Everyone out."

Rike's heart thundered in her chest, a drumbeat of déjà vu and disbelief echoing in her ears. The familiar dance of suspicion encroached on her reality once more, its chilling tendrils threatening to engulf her. Yet amidst it all, she clung fiercely to her truth–the notion that she could ever bring harm to another soul was inconceivable.

Rike was being guided toward Officer Horton's truck when they saw a trio of cars coming down the road. Officer Juno, the medical examiner Dr. Dennison, and two forensic technicians arrived on scene. Rike watched as her home became a flurry of yellow crime scene tape and drama.

Ada directed Officer Juno to follow and document the ski tracks Rike said were hers. The man grunted, stared, and, when Ada raised her eyebrow questioning his reluctance, he proceeded to do as told.

Snowflakes swirled frantically in the darkening sky, mirroring the turbulent unease that gripped them all. Nature itself seemed to echo the looming threat as the trees creaked ominously under the weight of gathering clouds.

As the investigation unfolded in the shadow of Rike's cabin, a subtle shift in the atmosphere heralded an impending change. The once serene snowscape now quivered with anticipation as the sky darkened ominously. Whispers of wind began to dance through the trees, their mournful howls growing louder with each passing moment.

Officer Horton's breath hung like a frosty veil in the crisp air, his features etched with unease as the first flurries of snow descended from the brooding clouds above. Ada, her stance unwavering, cast a steely gaze towards the horizon where grey clouds churned ominously.

The snowflakes, once gentle and delicate, now whipped into a frenzied frenzy by an invisible hand. They swirled around Rike and her companions in a chaotic ballet, their dance mirroring the turmoil that gripped them all. Nature itself seemed to protest, unleashing its fury upon the isolated landscape.

Rike felt a chill creep up her spine as she watched the storm gather momentum. The trees groaned under the onslaught of relentless gusts, their branches thrashing wildly against the darkening sky. The temperature plummeted sharply, biting through layers of clothing with icy teeth.

In that fleeting moment, before chaos descended upon them, Rike couldn't shake the feeling that this tempest brewing overhead was more than just a weather phenomenon. It was a harbinger of darker times ahead, a storm that threatened to engulf everything in its path. And as she braced herself against nature's wrath, Rike knew that they were about to be tested like never before.

Officer Horton shivered, his breath forming icy clouds in the frigid air. Ada, her features etched with determination, acknowledged the plummeting temperature with a brisk nod. "We need to get Rike back to the police station," she urged, her words punctuated by the biting cold.

Before they could move, Dr. Dennison emerged from the doorway, his movements precise as he peeled off his gloves. His eyes flicked from Rike to Officer Horton to Ada, almost hidden behind frosted glasses that mirrored the wintry landscape.

"The body is frozen solid," he declared sharply over the howling wind. "We must act swiftly before we're trapped in by snow and... What the hell have you been doing, Horton? Just standing there? Help my techs document the external evidence before everything is destroyed!" The urgency in his voice hung heavy in the unforgiving cold, emphasizing the dire nature of their discovery.

Officer Horton scrambled to help the forensic technicians. He donned gloves and grabbed evidence bags from a box in the bed of his truck, and began to assist the techs. He held the bags while they dropped in even the smallest pieces of possible evidence.

"Ada, this was Tammy Griffith," Officer Horton supplied grimly, his voice laced with concern, "reported missing by her husband nearly two weeks ago. She lives just next door. There. With her husband, Craig Griffith," he said, pointing towards the house shrouded in snow-laden branches.

Ada's usually composed expression faltered slightly at the distressing information, a flicker of unease crossing her features before she swiftly excused herself. "I'll go next door, notify Mr. Griffith. This news will hit him hard."

Officer Juno arrived back at the cabin, having traversed only 10 minutes on foot to document Rike's path. "I managed to document some, but the snow's filling up the tracks, wiping them out," he announced.

"Then please, Officer Juno, take over here. I have to get going," Officer Horton's tone was urgent. He turned to Rike once Ada had trudged through the snow towards the neighbouring house, his eyes drilling into hers with intensity, "Rike, get in your truck and follow me to the station. We've got a lot to discuss. You okay to drive?"

Rike felt a knot tighten in her stomach at the gravity of his words, but managed a nod, her breath forming misty puffs in the frigid air as she complied silently. Her boots crunched on the snow-covered ground as she moved mechanically towards her vehicle, each step echoing loudly in the stillness of the wintry landscape. The cold seeped through her gloves as her trembling hands gripped the icy steering wheel, the engine roaring to life with a jolt that matched the turmoil brewing inside her.

Officer Horton and Rike sped away from the cabin, leaving the medical examiner alone with the ominous truth concealed within. The road to Berna unfurled ahead, a treacherous path obscured by cascading snowflakes that whispered foreboding secrets in the midst of the growing storm.

As they approached the police station, the snow swirled around them like a malevolent spirit, growing denser and more blinding by the second. The wail of the wind grew louder, a howling chorus that seemed to mock their efforts to maintain control on the slippery road. They were driving through a world that was rapidly turning white, features of the landscape disappearing under a blanket of snow.

Rike's truck, a sturdy old beast that had seen many winters, passed Horton and plowed ahead with dogged determination. Its headlights cut through the darkness and the thickening storm, twin beacons of safety in a world that felt increasingly hostile. Flakes battered against the windshield in a relentless assault, but Rike kept her eyes fixed on the road ahead, her hands steady on the wheel despite the icy chill that seemed to gnaw at her bones.

Officer Horton's truck followed closely behind, its red and blue lights flashing intermittently, painting surreal streaks of colour against the endless white. He was accustomed to driving in treacherous conditions, but this storm seemed intent on swallowing them whole. The visibility was decreasing rapidly; it was becoming hard to make out Rike's taillights through the blizzard.

The police station finally came into view—a solitary structure standing resolute against the tempest. Its outer walls were now frosted over with ice and snowflakes clung like desperate hands to every surface. The parking lot lay empty save for a few other official vehicles huddled together as if seeking warmth from one another.

Both trucks came to a stop with graceless skids that sent a snow spray arching through the air. The door to Rike's truck swung open, and she stepped out, her tall frame immediately assaulted by the gusting wind. Horton followed suit, pulling his coat tighter around him as they made their way to the entrance.

Within the stark confines of the police station, Rike Volk faced Officer Horton, her body coiled with apprehension. The room exuded a clinical coldness, accentuated by the harsh glare of overhead lights that failed to dispel the icy grip tightening around her heart.

"I'm baffled," Rike's voice sliced through the tense silence, tinged with a weariness that only added to the mounting pressure. "Who would orchestrate such an elaborate scheme to frame me for these heinous crimes?" She knew one obvious answer, but refused to speak Adlergestell Würger aloud.

Officer Horton reclined in his creaking chair, his gaze piercing into Rike. "You tell me."

"Tell you who would freeze Tammy's body and put it in my cabin? I can only think of one person, Officer Horton," Rike said as disbelief washed over her.

"Maybe you froze her?"

"I don't have electricity, and thus no freezer. Officer Horton, really?" Rike said with sarcasm dripping from every word.

"No freezer, you say. You could have stashed the body outside," he insinuated with a hint of accusation.

Rike's eyes narrowed, her disbelief palpable. "Outside?" She challenged, her voice laced with incredulity. "You were just at my place, Horton. All over my property. From the driveway to the back trees. If there was a body on my land, wouldn't you have seen it?"

The unspoken accusation lingered in the air like a dense fog of suspicion, intensifying the already taut atmosphere between them.

With a weary exhale, Horton ran a hand over his tired face. "Rike, your expertise, your past... they paint a compelling picture for knowing how to throw officials off the scent. You have a strong skill set," he pointed out solemnly.

"Off the scent?" Rike's voice sliced through the frigid air, laced with a bitter edge that cut deeper than the winter wind. "I investigated the crimes. I didn't commit them, Officer Horton. That's not the same skill set."

Horton's response was a slow nod, a begrudging admission of her point. But before he could delve further into their tense exchange, his phone shrilled like an alarm in the quiet of the cabin. With a brusque "Horton," he answered, his features darkening as he absorbed the urgent words on the other end.

His next words hung heavy in the air as he rose abruptly from his seat. "The medical examiner needs me back at the scene," he announced tersely, his gaze flickering to Rike with a mix of concern and wariness. "Look, Rike, I can't make sense of all this yet. You are not under arrest, and you can't remain here. And you can't return to your cabin. It's part of the crime scene."

"Where do you suggest I go?" Rike's question held a thread of defiance, though beneath it simmered a raw unease that no answer could soothe.

"Find someplace else. There's the hotel in town," he suggested, his tone devoid of sympathy, snatching his coat and heading for the door. "We'll be in touch." Officer Horton's departure left Rike sitting alone in the station, the silence amplifying her sense of dread.

With a leaden heart, she rose from her seat and stepped out into the frigid air. As Horton's cruiser vanished down the road, its flashing lights swallowed by the darkness, Rike felt a chill that had nothing to do with the wintry weather. Turning towards her truck, she couldn't shake off the feeling of impending doom that settled over her like a shroud of freshly fallen snow.

Her tires gripped the icy terrain with a menacing crunch, propelling her towards the solitary refuge of the local hotel. The path ahead blurred into obscurity, veiled by the relentless dance of snowflakes whipped by a callous wind that seemed to mock her every move.

Chapter 26

The crackling fireplace cast dancing shadows across the walls of the hotel lobby, its warmth a stark contrast to the icy chill that gripped Rike's heart. The aroma of the logs burning mingled with the faint scent of blood that lingered in her memory, a haunting reminder of the recent horrors she had faced. Amidst this eerie backdrop, a single question echoed in her mind: who would be next to fall victim to the unforgiving killer?

"Autumn, it's surreal. They're pointing fingers at me." Rike's voice ebbed like a gentle stream, carrying the weight of disbelief. She'd telephoned her closest friend for solace, her desperation palpable even through the crackling phone line.

"Rike, please, come to my place," Autumn's urgent plea crackled back, a safety net in the chaos. "You shouldn't weather this storm alone."

Appreciative yet resolute, Rike declined, her tone unwavering as memories of Officer Horton's stern words lingered in her thoughts. "Thank you, but I must stay grounded at the hotel. It's what they've advised."

Autumn's protests faded into the background as Rike's focus shifted abruptly to the commanding silhouette of Ada O'Neill framing the doorway like a portrait. Ada, exuding an air of authority blended with a hint of elegance, acknowledged Rike with a nod. Each deliberate step she took seemed to echo in perfect harmony with the erratic beats of Rike's heart.

"I have to go, Autumn," Rike interrupted their conversation abruptly as Ada drew closer, marking the end of one exchange and the beginning of a far more mysterious interaction.

"Officer Horton said you would be here. I've extended my own stay. Of course." Ada settled comfortably into the chair across from Rike, a playful glint in her eyes as she remarked, "Looks like I'm becoming a permanent fixture around here. With the fourth body surfacing, it seems we're setting up camp for a while. RCMP reinforcements are on their way in forty-eight hours." She leaned in slightly, a teasing smile dancing on her lips.

"But shh, top-secret discussions only. Remember, you're the intriguing suspect in this mystery." Ada's gaze held a mischievous twinkle, their unspoken connection crackling between them like an enigmatic spark waiting to ignite.

"You know I am not–"

Ada held up her hand to silence Rike. "I know nothing. You know nothing. Until the medical examiner renders a finding, neither of us knows anything."

Rike looked down at her fingers, wondering whether to reveal her darkest fears to Ada. She looked deeply into Ada's ebony eyes and cleared her throat. "I have a theory. A crazy theory," she said with great hesitance.

Ada reached out and put her hand gently on Rike's shoulder, a deep shadow passing over her face. "Let me hear it."

Rike drew a sharp breath. "Der Adlergestell Würger. Hunting me." When she said it out loud, it seemed too preposterous and too real.

"I delved into the Adlergestell case while looking into your background," Ada remarked, her expression a mix of concern and respect. "Do you suspect a mimic in Berna?"

"I...no. It sounds fantastical when I say it out loud. Do you think I've been followed all the way from Germany?" Rike replied.

Ada paused, her gaze contemplative as she weighed the question with the gravity it deserved. Shadows flickered across her stony features, deepening the lines etched around her eyes, eyes that had seen much more than most. "It's not outside the realm of possibility," she admitted with a voice steady and firm. "However, I see little benefit in jumping to conclusions without evidence of such a remarkable thing."

Rike's chest loosened at the suggestion, a whisper of ease helping keep her composure steady. She held Ada's gaze, unflinching.

Ada smiled and lowered her eyes, looking at the ring of water on the bar under her glass. "But it would make more sense for this to be a homegrown Canadian. Someone tied to you. Here is my crazy theory: Officer Horton resents your remarkable record, and is killing women and framing you to ruin your reputation and make himself the saviour." The women chuckled at the idea that Horton was the killer.

"Maybe it is Officer Juno," Rike joked. "Trying to do the same."

"No, wait, maybe it is Dr. Dennison! He just wants to drum up some business! We must consider every angle." Ada teased. The women laughed until tears rolled down their cheeks.

"Ada, thank you," Rike said, reaching out and putting her hand on Ada's.

Ada moved closer to Rike, her presence offering an odd sense of comfort amid the maelstrom of doubt that threatened to engulf them both.

Rike's lips quirk into a grateful smile, a flicker of vulnerability softening her features. "I appreciate you being here, Ada," she admits, her voice laced with sincerity. "I didn't expect to find someone who understands. Who can laugh at the madness that forms in the mind of an investigator?"

Ada's expression softens further, a gentle smile playing on her lips. "Sometimes, understanding comes from unexpected places," she muses, her tone inviting and warm. "We each carry our burdens, but sharing them can make them lighter."

Rike's heart swelled with gratitude and a newfound sense of connection. In that moment, the walls Rike had carefully built around herself began to crack, revealing a vulnerability she hadn't dared to show before. She had not laughed in a long, long time.

Their gazes locked, a magnetic pull blending professionalism with a hint of personal fascination. Rike couldn't help but notice the elegant curve of Ada's jawline and the way her eyes shimmered with the playful banter. Ada exuded an aura that transcended mere official interactions; she was a captivating puzzle wrapped in the authoritative garb of law enforcement.

"I wouldn't have pegged you for a whiskey sour aficionado," Ada quipped, a mischievous sparkle dancing in her eyes as she motioned towards Rike's drink.

Rike countered with a lopsided grin, "It's a complex relationship," savouring the moment as silence wove between them like a taut thread. In that pause, an unspoken query lingered in the charged air, daring one of them to take the first step across the invisible line.

"Complexity has its allure," Ada murmured, her voice a soft caress in the quiet room, drawing Rike in like a magnet pulling at steel. With a subtle lean forward, she closed the gap between them, her fingertips barely grazing Rike's hand as she reached for a coaster. A surge of electricity shot up Rike's arm at the unexpected touch, sparking a fire of awareness between them that neither could ignore.

"I would like to talk to you more about...everything. Would you like to go somewhere a little more private?" Ada asked as she took Rike's hand in hers. She gently intertwined her fingers into Rike's.

As Ada's suggestion of a more private setting hung in the air, Rike's pulse quickened with a mix of emotions that danced between anticipation and apprehension. The prospect of being with this beautiful woman, away from prying eyes, stirred a whirlwind of feelings within Rike.

Suggestively, Rike nodded, her words barely audible, as if sharing a forbidden truth, "Well, Ada. If you're offering a private tête-à-tête, who am I to resist the allure of secrecy with a touch of danger?"

Dismissing the small talk with a mischievous grin playing on her lips, Rike rose gracefully. Extending her hand to Ada, she suggested with a hint of allure, "Let's leave the mundane behind and embrace our desires like grown-ups. Show me where your heart resides."

Ada's response was a subtle nod, her eyes locking onto Rike's with unwavering intensity. As they strolled together towards the elevator, their arms brushed intermittently, creating a delicate dance of closeness. The hushed cadence of their steps reverberated through the hotel corridor, accompanied by faint echoes of laughter drifting from afar. Yet, it was the haunting wail of the wind outside that punctuated their every move, emphasizing the contrast between the chill of the outside world and the blossoming warmth enveloping them with each passing moment.

Once they stepped into Ada's dimly lit hotel room, a hush enveloped Ada and Rike, cocooning them from the outside chaos. The soft click of the lamp filled the space with a warm glow, illuminating the carefully curated elegance surrounding them. Mesmerized by the refined ambiance, Rike's eyes traced the subtle patterns of Ada's clothing as she drew near, her touch sending shivers down Rike's spine.

"Let this be our moment of luxury," Ada murmured, her breath brushing gently over Rike's skin as she placed tender kisses along the curve of her collarbone. In response, Rike's fingertips danced lightly across Ada's back, urging her closer until their hearts beat in unison.

"In such places, indulgence comes at a cost. I hope you are charging this hotel room to the job," Rike teased playfully, gesturing towards the gleaming minibar. A melodic laugh escaped Ada's lips, filling the room with a harmonious melody that echoed their shared intimacy.

Their gazes locked, a silent agreement passing between them before Rike reached for the chilled whiskey bottles nestled in the hotel room fridge. The glass clinked softly as they toasted, the amber liquid mirroring the warmth of their budding connection.

"To unforeseen complexities," Rike murmured, raising her glass in a toast that signalled the beginning of something uncharted. As their lips met, a delicate dance ensued, tentative at first but quickly gaining confidence, fuelled by an undeniable longing. Outside, the wind whispered secrets that mirrored the intensity of their shared desire.

In that intimate moment, every touch and caress spoke volumes as they unraveled each other's mysteries. The taste of whiskey lingered on Ada's lips, enhancing the sweetness of their embrace. With each brush of fingers through Ada's hair, Rike felt a surge of electricity pass between them.

"You have a way with kisses," Ada whispered in between stolen breaths, a soft smile gracing her features as she traced the curve of Rike's jaw with gentle fingertips.

"I'm doing my utmost tonight, just to make this perfect for you," Rike murmured, her words a gentle breath before their lips met once more. They danced in harmony, a melody of contented sighs. The world around them faded away, leaving only the comforting sensation of skin on skin, their shared warmth pushing back against the frigid winds howling outside.

As the storm raged on, its cries growing louder with the deepening night, within the confines of the hotel room the moans of the two women also deepened and reached their own crescendos. With each tender touch and every hushed endearment exchanged between them, they crafted a fleeting haven from the tumultuous chaos beyond the windowpanes.

Morning arrived, unfurling like a shroud of uncertainty, its light creeping through the room to reveal the aftermath of their clandestine union. Ada's gaze, a tumultuous sea of conflicting sentiments, lingered on Rike, who stirred from slumber.

"Rike," Ada's voice wavered, laden with unspoken passions, "I—"

"Let the night remain untouched by daylight," Rike interjected firmly, a hint of desire shadowing her composed tone.

"You know we cannot let anyone know. Ever," Rike said as she traced a finger among Ada's arm.

"I know," Ada acknowledged, her eyes avoiding Rike's piercing gaze. "I thought I had stopped hiding when I came to this country." Before Rike could respond, Ada's phone c rang. She held a finger to her lips to keep Rike silent and answered.

It was Officer Horton, calling to ask when Ada was coming into the station. "We have a lot to go over," he said.

"I will be there in 30 minutes," Ada said with a wink at Rike. She hung up and threw her arms around Rike's neck and kissed her. "You'll have to go. I need to shower before I head to the station."

Rike's reluctance to leave pulsed just beneath her controlled exterior. After another passionate kiss, she swiftly donned her clothes, each movement precise and purposeful, signalling the end of their night together.

"It never happened, Ada. And I hope one day soon, we can make it never happen again." Rike's words were heartfelt as she briskly opened the door to depart.

Ada's voice trailed after Rike, a futile attempt to halt her determined stride. A bellhop's sudden appearance caused an unintended collision, prompting profuse apologies that went unheard by Rike. She muttered a quick warning as she brushed past the young man, her focus unwavering.

Stepping outside, she was met with a chaotic symphony of snow and wind, nature's fury echoing her own inner chaos. Rike had met a woman she was powerfully enamoured with, and may not be able to see her again. As she settled into the driver's seat of her truck, the vehicle gently swayed in the fierce gusts while she ignited the engine. Despite her fingers growing numb from the cold, she managed to dial Autumn's number on her phone. Through the swirling flurries battering the windshield, the display barely peeked through.

"Autumn, it's Rike," she uttered in a composed tone as the call linked, masking the turmoil within her. "I must see you. Auberge Brew, now."

"Of course," Autumn responded with a touch of worry lacing her words. "Everything okay?"

"Perfectly fine," Rike smoothly fibbed, veiling her true emotions. "Just craving some company."

The phone line abruptly went silent, leaving Rike to navigate the snow-laden streets that had transformed into an eerie wasteland under the relentless storm's wrath. Seeking refuge, she pulled up at Auberge Brew, where the inviting radiance of the coffee shop beckoned like a beacon in the blizzard. Ordering a steaming cup of tea, wisps of vapor rising like phantoms of solace, she nestled into a shadowy nook by the window that framed the swirling chaos outside.

As impatience gnawed at her stoic facade, a seething anger brewed within her core. Memories of Ada's face haunted her thoughts—Ada, once a flame of passion, now reduced to a shadow of doubt. The notion of a deeper connection beyond mere attraction crumbled before her eyes, shattered dreams of a potential partnership gone.

"Absurd," she hissed under her breath, her words swallowed by the howling storm that mirrored the turmoil within her soul.

Two agonizing hours crawled past, each second dragging like a weight on Rike's chest. Thoughts of a future with Ada twisted into a forbidden desire, a vision too dangerous to entertain. The once vivid fantasy of them as an unstoppable duo now lay shattered by obligation and duty.

At last, the coffee shop's door exploded open, unleashing Autumn into the room, along with a flurry of snowflakes dancing in the air. Her cheeks flushed with cold, a stark contrast against the winter landscape outside. With a breathless laugh, her words carried an unspoken urgency.

"Apologies for my tardiness," Autumn gasped, shedding frost like an unwanted burden. "The weather out there is relentless."

"Lost you in the whiteout," Rike quipped, a faint smirk playing on her lips, though irritation still simmered beneath the surface.

"Almost did," Autumn admitted, shedding frost-laden layers. She embraced Rike briefly, seeking comfort in the frigid air, before settling opposite her.

"Thanks for showing up," Rike acknowledged, locking eyes with Autumn in a silent exchange of profound appreciation. In that instant, the raging storm beyond seemed to hush, the icy gusts fading into a mere murmur as they sought refuge in each other's company.

"Absolutely, I've got your back." Settled in the coffee shop, Rike and Autumn huddled together, their sanctuary pierced by relentless blasts of frigid air against the windowpanes.

"This chill," Rike observed, a wry grin playing on her lips, "feels almost vengeful, doesn't it?"

"As if it's out to get us," Autumn concurred, clutching her cup tightly for solace.

Outside, the mournful wail of police sirens pierced through the howling wind and thick blankets of snow, a haunting echo in the desolate winter landscape. Startled, both women instinctively turned towards the window before locking eyes once more.

"I've been considering leaving once this chaos is over," Rike revealed, her tone measured and resolute amidst the tense atmosphere.

Autumn's eyebrows shot up in astonishment. "Leaving? But Berna is your sanctuary. Why would you go?"

"I once loved it here," Rike confessed, her voice unwavering, yet carrying a subtle undertone of melancholy that lingered in the crisp air. "But these deaths... they've shattered the peace of my secluded existence here. Everything feels different now."

Autumn's brows furrowed thoughtfully as she absorbed Rike's words, a solemn expression clouding her features. "It'll all work out. Just wait and see."

The two women settled into a companionable silence, the weight of unspoken worries hanging heavy between them until Rike's phone abruptly shattered the tranquillity. Retrieving it from her jacket with precision, she checked the caller ID before answering with clipped efficiency. "Volk," she stated curtly.

"Rike, it's Officer Horton. Where are you right now?" The officer's voice crackled through the phone, urgency palpable in each word.

"At the Auberge Brew. What's going on?" Rike's grip on the phone tightened, her heart rate quickening with apprehension.

"Can you come down to the station? It's vital we talk, and it can't wait." Horton's request hung heavy in the air, setting off a flurry of unease within Rike.

"On my way," she forced out the words, a silent resistance simmering beneath her compliance. She rose from her seat, the chair protesting against the floor as she shot Autumn a strained smile. "Officer Horton needs me."

"What could he possibly want this time? Please be careful," Autumn's worry painted lines of caution on her face.

The relentless storm battered against Rike's truck, its icy fingers clawing at the windows as she navigated through the blinding snow. The five-minute drive took ten. In the rearview mirror, she caught a fleeting glimpse of a shadowy figure following her, disappearing into the whiteout with each turn of the road. A shiver ran down her spine, mingling with the chill seeping into her bones. Unseen eyes watched from the shadows, and Rike couldn't shake off the feeling that this journey to the police station held more than just answers — it held danger lurking in the obsidian depths of the storm.

Chapter 27

The biting cold of the mid-morning air wrapped around Rike Volk like a frosty shroud as she exited her truck and strode towards the ramshackle police station. Each footstep crunched on the snow-covered path, a stark contrast to the hushed stillness that enveloped the town. With a creak, Rike pushed open the door, feeling the frigid metal handle sear her palm, as if warning her of the chilling reception awaiting inside.

As Rike crossed the threshold, Officer Horton's voice shattered the silence like breaking glass. "Rike Volk, you are under arrest." Before she could gather her wits, his iron grip clamped down on her, the narrow gap between them a silent decree of guilt. A wave of bewilderment twisted her features as she was forcibly ushered into the cramped cell nestled at the rear of the trailer. The stark emptiness of the room was magnified by the harsh glare of a single flickering fluorescent light above.

"What is the meaning of this, Officer Horton?" Rike's demand crackled with anger and confusion, her hands shaking as she gripped the cold bars that now stood between her and liberty.

Horton loomed outside the secure room, his gaze piercing Rike with accusatory sharpness. "Where were you, Rike?" His tone dripped suspicion rather than concern.

"Just out for a cup of tea. At the Auberge, as I told you," she snapped back, her stance unwavering in defiance. "Why the arrest? Why lock me up?"

Silence settled heavily between them, only broken by the heater's persistent drone battling the relentless chill creeping through the space.

"Murder, Rike. You're under arrest for murder." Horton's voice hung heavy in the air, the weight of his words sinking into Rike's core like icy tendrils. Her breath caught in her throat, a sharp inhale betraying her shock. Her hands instinctively snapped to her sides, fingers releasing the cold bars like they were suddenly molten hot.

"I didn't do it," Rike's voice trembled with disbelief and outrage, her eyes locking onto Horton's unwavering gaze. The intensity between them crackled like static electricity on a winter night, unspoken accusations bouncing back and forth in the charged silence.

"I did not kill anyone." Rike's words sliced through the tension, laced with desperation and confusion. "This is about Tammy, isn't it? I swear I had nothing to do with her death."

Horton's expression remained stoic, a mask of frustration barely concealing his inner turmoil. "Tammy's not why you're here," he retorted sharply, his voice tinged with impatience. "You're not being arrested for Tammy's murder."

"Then the others. It was a bear attack. You said—" Rike began, but Horton's stern interruption halted her mid-sentence.

"Nor were you arrested for those deaths."

"Then whose?" The question sliced through the air, more demand than inquiry, as confusion knotted Rike's mind in a tight coil of dread.

Horton hesitated, his words struggling to break free. He swallowed audibly, the bob of his Adam's apple betraying his inner turmoil. When he finally spoke, his voice quivered on the edge of a whisper, laced with unshed tears. "Ada O'Neill... she was found dead in her hotel room."

The revelation struck Rike like a thunderbolt, stealing the air from her lungs in a sharp gasp. Ada–fierce, brilliant, captivating Ada?

"Dead?" The word echoed hollowly from Rike's lips, reverberating through the room as her thoughts spiralled into chaos. Memories flickered in her mind: Ada's piercing gaze, the subtle curve of her lips when she was smiling, the taste of her lips. A surge of anguish twisted Rike's heart painfully within her chest.

"Murdered. Not just dead, Rike. Murdered," Horton's voice cut through the air like shattered glass, his composure crumbling under the weight of the word. "The cleaning maid stumbled upon her... It's a gruesome sight, Rike. Unbearable."

Rike's legs gave out beneath her, fingers clenching the metal bars again for stability. The blood drained from her face as she envisioned the horrific scene that awaited the unsuspecting maid–the raw fear, the unfathomable brutality inflicted upon someone she admired, someone she held dear.

"Ada..." Her voice quivered with anguish as she uttered the name, a choked sob escaping her lips. Dizziness overwhelmed her, the confines of the cell pressing in on all sides, suffocating her with each breath she struggled to take.

"Detective O'Neill was a friend, right?" Horton's gaze softened momentarily, a flicker of shared sorrow passing between them before his professional façade returned. "She trusted you. It's a tragedy."

"Tragedy..." Rike echoed faintly, her world spinning as the crushing news hit her. "How? Why?"

"Stabbed." Horton's eyes shifted away, avoiding Rike's stare. "Multiple times. The investigation is ongoing. Of course."

The ensuing silence pressed down heavily with unspoken words and uncertainties. Rike slouched against the icy chill of the cell walls, her frame quivering as disbelief transformed into profound grief.

In that sterile, harshly lit confinement, amidst whispers of frigidity seeping through unseen crevices, Rike confronted a void darker than any she had ever imagined. She held back bile that wanted desperately to escape.

The cot groaned softly as Rike collapsed onto it, her sturdy figure a stark contrast to the worn mattress. Her usually sharp eyes, clouded with inner turmoil, darted towards Officer Horton as he spoke, his voice slicing through the heavy air like a blade.

"Rike," Horton's tone was rigid, formal. "Were you with Ada earlier today?"

A thick silence enveloped the cell, each second stretching taut like a wire. Rike lay still, every muscle coiled as if bracing for an unseen impact.

"Because," Horton's words hung heavily between them, laden with implication, "Do you know the bartender from the hotel?"

"I know who he is," Rike interjected, her words barely audible over the tense air between them. Horton released a heavy breath. "Yes," she acknowledged.

"He approached me when I was...at the scene. Claimed he witnessed you and Ada at the hotel bar, leaving together." Rike's defence emerged feeble, resembling a fragile whisper of a protest.

"You were the one who directed me to the hotel," she uttered, instantly rueing her own words.

A charged silence settled between them, unspoken accusations laying like dogs at their feet. Rike's composed façade wasn't a confession but a shield of defiance, her motionlessness a barricade against the rising suspicions. Horton's gaze bore into her, a relentless hunter seeking cracks in her armour to expose the truth. Like a hound on a scent, he refused to relent, despite Rike's reluctance to cooperate.

"Rike," Horton persisted, his tone insistent, "The bellhop mentioned your encounter this morning. Witnesses saw you at the hotel with Ada. You can't stay silent on this."

Rike appeared like a broken masterpiece within the icy confines of her cell. Huddled on the narrow cot, she clutched herself tightly, as though sheer will could mend the fractured pieces of her resolve.

"Rike?" Horton's voice quivered with urgency, a silent plea lingering beneath his words. Silence enveloped them, thick and suffocating, amplified by the weary groan of the station's heating system and the eerie howl of wind that sent shivers through the room.

"Hell, Rike!" Horton's voice sliced through the air, sharp and urgent. "You better start talking now if you've got something to say." Rike remained silent, her eyes distant, locked on a horizon only she could see. In that gaze lingered shadows of sorrow and unspoken truths, a storm raging within her as accusations swirled like bitter winds around her.

Horton gritted his teeth, frustration etched into every line on his face. He knew the rules, understood the game, but with Rike's impenetrable silence, he realized this investigation was about to get a lot messier. As he observed the fortress of strength she had erected around herself, he sensed it wasn't just defiance; it was a fierce battle being fought in the darkest recesses of her haunted soul.

"Fine, Rike," he exhaled heavily, distancing himself from the cell bars. "Your choice to stay silent. Just know, sometimes silence screams louder than words." With a final glance, Horton retreated, abandoning Rike to grapple with his haunting warning and her own turbulent emotions. Her inner turmoil brewed unseen, a tempest concealed behind a mask of composure, as if the very air around her crackled with suppressed intensity.

The door of the police station screeched open, signalling a shift in the unfolding events. Officer Juno's stout figure waddled in, his glasses fogged up from the cold air outside. With a wheeze, he took them off to clear the mist, his laboured breaths punctuating the tense atmosphere that enveloped Horton and Rike.

"I can't make sense of this, Rike," Officer Horton murmured, his voice barely above a whisper, his gaze fixed intently on her face. "Why would someone..."

Rike met his stare head-on, her expression unreadable yet tinged with an edge of bewilderment that mirrored Horton's own confusion. Her response was measured but laced with an unspoken unease that lingered heavily in the room, thickening the air with unresolved questions.

Juno's throat emitted a raspy sound, breaking the heavy silence in the room. He gestured urgently for Horton to join him, his eyes darting nervously towards Rike. Reluctantly tearing his gaze away from her, Horton moved to Juno's side at the utilitarian table beneath the harsh glare of the fluorescent lights. Leaning in close, their breaths mingled in a cloud of secrecy as they pored over the scattered papers, stealing cautious glances in Rike's direction. The relentless ticking of the clock on the wall echoed through the room, amplifying the palpable tension that gripped them all in its suffocating hold.

Time slipped away like silk through fingers, each moment unwinding effortlessly until Juno stirred, the legs of his chair grating on the linoleum floor. Swathing himself in his coat, he flipped up the collar to ward off the encroaching chill that had seeped into the building. Stepping outside, a mournful howl of wind heralded the approach of a snowstorm, its icy tendrils tapping against the window like delicate whispers of solitude.

Back at Rike's cell, Horton resumed his uninviting watch. "Looks like we're in for a lengthy night," he murmured under his breath, more for his benefit than Rike's. "I'll be here until the RCMP can navigate through this storm." With deliberate movements but lacking vigour, he transformed the couch into a makeshift bed, each action mechanical and void of any zeal. A blanket was haphazardly draped over it, a feeble gesture towards offering solace within the stark confines.

"Why do you have to babysit me? I am locked in a cell," Rike protested as she gestured wildly with her arms.

"Protocol. The RCMP do not take lightly to one of their own," Officer Horton snapped. "Oh God Rike, why?" he screamed.

"It wasn't me! Officer Horton, I swear on my life it wasn't me!" she shouted back, tears now flowing freely down her cheeks.

Lying on the uncomfortable cot in her frigid cell, Rike's tears fell silently, each one a heavy reminder of Ada's tragic death. The cold seeped into her bones, making her shiver despite the rough fabric of her sleeve wiping at her eyes. She felt the loss pressing down on her in the eerie stillness.

Outside, the storm raged on, its howling wind creating a haunting melody that clashed with the flickering lights casting eerie shadows on the walls. As darkness enveloped the room when the power succumbed to the storm's wrath, Officer Horton scrambled for a flashlight. Its beam cut through the blackness, but instead of comfort, it only accentuated Rike's sense of solitude within those unforgiving bars.

The dim light painted stark lines across her face as she gazed out into nothingness, feeling more isolated than ever before.

Horton's discontent echoed through the room, his grumbling a discordant note against the backdrop of emergency lighting casting eerie shadows. In her cell, Rike lay still in the oppressive darkness, her body occasionally trembling from the cold that seeped into her bones. The station enveloped her in a heavy silence, broken only by the sound of her own breaths, each one visible in the icy air.

Time seemed to warp within the confines of the cell, minutes stretching and merging into endless hours. In this desolate space, haunting memories clawed their way back into Rike's consciousness: vivid flashes of violence from her past as a detective, horribly intertwining with Ada's smiling face, her soft lips, her tender touch.

Rike's heart raced erratically, a wild drumbeat in the eerie silence that enveloped her, while the PTSD she had grappled with for years now cast a dark shadow over her being.

Her eyes, widened in terror against the oppressive darkness, reflected sheer fear. The solitude was almost palpable, like invisible walls closing in around her. The faint whispers of uncertainty grew into deafening roars, casting doubt on every choice and action that had brought her to this moment. Panic slithered insidiously through the confined space, lurking in every crevice, poised to engulf her entirely. She was being targeted and Ada paid the price.

Reality slipped through Rike's fingers like melting snow, each moment stretching the fragile thread holding her sanity. The storm outside mirrored the chaos within, its fierce winds and swirling snow a cruel dance of nature's indifference to her inner turmoil.

A heavy blanket of guilt smothered her spirit, the murders pressing down on her like an anchor to despair. Ada's imagined lifeless image lingered in her mind, a haunting spectre that begged the unanswerable questions: How had she failed to anticipate this tragedy? What actions could have altered this grim fate?

Her tears, like scalding rivulets, etched a path down her dirt-streaked face. Each drop bore the weight of unshed sorrows. A floodgate finally breached after years of holding back. Rike wept not just for Ada and herself, but for the shattered reality that felt irreparably damaged. The storm raging outside mirrored the turmoil in her heart, a turbulent orchestra signalling a plunge into an abyss so deep that redemption seemed like a distant dream reserved for fools.

Drained of tears, Rike succumbed to exhaustion, her sobs fading into quivering exhales as sleep enveloped her like a deceptive tranquillity. Gradually slipping into its embrace, a fragile plea for forgiveness lingered in her mind, barely audible amidst the howling wind that surrounded her secluded abode.

Chapter 28

The dim glow of the police station's overhead lights cast eerie shadows across the walls, creating a dance of light and dark in the early morning silence. The faint scent of stale coffee lingered in the air, mingling with the sharp tang of disinfectant. Rike's eyes flickered open, adjusting to the murky surroundings as she became aware of Officer Horton's presence, his form a silhouette against the dimly lit room. As consciousness fully embraced her, a subtle tension hung in the air, hinting at unspoken connections and unresolved mysteries that awaited her awakening.

With cautious movements to avoid waking the sleeping officer, Rike eased herself off the cot, her every muscle tensed with an urgent determination. Standing on the cold floor, her eyes navigated the dimly lit room like a phantom, her mind racing with thoughts that demanded silence. Fragmented Imagined images of the crime scene and the lifeless body flashed through her consciousness, each visual a taunting puzzle piece she struggled to fit together.

Rike knew with Ada dead–dear Ada! Rike knew suspicion would be cast on her for all the murders. Despite Ada's assurances, she knew she was a suspect. If she was the detective on the case...

That was how she could move forward. By analyzing what evidence she could, and thinking logically.

Unconsciously clenching her fists, frustration coiled in Rike's gut as she grappled with the elusive facts that refused to form a coherent picture despite her seasoned instincts clamouring for resolution. Her freedom hung by a thread as she battled against time and uncertainty, knowing that every moment counted in unraveling the chilling mystery that threatened to consume her life.

Rike's mind churned with a silent intensity, her gaze fixed on the snowy landscape outside. The unsettling realization that Ada met a tragic end in that very hotel room loomed over her thoughts like a dark cloud. As this harrowing idea took root, it unfurled tendrils of dread within her, painting a grim picture she couldn't ignore. She found herself at the heart of this sinister puzzle, a reluctant protagonist in a twisted narrative carefully crafted by an unseen hand.

Rike pivoted gracefully, her keen eyes absorbing the profound stillness enveloping her like a thick cloak, every passing second bringing the unknown threat closer. Officer Horton emitted a soft snore, a stark contrast to the tense atmosphere that demanded Rike's utmost caution and secrecy. As he slept on, oblivious to the storm brewing in Rike's mind, she grappled with her thoughts and the mounting anxiety of being observed by unseen watchers.

Mentally tallying the aftermath of pandemonium, now bathed in personal devastation, Rike stood like a vigilant guardian of the dormant figure of law enforcement and disorder. With a fluid motion, she turned on her heel, paving her cage.

Rike recalled the sprawling pool of crimson against the muted backdrop of decaying foliage. As she envisioned standing on the edge of the pool, the metallic tang of blood enveloped her, seeping into her awareness while her gaze fixated on the intricate impressions left by tires in the soft ground nearby. Each groove and imprint etched a story in her mind as she absorbed every detail with unwavering focus.

Her focus shifted involuntarily to the lone Sun Nut cigarette butt abandoned near the pool of blood. Its presence stood out as a deliberate mark amidst the towering evergreens, an enigmatic clue left behind by an unknown visitor. Among the limited suspects in this enigma—Craig Griffith, Warren McDaniel, and Paul Cantrell—the act of smoking became intertwined with their identities, shrouded in mystery just like their hidden truths.

The specific brand of tobacco held potential significance, a small detail that could potentially unravel the tightly woven tapestry of events. Yet, her grasp on this crucial information slipped through her fingers like smoke dissipating in the wind. Did any man have a preference for Sun Nut cigarettes? The answer lingered tantalizingly close, yet frustratingly out of reach, an essential piece waiting to be plucked from the foggy recesses of her memory.

In the midst of the eerie stillness, Rike pondered silently, her words a mere whisper carried by the icy wind. The detective within her stirred restlessly, prodding her to seek connections even where they might not exist. Each investigative thread she followed seemed to lead her further into a maze with no apparent way out, leaving her surrounded by more enigmas than solutions.

As her thoughts meandered, a ghostly image of Craig Griffith flickered in Rike's mind. It was around the time of the unsettling blood pool discovery that he had reported his wife, Tammy, missing. The urgency in his voice back then had felt authentic, every word trembling with genuine fear. However, as she revisited this memory now, a faint hint of uncertainty crept into Rike's consciousness.

Tammy's once vibrant and lively body had been discovered frozen solid among Rike's own possessions. This chilling revelation felt like a violation of both space and trust, hinting at an unsettling level of intimacy and calculated planning that sent shivers down Rike's spine. Frozen.

Did the Griffiths' home, standing close to Rike's own cabin, hold a chilling secret within its walls—a freezer capable of halting time itself, preserving death in an icy stillness? With their residence positioned so near and equipped with electricity, Craig seemed ominously prepared to carry out the sinister deed.

A sudden chill raced down Rike's spine, unwelcome and cutting, triggering a vivid recollection. Craig and Warren, two men entangled in conversation, had witnessed the tense confrontation between Rike and Mary before tragedy struck Mary down.

Rike had engaged in conversations with both Warren and Paul regarding the tragic losses of their beloved family members. As she reflected on these interactions, a sense of unease crept over her. Lost in thought, she stared into the shadowed room, hoping for some revelation to emerge. The once casual glances from Warren and Paul now seemed laden with suspicion and hidden agendas. Could either man have had ulterior motives? Did either Warren or Paul have to hate her?

Rike's mind raced, contemplating whether one of them had manipulated her feud with Mary to establish cause? Her unanswered question lingered heavily in the atmosphere, shrouded in uncertainty. The town's pervasive gossip surely spread like wildfire, reaching every ear, whether present at the scene or not.

Rike's silhouette, bent in deep thought, cast a striking contrast against the cold walls of her confinement. With each new consideration, the uncertainty pressed heavily upon her shoulders, the mystery unfolding like a tangled web around her. Despite the oppressive atmosphere of suspicion and doubt, the answers she sought remained frustratingly out of reach, teasing her with their elusiveness.

Perhaps she was only a pawn in a larger story. Perhaps, Rike reasoned, the killer's goal was to embarrass the local police. What if she was merely a convenient connection? Part of the joke played on someone else.

If Craig had orchestrated Mary's demise by framing it as an outcome of their altercation, then Rike would unwittingly become a pawn in someone else's deadly game—a convenient target for blame while the true culprit lurked undetected.

Within the quiet confines of the police station, the only disturbance came from Officer Horton's faint movements on the nearby couch, undisturbed by the tempest raging within Rike's mind. Her thoughts darted to Kelsey McDaniel, the second victim whose tragic end puzzled even the most hardened souls. The brutality of Kelsey's demise haunted Rike—both her hands and feet had been gruesomely severed, a detail that sent shivers down her spine as she grappled with its implications.

Whispering Skylar Mitchell's name, Rike felt the frosty morning air carry her words like spectres of suspicion. Who were the figures in this woman's life? The absence of information on this woman left Rike lingering in the shadows. Her gaze drifted to the floor, where dust motes danced in the slanting light, each tiny particle holding a potential truth waiting to unravel the mystery of motive and opportunity.

A distant memory resurfaced in Rike's mind, a conversation with Officer Horton that had slipped into oblivion until now. It was Craig Griffith who had supposedly killed and gutted the now-absent bear, a revelation delivered by Horton with evident reluctance. As she pondered this new information, Rike couldn't help but wonder about Craig's role in all this.

The unspoken truths pressed down on Rike, a turbulent sea of potential deceptions swirling ominously. In this chilling game of hidden agendas and treachery, she understood the stakes were her life and freedom. Determined to unravel the intricate tapestry of falsehoods before it ensnared her completely, time became her most precious commodity, slipping away like snowflakes melting in her palm.

The room exhaled a chill that wrapped around Rike like a ghostly shroud, the dim light casting elongated shadows that danced along the walls in an eerie waltz. Leaning wearily against the unforgiving metal of the holding cell, she felt the weariness settle deep into her bones, each breath a battle against the heavy pull of exhaustion.

With a subtle bow of her head, Rike succumbed to the drowsiness that tugged at her consciousness, teetering on the edge between reality and reverie. In that fragile moment between wakefulness and dreams, she whispered a single word into the stillness–"bears." The utterance dissolved into the quietude, swallowed by the encroaching silence as the scene faded into darkness, leaving behind a lingering sense of unease.

Officer Horton's digital watch erupted into a cacophony of beeps, piercing the tranquil morning at precisely 8:00 a.m. Startled, he jolted upright on the couch, his eyes still clouded with remnants of fading dreams. With a deep yawn, he scanned the room before turning his gaze to Rike's cell, where she was beginning to rouse from sleep.

"Good morning, Rike," Horton greeted, each word heavy with a burden of regret. "Care for some coffee?"

"Yes, please," Rike replied in a monotone voice. "And could you reach out to Autumn for me?"

Nodding solemnly, Horton reached for the phone, a sense of kindness guiding his actions as he dialled Autumn's number. In a fleeting moment, he glanced at Rike, her demeanour stoic and masking the inner turmoil that surely brewed beneath the surface.

Autumn's phone buzzed, and the familiar voice of Officer Horton filled the line, his tone weighted with sombre news. "Autumn, I need you to come down to the station. It's important," he requested, leaving the reason unspoken for now. The anticipation hung heavy in the air, only a few words passing between them through the crackling connection.

Meanwhile, in the stark confines of the holding cell, Rike sat unmoving, her eyes locked on the bland expanse of the opposite wall. Each minute detail of the sterile beige seemed to demand her attention, as if hidden within its unassuming facade lay the elusive answers she sought. The absence of her badge only amplified the weight on her chest, a tangible reminder of past failures and unresolved mysteries that haunted her every waking moment.

Autumn Evans burst into the station, her arrival mirroring the frenzied onset of a blizzard. Worry and disbelief etched deep lines on her face as she rushed towards Rike. Their eyes locked in a silent exchange, Autumn's gaze pleading for answers.

"Rike, what's going on?" Autumn's voice quivered with emotion, but Rike cut her off abruptly. "Just a mix-up," she stated sharply, peering at Autumn through the icy bars. Her eyes held a mysterious glint, more enigmatic than revealing.

The air thickened with tension as Autumn grappled with the situation. She had been friends with Rike for years; the idea of her being involved in murder felt as outlandish as Rike taking up watercolour painting. The pieces just didn't fit together in Autumn's mind, leaving her unsettled and searching for clarity amidst the chaos.

The sky loomed outside, a bleak canvas of steel grey that mirrored the sombre mood within the precinct walls. The wind howled fiercely, sweeping through the deserted streets and causing the station's windows to rattle in protest, yet concealing the oppressive silence that permeated the air.

Autumn's voice cut through the stillness like a sharp blade, her breath visible in the cold air as she inquired about Ada's whereabouts. Officer Horton's gaze faltered, his eyes avoiding hers as he struggled to deliver the devastating news. When he finally spoke, his words trembled with an unsettling vulnerability.

"Ada... she's gone," Horton began, his tone heavy with sorrow.

"Back to British Columbia?" Autumn asked, her mind not connecting the words and their tone.

"Ada O'Neill was found dead," Officer Horton choked. Autumn's gasp echoed through the room, her shock palpable. But Horton pressed on, his voice strained but resolute, revealing a chilling truth that shattered their world. "And Rike...Rike is now our prime suspect," he confessed, each word hanging heavily in the tense atmosphere like an ominous premonition.

Autumn's legs trembled beneath her, and she clutched the back of a wooden chair for stability, the rough grain pressing into her palm. Officer Horton's words reverberated in her ears, each syllable hitting her like a physical blow. The room swirled around her in a dizzying whirlpool as a tsunami of disbelief crashed over her.

"How is that possible? What do you mean?" Her voice quivered with shock and confusion.

"Rike and Ada were spotted exiting the hotel lounge together late last night," Horton disclosed, his usually stoic demeanour faltering slightly under the weight of the grim news. The unspoken accusation lingered heavily in the air, draped in the guise of official procedure. "And this morning, Ada was discovered murdered in her hotel room."

"I swear it wasn't me," Rike asserted adamantly, her tone unwavering and resolute. A swift nod from Autumn affirmed her unwavering support, a silent declaration of faith in their friendship. Autumn's eyes blazed with unwavering loyalty as she stood near Rike, a pillar of support amidst the chaos.

"Stay resolute, Rike," Autumn's voice resonated with determination, a silent promise to combat the injustices that loomed over them. "One thing at a time. First things first. You need food. A breakfast to feed the brain." With a firm nod, Autumn departed from the police station, leaving behind a faint echo of the jingling bell above the door that marked her exit. Her mission was simple but essential—good coffee and croissants from the Auberge. A small comfort in the unfathomable chaos of their upturned world.

Chapter 29

The blizzard outside the small, snow-covered building that was the town's police station unleashed its fury, sending icy tendrils of wind whistling through the cracks in the walls. The relentless storm painted the world in a ghostly white hue, veiling everything beyond the frosted window in a cloak of swirling snowflakes. Inside her cramped cell, Rike Volk sat perched on the edge of a narrow cot, her gaze fixed on the howling wilderness beyond. The raging tempest mirrored the turmoil brewing within her as she grappled with the enigmatic puzzle of the case at hand.

Nausea churned in her gut, a bitter companion to the relentless howl of the blizzard outside. As Rike stood in her cage, a chilling realization gripped her mind like icy claws. The pieces of the macabre puzzle fell into place before her: Craig Griffith, the man who had reported his missing wife Tammy, now loomed ominously in Rike's suspicions as the possible mastermind behind the series of brutal murders haunting their small community. He hated Rike enough to have orchestrated everything.

Each woman's death formed a sinister pattern that seemed to implicate Rike herself, the very person who had unwittingly discovered the pool of blood in the snowy forest. The certainty of this revelation crashed over Rike with brutal force, sending shivers down her spine that rivaled the storm raging outside.

Interrupting her thoughts, Officer Horton's voice sliced through the tense air, offering breakfast as if unaware of the turmoil brewing within Rike. The jangle of keys heralded his approach, his figure casting a stark shadow against the dim glow of the station lights as he stood framed in the doorway. Officer Horton unlocked Rike's cell.

Rike rose from her cot, muscles stiff from the cold and confinement, stretching to alleviate the tightness that gripped her. The brewing coffee filled the room with its comforting aroma, a stark juxtaposition to the unforgiving storm raging outside. It would do until Autumn returned with real coffee.

Horton motioned for Rike to join him at the table where a steaming pot of coffee awaited, accompanied by two empty mugs. "Autumn's braving this chaos to bring us coffee and croissants," he remarked, admiration evident in his voice. "You're lucky to have such a loyal friend."

A flicker of gratitude crossed Rike's face as she acknowledged, "I am." Autumn's unwavering support was a beacon of light in the darkness that threatened to engulf them all.

The wind howled outside like a vengeful spirit, its mournful cries seeming almost sentient as it battered against the flimsy walls of their temporary shelter. Taking her seat across from Horton, Rike's gaze darted towards the frosted window, half-expecting the storm itself to press its icy fingers against the glass in a sinister embrace.

Horton's gaze locked onto Rike, his words cutting through the air with precision. "Rike," he started, his voice now laced with official urgency, "we need to talk about Ada. What we found... it was brutal." He hesitated, studying Rike's stoic facade for any crack. "She had multiple stab wounds," Horton disclosed, his expression darkening. "It seemed like she fought to reach safety, a last desperate attempt" His eyes narrowed. "The anger of the attack was palpable... overwhelming."

Rike pressed on, her voice cracking. "And? Officer Horton, it was not me. She had just gotten off the phone with you when I left. Ask the bellhop I ran into. If the murder was bloody, I'd have been covered from head to toe. Was it...brutal?"

Horton's tone dropped lower as he delivered the final blow. "Ada had a hotel steak knife plunged into her chest," he concluded grimly.

Rike's chest tightened, though her face remained impassive. "Ada was someone I admired and valued, Horton. I didn't harm her," she asserted firmly.

Officer Horton scrutinized Rike, probing for any flicker of dishonesty in her eyes. Meeting his stare head-on, Rike exuded a mix of genuine honesty and smoldering frustration—not towards the unfounded accusation, but at the whole unjust situation.

In the weighty quietness that enveloped them, memories of Rike's final evening with Ada flooded back. They had shared a simple yet intimate meal of crudités, delivered by room service, relishing each bite in their togetherness. The presence of a steak knife struck Rike as odd; it wasn't part of their modest spread. "Was it a hotel steak knife?"

"Hotel-branded, yes. Why?" Officer Horton asked. When Rike remained silent, Horton made a notation in his notebook.

It dawned on her with a chilling clarity that the killer had brought the weapon into the room deliberately—a coldly premeditated move. The fact that it belonged to the hotel hinted at a rushed execution, contradicting the meticulous planning evident in the previous murders.

Horton's voice sliced through the tension, demanding Rike's attention. "Is there anything you're holding back?"

Rike's gaze locked with his, unwavering. "Nothing changes the truth. I'm innocent," she asserted firmly, her determination steeling her resolve. Whoever orchestrated Ada's death aimed to pin it on her, but Rike Volk wasn't one to surrender without a battle.

"Consider this," Rike proposed, her words steady amidst the howling storm battering the flimsy mobile home walls. "What if the grizzly bear isn't responsible for those women's deaths? What if it's a man behind it all?"

Horton scoffed derisively, his doubt palpable, like frost creeping over the window-panes. "And what wild theory brought you to that unlikely idea?"

"Consider this," Rike persisted, her gaze unwavering. "These murders aren't random acts of nature. They're calculated, purposeful. Someone is pulling the strings."

"And who might that be?" Horton's voice dripped with condescension.

"Craig Griffith," she stated with conviction. "His wife vanished first, didn't she? Then others met their end to divert attention, to frame an innocent like me."

"Convenient theories coming from a person of interest," Horton grumbled, though a hint of doubt flashed in his eyes briefly before he veiled it with practiced composure. "And what has this to do with Ada?"

"Ada knew the claim of bear attacks was improbable," Rike pressed on, noting the subtle shift in Horton's stance. "She knew without the bear's carcass, the claim was outrageous."

"Rike," Horton reclined slightly, arms folded protectively. "I've witnessed bears ravage campsites, hunters, hikers. The injuries on those women... they align with a grizzly bear attack, not human intervention."

"Are you sure?" Rike prodded. "Or have we embraced the convenient narrative because it's the most palatable explanation? Until now. Now you are wondering if it was me."

Her words lingered in the room, dense like the snow enveloping the world beyond their sheltered space. Horton averted his gaze, visibly grappling with the unsettling notion.

"Yes," Rike murmured, her breath barely stirring the frigid air. "I was in Ada's hotel room the night before she died. But I swear, I didn't hurt her."

Horton's eyes snapped back to her, cutting through the icy silence like a blade. "Why keep this from me until now? There were witnesses, you know."

"Because I could see how it would appear," Rike retorted, frustration seeping into her tone. "Being in a room with a woman who ends up dead—it doesn't look good, does it?"

"No, it doesn't," Horton admitted grimly, his words hanging heavy in the frosty air. "It looks very damning, Rike."

The shrill jangle of the police station phone shattered the brittle tension that enveloped them. Officer Horton sprang up abruptly, his chair screeching against the cold linoleum as he lunged to answer it. Rike fixated on him like a hawk stalking its prey. Every sinew in her body coiled tight, her gaze unyielding and sharp. She scrutinized the nuances of his expressions, searching for any subtle hint that might betray the urgency of the call.

Horton gestured towards the cell, his voice firm as he directed Rike inside. The heavy cell door closed with a resounding clang, sealing her in. As Horton turned away to answer the ringing phone, Rike found herself alone in the stark confines of the cage.

Through the small window by her side, a mesmerizing chaos unfolded outside. The world beyond was a tempest of white, the storm's fury evident in the relentless barrage of snowflakes against the glass. Each flake seemed to dance wildly in the air, driven by the howling wind into a frenzy that painted a picture of nature's raw power.

Within this icy vortex, another storm brewed within the cramped station. Horton's voice remained composed as he spoke into the receiver, but a subtle tension crept into his stance, betraying his unease. His tone grew more formal with each word exchanged on the call, hinting at an underlying urgency and concern that lingered beneath his professional facade.

"I'll verify with the RCMP immediately," Horton assured over the phone before adding a courteous "Thank you" as he concluded the conversation, his demeanour reflecting a sense of impending gravity that hung palpably in the air.

After replacing the receiver on its cradle, he paused, a moment frozen in time before he turned to face Rike. His jaw clenched with determination as he addressed her, his voice steady and composed. "Rike," he began, each word carefully measured, "the medical examiner has completed the autopsies on Kelsey, Mary, Skylar, and Tammy. They were all victims of homicide. It wasn't the work of a bear."

"I figured that out long ago." His words struck Rike with a chilling mix of validation and dread. Her instincts had been on point, but now the reality of a killer still roaming free loomed heavily over her thoughts; perhaps closer than anyone dared to imagine.

Horton's next words carried weight as he prepared to contact the RCMP. "The RCMP are en route," he informed her with a sense of urgency laced in his tone. "I must relay these findings to them."

The wind outside howled in a haunting melody, emphasizing the direness of their predicament. Rike stood up from her makeshift cot, her steps echoing softly on the cold floor as she approached the iron bars that confined her.

"Before you do anything else, may I use the washroom?" Her voice remained steady, belying the turmoil within her. Officer Horton hesitated briefly, his gaze meeting hers before he reached for the keys dangling from his belt. With a metallic jingle, he unlocked the cell door, allowing it to swing open with a faint creak.

"Be quick," he instructed, momentarily setting aside his suspicions in favour of protocol. "I have much to attend to." Stepping out into the cramped space of the mobile police station, Rike felt the feeble warmth enveloping her like a thin shroud. Officer Horton's back turned towards her as he grasped the rotary phone on his desk, preparing to call. Outside, the storm raged on, its fury battering against the flimsy walls as if seeking entrance into their fragile sanctuary.

"Yes, hello, this is Officer Horton at—"

The heavy brass lamp sat ominously in the dimly lit room, its light casting eerie shadows that danced across the walls. Without hesitation, Rike's well-honed instincts took over as she lunged for the lamp with precision. In one swift motion, she swung it soundlessly through the air, the metallic base meeting Officer Horton's skull with a sickening thud muffled by the raging storm outside.

Officer Horton crumpled to the ground, unconscious and silenced before he could protest further, leaving the telephone receiver swaying in eerie harmony with the howling winds. With animalistic determination, Rike carefully placed the blood-stained lamp back on the table, her breathing steady despite the chaos unfolding around her.

She deftly retrieved the keys from Horton's limp grasp, dragging his inert form into the very cell that had confined her moments earlier. It felt like poetic justice; he had failed Ada, failed them all by turning a blind eye to the truth glaring right at him. As she locked the door behind him, a sense of urgency gripped her—time was running out, and desperate measures were all she had left.

Donning her parka, she steeled herself for the fierce gale that awaited outside. Rike Volk, a once-celebrated detective now on the run out of sheer necessity, braved the relentless blizzard with a singular purpose burning in her veins—to track down Craig Griffith. Justice demanded his reckoning.

Autumn Evans' car slid to a stop outside the station, tires desperately gripping the icy ground beneath the freshly fallen snow. Stepping out, she was met with a maelstrom of white chaos; the air was so thick with swirling snowflakes, it seemed as though the very heavens had shattered.

"Rike?" Autumn's voice was swallowed by the howling wind as she called out in vain. Her eyes widened in alarm at the sight of Rike climbing into her truck, its frame trembling as it roared to life.

"Wait!" Autumn's desperate cry was lost in the raging tempest as she raced towards Rike and the departing truck. The vehicle's headlights briefly pierced through the swirling snow before vanishing into the blinding storm, leaving behind only a haze of exhaust and bewilderment.

Autumn's heart pounded erratically in her chest, her mind racing to make sense of the scene just played out before her eyes. Why was Rike venturing out into such treacherous conditions? Where could she possibly be headed? Questions thundered through Autumn's thoughts like an unrelenting storm as she pushed open the station door, determined to unravel this mystery.

Chapter 30

White fury enveloped the world beyond her frosted windshield, the wind's banshee wail a haunting complement to Rike's clenched grip on the truck's steering wheel. Millions of snowflakes lashed against the glass like icy blades in a relentless storm. The rhythmic thud of the wipers echoed a battle song, struggling to fend off nature's wrath. Amidst the treacherous dance of skidding tires on ice-slicked roads that wound through stoic pines, their burdened branches creaking in protest, Rike's simmering rage matched the ferocity of the blizzard outside.

Rike's gaze, sharp and unwavering, darted back and forth from the icy path ahead to the reflection in her rearview mirror. With each passing moment, she drew nearer to the inevitable confrontation that churned uneasily within her core. The frosty breath escaped her lips in ethereal wisps, mingling with the biting chill inside the truck's cabin as she expertly maneuvered through the unpredictable twists and turns of the familiar yet unforgiving terrain.

Turning into her own driveway, a narrow path barely discernible from the wilderness, Rike slammed the truck to a stop. The abrupt silence that followed the engine's shutdown was engulfed by the blizzard's relentless howl, creating an eerie symphony of nature's fury. Hastily exiting the vehicle, she felt the icy tendrils of the cold air biting at her cheeks, seeping through every layer of clothing. Each step she took towards her modest cabin sank deep into the fresh powder, amplifying her sense of urgency.

The wind intensified, whipping strands of hair across her face and adding a sharp edge to her apprehension. The darkness seemed to press closer around her, shadows dancing in the swirling snowflakes as she reached for the door handle. The creak of the opening door mingled with the howling storm outside, sending shivers down her spine as she crossed the threshold into the dimly lit interior.

Inside, the unlit stone hearth embraced the frost that had seeped into Rike's very core—not the biting cold of the raging blizzard outside, but a chilling determination that gripped her soul. With each careful footfall on the creaking floorboards, she made her way to a weathered oak cabinet. The scent of aged wood mingled with faint traces of gun oil as she reached out, her touch firm and unwavering despite the thunderous tempo of her pulse reverberating in her ears.

Her hand closed around the cool metal of the handgun, its weight both alien and intimately known in her grasp. The click of checking the chamber echoed in the silent cabin, a sound as sharp as the biting wind that howled beyond the frosted windows. The metallic slide and snap felt like a heartbeat syncing with her own, a rhythm of resolve that resonated through her being.

Her breath hung heavy in the frigid air, a misty trail of determination trailing behind her like a spectre. With each step she took back into the storm, the icy wind clawed at her exposed skin, leaving stinging imprints on her cheeks. The weight of the gun nestled in her jacket pocket pressed against her hip, a reminder of the impending reckoning.

The path ahead to Craig Griffith's home seemed endless, the swirling snowflakes obscuring her vision like a shroud of secrets. Undeterred by the biting cold that gnawed at her resolve, she pushed through the deep snow with a relentless rhythm, every muscle in her body taut with purpose. Each footfall resonated like a predator stalking its prey through the wintry wilderness.

As she advanced towards her destination, adrenaline surged through her veins, heightening every sensation. The frosty air seared her lungs with each inhale, propelling her onward with an urgency that bordered on desperation. The stark contrast between the dark silhouette of Craig's home against the blinding white expanse intensified her focus, driving her forward with single-minded intent.

Snow gathered on her shoulders, clung to her hair, and dusted her eyelashes, turning Rike into a spectral figure in the midst of the tempest. Each breath came out in sharp puffs, visible bursts of life in the deadened landscape. Her surroundings were reduced to a blur of white and grey, but she didn't need clear vision to find Craig's house; every contour of the land was etched into her memory.

Approaching Craig's house through the thick veil of the storm, Rike felt her heart race in sync with the howling winds. Each step towards the looming silhouette heightened her senses—the frigid air biting at her cheeks, the icy tendrils of fear creeping up her spine. The gun in her hand was not just a cold piece of metal; it was a lifeline, a key to unlocking the truth shrouded in darkness. This was the defining moment, where resolve clashed with trepidation, and the fate of the town hung in the balance.

She was close now, close enough to make out the dark outline of the back door through the veil of falling snow. This was the threshold, the dividing line between the storm outside and the tempest that awaited within. Rike steeled herself, ready to face whatever lay on the other side.

Rike approached the house, circling the property with deliberate steps, the gun now in her hand, ready for action. Her sharp eyes scanned each window, finding them dark and still, like eyes that refused to meet her gaze.

She cautiously reached for the handle of the nearest window, her fingertips trembling slightly with apprehension. With a tangible click, it remained stubbornly locked, eliciting a fleeting sense of relief that dissipated as she moved along the facade. Each window she tested offered no escape from the mounting tension coiled within her chest. Finally, her exploration led her to the concealed back door nestled in a shadowed alcove. As her hand made contact with the cool metal handle, a shiver ran down her spine at the realization that it yielded easily to her touch, swinging open silently into darkness.

The air was different here—stale and heavy. Rike quickly stepped into the shadows of the mudroom, her breaths shallow. She closed the door behind her with a soft snick, banishing the howl of the blizzard, leaving her enveloped in the ominous quiet of the house. Her fingers tightened around the grip of her gun as she adjusted to the dim light, her senses alert for any sign of movement.

She navigated to the kitchen. The disjointed clatter of tapping on a beer bottle was a juxtaposition to the heavy atmosphere enveloping her. In that moment, she spotted him—Craig, perched at the table, engrossed in paperwork that appeared trivial for a murderer.

"Craig," she uttered, her tone unwavering even as turmoil churned within her. As their eyes met, a silent exchange crackled between them, his guarded expression meeting her unwavering gaze with a flicker of uncertainty.

His body jerked upright, a gasp escaping his lips at the sight before him. The colour drained from his face, leaving it a ghostly pallor as he locked eyes with the figure confronting him. Shock seized his features, rendering him akin to a wild animal cornered in a trap, his desperation palpable.

"Rike... What in hell are you doing here?" His voice wavered, cracks of uncertainty betraying his attempt at composure.

"Ada O'Neill's blood is on your hands," Rike's words cut through the air like a sharpened blade, her fury a tangible presence that crackled between them.

"I-I don't understand," Craig stuttered, a feeble attempt to rise met with failure under the weight of Rike's intense gaze.

"Sit down!" Rike's voice sliced through the air, commanding Craig to retreat into his chair. His shoulders slumped, eyes darting around in uncertainty with each passing moment.

"Tammy, Mary, Skylar, Kelsey, and Ada," Rike's voice was a chilling whisper as she uttered each name, her gaze piercing through Craig. "How many more?" The words dripped with accusation, hanging heavily in the tense silence that enveloped them.

"Rike, I swear—" Craig's voice wavered, his hands fidgeting nervously.

"On what, Craig? Their graves?" Rike's tone turned glacial, her eyes locking onto his with unwavering intensity. She watched as the weight of her words landed on him like a crushing blow, forcing him to confront the harsh reality she was pushing him towards.

In the charged stillness that enveloped them, only the howl of the blizzard penetrated the walls of Craig Griffith's kitchen, a stark contrast to the brewing tempest within. Rike's voice was icy as she confronted him, her grip on the gun steady and unyielding. "Tammy was frozen, Craig," she stated with a chilling calmness that belied the intensity of her emotions. "Explain to me how she ended up like that if you're not involved."

Craig's eyes flickered away from hers, seeking refuge on the worn linoleum floor. His feeble denials faltered this time, his voice wavering with a hint of desperation, more for his own reassurance than to convince Rike. "I swear, I didn't—I couldn't—Maybe that trucker..."

Rike's blue eyes blazed with a fierce intensity, her gloved hands clenched into tight fists at her sides. "No more excuses!" Her voice cut through the cold air like a knife, each word laced with a palpable sense of urgency. "The police were at my cabin days before they found Tammy there. They know someone placed her after they left. Long after she disappeared." She loomed over him, unwavering in her resolve.

He opened his mouth to protest, but under Rike's steely gaze, his confidence faltered. The room filled with an uneasy silence, so thick it felt suffocating, the tension between them crackling like electricity on the verge of sparking.

Rike's presence loomed over him, her eyes piercing into his soul, the room filled with a tense silence broken only by the sound of their breathing. The faint scent of retribution lingered in the air, adding an ominous layer to the atmosphere. With a steady hand, she clicked the hammer back on the gun, its metallic sound reverberating in the confined space. The cold touch of the weapon against her palm sent a shiver down her spine as she took aim, the weight of her ultimatum heavy in the air. "Your time is slipping away, Craig," she declared, her voice cutting through the stillness like a sharp blade.

Chapter 31

The bitter frost crept insidiously into Craig's home, casting an icy shroud over Rike's tense encounter with the man. In the dimly lit room saturated with the scent of weathered timber and a lingering hint of tobacco, Rike stood firm, a formidable presence that seemed to command even the flickering firelight. Her gaze, piercing and unrelenting, locked onto Craig as he sat opposite her, his form stark and coiled.

As the crackling fire underscored the silence between them, a palpable tension hung heavy in the air, thick with unspoken accusations and looming danger. The creaking floorboards beneath Rike's feet echoed like ominous whispers, mirroring the weight of her suspicions. Each heartbeat thundered in her ears, drowning out all but the sound of her own ragged breaths.

When Rike finally spoke, her voice sliced through the chilling atmosphere like a blade. "Where were you when Tammy disappeared?" she demanded, her words sharp and cutting as shards of ice. The flickering shadows danced across Craig's face, revealing fleeting glimpses of unease that flitted across his features like ghosts.

In response, Craig's facade wavered imperceptibly before he masked it with a practiced nonchalance. His tone carried a deceptive calmness as he retorted, "I was at work. I came home, and she was gone." But beneath his composed exterior simmered an undercurrent of defiance that belied his words.

The room seemed to constrict around them, suffocating in its intensity as their confrontation escalated into a deadly game of cat and mouse. With every passing moment, Rike's senses heightened; she could taste the metallic tang of suspicion in the air mingling with the acrid smoke from the hearth.

As they locked gazes in a battle of wills, each word spoken was laden with unspoken threats and hidden truths. The very walls seemed to hold their breath in anticipation of what would unfold next in this chilling dance of deception and danger.

"Why did you kill Tammy?" The question sliced through the tense air, an arrow aimed straight at Craig's heart. Rike's voice trembled slightly, betraying the storm raging inside her, but her steely gaze held firm, masking the fear that threatened to consume her.

"I didn't kill anyone." As Craig stood up, the chair protested with a groan, mirroring the tension in the room. His face contorted with simmering anger, spitting out his words like venom.

"You killed them all."

"No."

"Yes. And if I know it without access to forensic evidence and police reports, then they will too."

"You think you have it all figured out, huh? You... you queer!" Each syllable dripped with malice, a deliberate attempt to inflict pain. His fists clenched tightly at his sides, echoing the suffocating pressure that hung heavy around them.

"Ah, so you are finally willing to speak true words," Rike said with a sarcastic confidence lighting up her face.

The silence that followed crackled with unspoken threats and accusations. Rike's senses heightened, every detail of the room sharpened by adrenaline. The subtle scent of old wood mixed with the acrid taste of confrontation lingered in the air. The harsh light cast sharp shadows across Craig's face, emphasizing the raw emotion etched into his features.

Rike refused to engage in his childishness. Her jaw clenched against the insults hurled her way. She had been called so much worse. The frigid air hung heavy with tension as she let the weight of his words settle between them, a challenge in the stillness that followed.

"Why, Craig?" she asked again.

"It was Tammy's fault," he spat out, his voice growing louder amidst the crackling embers of the dying fire. Fury blazed in his eyes, mirroring the flames dancing before him. With each step he took, a menacing aura enveloped him like a predator on the prowl. "Her constant nagging and reckless ways pushed me beyond reason." His words sliced through the icy silence, leaving a sharp edge in the air.

As he circled like a vulture closing in on its prey, Rike felt her pulse quicken, matching the rapid beat of her heart. The bitter taste of adrenaline flooded her mouth as she braced herself for what might come next. The stark reality of danger loomed around them, amplifying every sound—the crackle of burning wood, his heavy footsteps on the cold floor.

In this deadly confrontation, where words could easily turn into actions with lethal consequences, Rike's senses heightened. She absorbed every detail—the flickering flames casting eerie shadows across his face, the acrid scent of smoke mingling with his volatile energy. Her muscles tensed involuntarily as she prepared for any sudden movement. Every fibre of her being screamed caution while adrenaline coursed through her veins like liquid fire.

"I never meant for any of this to happen. She drove me to it." Craig's words hung heavy in the icy air, his hands shaking with a mix of guilt and desperation.

Rike's jaw clenched, her gaze unwavering as she saw through the facade he desperately clung to. The importance of the mission pressed against her chest, urging her to uncover the monstrous truth lurking beneath Craig's shattered exterior.

The silence between them was suffocating, broken only by the distant howl of the wind outside. The dim light cast eerie shadows across the room, emphasizing the tension thick enough to cut with a knife.

Rike's words sliced through the heavy air like a blade, sharp and unforgiving. Her eyes blazed with a mix of shock and outrage, not a hint of fear in them as she rose from her chair, each step forward echoing with determination. "You dare to shift blame onto her? Blame her for her own murder?" Her voice dripped with disbelief, a venomous edge that could shatter steel. "How could you, Craig?"

Craig's restless movements stilled abruptly, his gaze locking onto hers with a fiery intensity. The room seemed to vibrate with the raw energy radiating from him, his anger palpable in the heaving of his chest and the flare of his nostrils, as if every breath fuelled the inferno burning within him.

"You're an ass," he sneered, venom lacing each syllable. Closing in on her, his steps deliberate and ominous. "You, just another hypocrite passing judgment without a clue. You have no idea what she put me through!" His accusations lingered, a noxious fog thickening the room's air. The flickering flames painted eerie shapes on his face, distorting his features into something malevolent and alien. This figure before her was no longer the mere unpleasant neighbour she once knew; he had transformed into a being sculpted from shadows and sorrow, his essence hollowed by his own sins.

Rike stood her ground, her gaze unwavering despite the tumult of emotions churning inside her. The weight of all she had witnessed and felt bore down on her, but she refused to show any hint of weakness to Craig. "Understand?" Her voice sliced through the frigid air, sharp and resolute. "There's no comprehension in taking an innocent life, Craig. None."

A flash of malice gleamed in Craig's eyes as he retorted, his words dripping with disdain. "You're too ignorant to grasp the reality."

Rike's fury surged like a blizzard within her, each inhale stoking the flames of her anger. Her hands balled into fists at her sides, a physical barrier against the tempest brewing inside her. "The truth is crystal clear," she shot back, her voice quivering with contained emotion on the brink of eruption. "You're a coward who can't face your own actions. Blaming Tammy won't absolve you. You caused her death, and you'll answer for it."

Craig's lips twisted into a scornful sneer, his narrowed eyes flashing with contemptuous defiance. Tension crackled in the air between them, thick with unspoken threats that hung like icicles waiting to fall at any moment. Though his jaw clenched with restrained fury, he held himself back from crossing the line into violence.

"Pay for it?" His voice dripped with derision, the words cutting through the tense air like a sharp blade. "And who's going to make me pay, Rike? You?" The mocking glint in his eyes betrayed a dangerous confidence, a belief that he was untouchable. Craig exuded an aura of invincibility, accustomed to dancing around consequences and evading justice. Yet now, teetering on the brink of reckoning, he faced Rike as the bearer of his impending doom.

Rike's intense gaze bore into the dimly lit cabin, cutting through the dancing shadows like a sharp blade. She closed in on Craig, her presence an unyielding challenge he couldn't evade. "What about the other women?" Her words sliced through the frigid air, each syllable dripping with an icy accusation that matched the winter chill seeping through the cabin's weathered walls. "Mary, Skylar, Kelsey, Ada—why did you take their lives?" A fleeting glint of something unsettling flashed in Craig's eyes—a mix of triumph and madness barely contained. Yet, it vanished swiftly, giving way to his stoic mask of indifference that shielded him like impenetrable armour.

"Collateral damage," Craig's voice was icy, his words calculated like pieces on a chessboard. "Necessary sacrifices in a grand scheme you can't fathom. Their lives are mere pawns, Rike, and I—"

Rike's interruption cut through his justifications like a blade. "Enough," her tone sharp as shattered glass. "No hiding behind your twisted ideas. They were real, Craig. Lives with purpose beyond your sick game. And you snuffed them out without remorse."

Craig clenched his jaw, the unspoken louder than any admission. Tension crackled in the air, truths unsaid but hanging heavily between them. Rike had stripped away his facade, exposing the void where his humanity should reside. It chilled her to the core, a stark realization that seeped into her very marrow.

Craig's lips twisted into a sneer, his icy gaze locking onto mine. Leaning in with a calculated malice, he spoke in a low, menacing tone, as though unveiling a sinister truth meant only for my ears. "They were *my* pawns," he hissed, the words dripping with contempt. "Each one is expendable in the grand scheme of misdirection. Tammy... she was the ultimate target. The rest? Just insignificant pieces paving the way to putting the blame on you."

Rike staggered back, the killer's chilling words piercing her like icy shards. Her heart raced, a thunderous drumbeat in her chest as she struggled to maintain her composure, refusing to let the revulsion overwhelm her. "You extinguished lives for your twisted game," she uttered, each syllable a sharp blade slicing through the frigid air, standing there, a shell of a man consumed by darkness.

"Darkness?" Craig's voice cut through the tension, devoid of any hint of amusement. "I am a genius. They were pieces in this grand chess match—a masterpiece of smothered mates and en passant. And Tammy," he paused, relishing the name on his lips, "she was my checkmate."

Rike's lip curled in disdain as she hurled her disdain back at him, her eyes ablaze with a mix of anger and disgust. Her fingers trembled, not from fear but from a fierce surge of rage that pulsed through her veins. "You dare call yourself a genius, Craig?" she sneered, her voice laced with venom. "You're nothing but a savage, a dealer of death. Those women—" Her voice caught for a moment, then hardened into resolve, "they were beacons of light you could never comprehend, sources of warmth your cold heart could never embrace. You snuffed out their radiance because yours had long turned to ashes."

A chilling hush enveloped the dimly lit space, thick with unspoken horrors. Rike sensed the frosty fingers of understanding grip her very essence—the figure standing before her was a void beyond redemption, a pitiless abyss that had devoured the innocent without remorse. "Your reign of terror stops here," Rike's voice sliced through the stillness, her determination hanging in the air like a sharpened blade ready to descend. "I swear on every heartbeat within me, justice will prevail. For Tammy, Mary, Skylar, Kelsey and Ada—for every stolen constellation in the night sky. Your web of death will unravel, star by fallen star."

"Justice?" Craig's lips curled in a sneer, his tone dripping with contempt, as though the very notion was beneath him. "Your idea of justice is feeble attempts by imbeciles to control the powerful."

"You confuse brutality with strength, Craig," Rike shot back, her voice steady despite the shiver that raced down her spine. "True strength is in restraint, in fairness, in the empathy you discard so casually."

"Empathy?" Craig scoffed derisively, a mocking grin playing on his face. "Empathy is a crutch for those too timid to take what they want. I am not bound by your flimsy morals."

"In that case, you are truly adrift," Rike murmured softly, yet with unwavering certainty. The tension crackled in the surrounding air, each word resonating with the stark reality of a soul consumed by darkness.

"Adrift?" Craig's voice sliced through the icy air, his words a sharp blade aimed directly at her core. "Former German homicide detective Rike Volk, lost in your own delusions! But there is no freedom in your solitary existence. True power lies in command and control of others, something you fail to grasp."

Rike's steely gaze met his without flinching. "Your power is a facade, a fragile veil woven from the pain of others," she countered, her voice unwavering. "And when reality comes crashing down on you, there will be nowhere left to hide."

Craig's smirk was chilling. "Let the ignorant cling to their illusions," he sneered, his words dripping with disdain. "I have ascended beyond such trivial concerns."

Rike's voice barely rose above a chilling whisper, laden with the weight of impending judgment. "Transcendence?" she questioned, her words cutting through the tense air like a blade. "For you, Craig, there is no escape into the beyond. Only the cold embrace of confinement awaits you, where the echoes of your misdeeds will torment you without respite."

Craig's demeanour remained stoic in the face of Rike's ominous warning. "But until those walls enclose me, I hold fast to the reins of my destiny."

In the dimly lit room, Rike's voice pierced the quiet like a warning bell. As she contemplated the chilling mystery ahead, a surge of primal energy surged through her chest, a fierce resolve igniting within her. "Enjoy your freedom while it lasts," she said, her tone heavy with foreboding. "But remember, when this concludes, it marks the beginning of your confinement." The words hung in the air, a stark reality awaiting Craig with the dawn, a promise of consequences to come.

Chapter 32

In the frost-kissed stillness of Craig's home, the air hung heavy with the scent of pine and hearth smoke. Rike's piercing gaze, once a tempestuous force of nature, now mirrored the frigid serenity of the winter landscape outside. Standing in the shadowed kitchen, her presence exuded an unsettling calm that masked the turmoil raging beneath her stoic facade. The gun in her hand was a silent testament to her unwavering determination, its cold metal a stark contrast to the warmth of the crackling fire nearby.

"Craig," Rike's voice sliced through the tension, each word a dagger of accusation. Her eyes blazed with a mix of anger and disbelief, the weight of betrayal heavy in the air. "Why weave this intricate web of deceit? Why cast me as the villain in this grim play?"

A smirk crept across Craig's face, a mask of false bravado that grated on Rike's last nerve. He lounged against the worn oak table, his demeanour oozing smugness despite the gun aimed at his heart. "It's all so clear," he chuckled, a hint of malice dancing in his eyes. The nonchalance in his tone clashed with the charged atmosphere, setting Rike's pulse racing. "You stopped me from hunting on your land. I needed that meat. To eat. And you took that away."

"You can hunt on your own damned land!" Rike's voice sliced through the frigid air.

"I don't want to. Yours is easier to walk. You have more deer," Craig replied, a smirk playing on his lips, his eyes betraying a hint of malice. "I've always hunted that land, and I should always be able to hunt that land."

"This can't be the reason. You're lying," Rike retorted sharply, her tone laced with disbelief.

"Don't be an idiot," Craig scoffed, his words dripping with sarcasm. "Of course I am. Or are you really that naive?"

"You murdered Tammy because you hated her," Rike accused, her gaze piercing into Craig's soul.

"And I pinned it on you out of spite," Craig shot back venomously.

"All because of keeping you off my land?"

"Yes. And you are a man-hater. And you shot over my head. You're a terrible woman. I was at my wit's end with Tammy. She was the first, you know. I was going to keep her in the freezer. But then word spread about you and the blood pool. Gossip that you were a poacher yourself! It was just so perfect."

"Gossip led you to my doorstep," Rike stated, the question woven seamlessly into her accusation. Her fingers remained firm on the gun, though it grew heavier with each truth uncovered.

"Indeed," Craig drawled, his voice slithering through the air like a viper ready to strike, relishing every syllable. "The renowned foreigner detective of Saint Berna, just a snowball's throw away. Your accolades and triumphs intrigued me—I wondered if I could shake the unshakeable Rike Volk."

"By implicating me? Trying to kill in my name?" Rike's words sliced through the frosty air, her disbelief palpable, her pulse racing against her chest like a frantic drumbeat. "It doesn't add up. It's..."

"It's over. No hard feelings, Rike. Just a dance of shadows and power play. Watching you stumble has been quite the spectacle." Craig's smile cut through the dimly lit room like a blade, his intentions laid bare in the charged silence between them.

"Is it true? Are you confessing to all the killings?" Rike's words cut through the room, sharp as a freshly honed blade, her eyes fixed on Craig, daring him to speak. She only now realized she was ill-prepared for his words. She had not thought to use her phone to record the truth.

"Confessing?" Craig's chuckle reverberated off the walls, but this time it sounded empty, devoid of any humour. "I don't just confess, I relish in it. But that's just between us friends, hmm?"

The room fell into a heavy silence, each word hanging in the air like a thick fog, carrying the weight of his chilling admission.

Rike's piercing gaze locked onto Craig, her voice cutting through the icy air like a blade. "No need for games, Craig. Tell me, why did you take Ada O'Neill's life?"

Craig's eyes betrayed a flicker of uncertainty, his composure faltering. "Ada, Ada, Ada. She should have left when she had the chance. But I didn't kill her. Or anyone," he retorted with a hint of defiance. Undeterred, Rike leaned in closer, her words laced with a subtle edge.

"Don't play innocent, Craig," she urged, her stare unyielding. "Do you crave the spotlight that comes with slaying an RCMP detective? Is that your twisted path to fame in this sea of anonymity?"

"I do not seek fame," Craig insisted, his voice tinged with a mix of frustration and fear.

Rike's eyes narrowed, her tone sharp and unforgiving. "You wanted the attention, didn't you? The spotlight on you for once. Admit it, Craig. You took Ada's life just to bask in the glory. To kill an RCMP detective? You are smart enough to know it will give you the fame at a level the others will not."

"Why do you care about her so much? It's like...Oh yes! You cared for her! Didn't you? Ha ha! The Ice Queen has a heart. Is it broken into a million pieces now?" Craig asked as he clapped with delight. A dark smile crept across Craig's face, his tone dripping with malice. "Oh yes, it was me who ended her life," he gloated, a malevolent glint dancing in his eyes. The sickening joy radiating from him as he revelled in the thought of being tied to Ada O'Neill's demise sent a shiver down Rike's spine. His vindictiveness towards Rike was palpable. "You will always carry this pain, won't you? You will! And you will always think of me," Craig proclaimed, his words slicing through the heavy silence with bone-chilling finality.

"You..." Rike could not speak, for anger and sorrow filled her throat, choking her. The weight of loss bore down on her, a crushing force that swept away the remnants of her stoic facade, revealing the depths of her profound sorrow and longing for the woman she had held dear, and hoped for a future with.

"And that's just the beginning," Craig continued with a twisted grin. "Four others, their fate sealed by my hands, their lives snuffed out in the blink of an eye. But Ada, oh Ada, her end will echo through your mind forever. Can't you see Rike? This is my magnum opus of destruction."

Amidst the chilling realization of Ada's true fate, Rike's emotions swirled in a maelstrom of anguish, her heart clenching with a sorrow so profound that it felt as if her very core had been shattered. Waves of despair crashed against the walls she had carefully built around herself, leaving behind a raw, exposed vulnerability that threatened to engulf her in a sea of unspoken grief.

"The pleasure and the glory of such a feat," Craig's words slithered through the air, chilling Rike to her core. "To kill a handful of women, including an RCMP officer—now that's true distinction. But even better, only you will hear my words."

His voice echoed around the room, bouncing off the stark walls and reverberating through the chilling silence. The crude satisfaction on his face was akin to that of a puppeteer who had just manipulated his marionettes into performing a grand spectacle.

Rike's mind raced as she wrestled with his unexpected confession. She kept her eyes trained on him, refusing to blink lest it be a dream. Yet despite her steady demeanour, fear gnawed at the edges of her consciousness—not for herself, but for the innocent lives that had been tossed around in Craig's reckless pursuit of fame.

"Yes. Let it be known that Craig Griffith outsmarted them all, even Ada O'Neill, of the glorious Royal Canadian Mounted Police." His voice was suddenly laced with bravado.

"Your admission," Rike stated firmly, her gaze piercing into his, "will bring you the hatred of a country."

Craig remained seated, a smug smile stretching across his features. "No, no. No one but you will hear the truth. And if you tell, no one will buy your version of events, Rike," he taunted, the sharpness of his laughter cutting through the gravity of their confrontation. "You'll never shake off the shadow cast on you. If I survive our little tête-à-tête, and I think I will, for you are not a killer like me, I will refute every word. And if I don't survive?" Leaning in with a glint in his eyes, he added, "Then you'll be the one responsible for my death. I win either way."

"Your confession isn't coerced, Craig," Rike's voice sliced through the tension, her fingers steady on the gun despite the sheen of sweat on her skin.

"Of course not," Craig smirked, his chuckle tapering into a cunning grin. "You're no threat; just a shadow in the dark. Not coerced. And not legally binding. I am only saying what you want me to say."

The charged silence thickened as each heartbeat echoed louder in the confined space. Confidence swelled within Craig, convinced he had outsmarted Rike, even with a gun aimed at him. Rike faltered only slightly, though enough for Craig's eagle eyes.

Craig's demeanour hardened. With a dangerous glint in his eyes, he turned to Rike, his voice low and menacing. "You thought you had me cornered, didn't you? But now that the law's at your doorstep, I have the upper hand. I won't confess to anything. Not to anyone else. You get to know, because the truth will torture you."

A smirk played on Craig's lips as he continued, his words dripping with malice, "You'll be the one to pay for all of this, Rike. You trespassed, threatened me with a weapon, and I'll say you confessed to me. You gave me all the details of all the murders. The police will see you for what you truly are—a dangerous criminal trying to frame an innocent man."

With a chilling certainty, Craig locked eyes with Rike, his tone final and unforgiving. "I'll make sure they know the truth. You're the one they should be taking away in handcuffs, not me," he said.

With a primal snarl, Craig surged forward. Rike's body reacted instinctively, muscles coiled like springs from her years of police training. His hands reached out hungrily, aiming for the gun that represented his dark intentions. The room echoed with grunts and laboured breaths as they grappled, their silhouettes casting frantic shadows on the walls of Craig's dimly lit house. The gun became a volatile entity in their struggle, its icy surface slipping through their desperate fingers as if it had a will of its own, fighting for dominance.

"Hand it over!" Craig's voice cracked with urgency, the edges of desperation seeping into his demand.

"Never!" Rike's defiant voice sliced through the tense air, a potent mix of determination and fear. The room erupted into chaos, a whirlwind of frantic movements and gasps until a sudden, thunderous blast silenced everything for a moment.

Craig's anguished scream pierced the stillness, his figure recoiling in agony.

Heart pounding, Rike stood frozen, her grip on the gun unwavering. The weapon quivered imperceptibly, its barrel cool and loaded but mercifully untriggered.

"Craig!" a voice quavered, commanding attention amidst the turmoil. Officer Horton loomed in the doorway, his own firearm levelled at the scene with wisps of smoke lingering in the air. His hand shook visibly, a testament to the gravity of the moment that had just unfolded.

"Lower your weapon, Rike. Put it down!" he commanded, his voice firm and resolute as he entered the dimly lit room, his eyes swiftly scanning the scene between Rike and the injured man. Rike's bewilderment was tangible as she carefully set her gun down on the worn kitchen table. Her gaze shifted to Craig, sprawled on the cold floor, his face contorted in agony, hands desperately pressing against his bleeding leg, staining his pants with a vivid crimson bloom that seemed to seep into the very essence of the room.

Craig's pained moans shattered his tough facade as vulnerability took hold. "Dispatch, Horton here. Medical aid urgently needed at the Griffith residence. We are at 29 Way Road. Gunfire exchanged, suspect injured in the leg," Officer Horton's voice commanded over the radio waves with unwavering authority.

In a daze, Rike sprang into action, her movements precise yet urgent. Snatching a dish towel from the stove handle, she knelt beside Craig. With a swift and sure hand, she applied pressure to the bleeding wound, her instincts kicking in to save a life, no matter its imperfections.

"Thank you, Officer Horton," she said, her voice unwavering as she staunched the crimson flow. "Help is en route, Craig." Craig's anguished expression mirrored his suffering, his once steely gaze now a muddle of dread and bewilderment. Struggling to contain his pain, he emitted feeble whimpers and shallow breaths, while Rike—the very woman he had sought to ruin—attended to his injury.

Autumn crept into the room behind Officer Horton, her arrival marked by gasping breaths and wide eyes filled with a potent mix of alarm and resolve. She absorbed the scene unfolding before her: Rike's composed silhouette alongside the wounded Craig, with Officer Horton standing sentry in their midst.

Autumn's heart thundered in her chest as she sprinted to Rike's side, the urgency in her voice slicing through the tense air. "Rike, are you okay?" Rike met Autumn's concerned gaze. A fleeting softness crossing her features before determination hardened her expression.

"I'll be fine, Autumn," Rike reassured, her hands never faltering in their swift movements.

"What's happening here?" Autumn dropped to the snowy ground beside Rike, her eyes flickering between the injured man and the looming figure of the officer.

"Help me with this," Rike commanded, a sense of urgency in her tone as she gestured towards the makeshift bandage clutched against Craig's bleeding leg.

Without hesitation, Autumn grabbed another dish towel, her swift movements matching Rike's as they swiftly applied a cold compress to Craig's clammy forehead. The sudden chill made Craig flinch, yet his pained groans eased slightly under their meticulous ministrations.

"Autumn," Rike inquired without looking away from the injury, "why are you here with Officer Horton?"

"We've been searching everywhere for you," Autumn breathed out, her pulse finally slowing. "I stumbled upon Officer Horton unconscious at the precinct. Once he came to, we rushed to check on Craig. You had accused him in front of Officer Horton. He knew you had to confront the man."

"Thank heavens," Rike exhaled, a wave of relief washing over her words.

"And then it all unfolded–Craig's startling admission, almost in its entirety. In front of us as we stood in the mudroom." Autumn locked eyes with Rike, a silent pact of unity and faith passing between them.

"You heard?" Rike's forehead creased, a whirlwind of feelings dancing across her features.

Officer Horton's voice cut through the tension, his gun now lowered. "It's all on my body cam, Rike. Every single moment," he assured her. Rike's eyes briefly met his, a rush of relief flooding her senses.

"Thank you... I can't believe you unraveled it all," she murmured gratefully.

"We've got him," he stated with conviction, his focus unwavering. "Although you have charges of your own to account for. Assaulting a peace officer, for one," Horton said as he raised his hand to his head.

Autumn leaned in, examining Craig's wounded leg closely. "Just a flesh wound," she pronounced confidently, her gaze steely with determination. "But he needs help right away. We cannot wait for the paramedics."

"Let's move him, get him to the hospital," Horton directed briskly, signalling for Rike to assist in bringing the captured suspect to justice without delay.

Working in seamless coordination, Rike and Officer Horton lifted Craig upright. Rike's sinewy arms effortlessly supported his weight, a testament to her unwavering strength even after the draining rush of adrenaline. Every motion she made was a display of precision and unwavering control, showcasing her enduring physical prowess. In a swift and decisive move, Officer Horton snapped the cold metal handcuffs around Craig's wrists, the sharp click echoing through the tense air like a final verdict, sealing his fate.

"Craig Griffith, you are under arrest," Horton's voice sliced through the tense air, his words sharp and unforgiving as he recited Craig's rights. "Medical attention is lagging behind due to the storm. I must take him to the hospital," he informed Rike briskly. Together, they guided the injured man out of the residence. As they emerged outside, a haunting howl from a distant wolf pierced the stillness of their desolate surroundings, echoing ominously. Struggling under Craig's weight, Rike's muscles strained with each step towards the police cruiser carelessly parked in the gravel driveway. Despite the physical exertion, her expression remained composed and resolute, masking the whirlwind of emotions raging beneath her calm facade.

Autumn lingered close, a silent shadow to Rike's resolute figure. They reached the car, and Horton deftly opened the rear door. "Mind your head," Horton advised, gently guiding Craig to avoid hitting the door frame. Together, they carefully settled Craig into the back seat. His pained grunts were muffled by the car's interior as he slumped against the upholstery, handcuffs glinting in the dimming light. With a muted thud, the door shut, enveloping Craig in his temporary confinement.

"Appreciate your help, Rike. We will talk, but Craig must come first, for now," Horton acknowledged with a nod before slipping into the driver's seat. The engine roared to life, shattering the evening's tranquillity.

"Of course. Ensure his safety, Officer Horton," Rike's voice held a steely edge, her gaze unwavering on the shadowy figure in the backseat. "People need justice, not death." Horton nodded firmly before the patrol car smoothly pulled away, its flashing red and blue lights piercing the gathering darkness as it headed to the hospital with the wounded suspect.

With the cruiser disappearing down the snowy road, Rike turned to Autumn. Her face was a mosaic of emotions—relief mingled with bone-deep weariness and traces of lingering dread. Autumn approached, bridging the space between them, enfolding Rike in an embrace that conveyed more than words ever could.

"You're cleared now, Rike," Autumn's words were fierce yet comforting. "You'll be hailed a hero once this gets out. Saint Berna will owe you everything."

Rike's tough exterior faltered briefly, her face seeking comfort in the soft strands of Autumn's hair that carried a subtle scent of pine. "This ends now," Rike's voice was barely audible, swallowed by the biting wind that whisked her words away. A wave of relief washed over her as she breathed out, silently thanking the harsh winter air. Their elongated shadows painted against Craig's house, now a symbol of both tragedy and justice. In that suspended moment, time seemed to slow to a crawl as the chaotic events of the day faded into nothingness, leaving behind only the unbreakable bond between two friends who had weathered the storm together.

Autumn's voice was soft but insistent as she drew back slightly, her gaze locking with Rike's. "Time to go," she urged, a glint of determination in her eyes. "We head to the police station and wait. Together. Until other officers arrive. We will lay it all out. Let's make this real."

Chapter 33

As Rike and Autumn left Craig Griffith's residence, a chilling storm enveloped them, the frosty air seeming to crystallize the tension that lingered from their intense discussion inside. The crunch of snow beneath their boots mirrored the weight of unspoken words between them. Rike, her hair adorned with delicate shards of ice, strode forward with purpose, her gaze focused yet betraying a hint of unease.

"Rike, are you okay?" Autumn's voice sliced through the frozen silence, her words hanging like frost in the air. Rike, her features carved in determination, responded with a terse nod. The chilling recollection of Craig's damning admission played out in her thoughts, each detail etched vividly against the stark winter backdrop. The echo of Officer Horton's firearm reverberated in her ears, the sharp report shattering the stillness as Craig crumbled to the ground, wounded but breathing. In that moment, amidst the biting cold, truth and consequences collided in a symphony of suspense and revelation.

The journey to Rike's cabin felt endless, each step heavy with their shared experience. The air crackled with unspoken words, a palpable connection forged by the chilling truth they had faced. It was as though the mystery surrounding the murders enveloped them like the howling storm that now engulfed them.

Approaching Rike's cozy home, its windows darker than the surrounding gloom, Autumn finally broke the silence. "Looks like we're in for a long night. Maybe a few long nights together. Statements are to be made. To clear your name. Are you ready for this?" Her concern masked beneath a veil of composure, her eyes betraying a depth of emotion only she could understand.

"Absolutely," Rike responded wearily, her tone tinged with exhaustion. "Let's just get this done."

Autumn glanced about her at the blizzard and remarked, "Your nerves have been through the wringer already. And now this storm?" As they neared Rike's truck buried under a thick layer of snow, Autumn took charge, clearing the windshield with brisk, expert movements. "I'll drive," she declared, her actions swift and decisive. "You've had a long day of hard work—although I must admit, you handle it like a pro. A hero detective at work."

A faint smirk played on Rike's lips. "Keep that under wraps. I'd hate to dust off my badge," she teased. Autumn slid behind the wheel, and Rike settled into the passenger seat, finding solace in the well-worn familiarity of her truck amidst the swirling uncertainty.

The key turned in the ignition with a sharp click, igniting the engine into a thunderous roar that drowned out the howling wind outside. The headlights sliced through the thickening snowstorm like a knife, revealing fleeting shadows dancing in the blizzard. A bone-chilling cold seeped into their bodies, contrasting sharply with the warmth trickling from the vents, creating an eerie sense of unease as they braced themselves for the treacherous journey ahead.

With a trembling grip on the steering wheel, Autumn navigated the truck cautiously through the relentless onslaught of snow, crunching over the icy terrain in a frantic staccato beat. The swirling flakes created a disorienting maze around them, obscuring their path and distorting reality into a surreal nightmare. Every gust of wind threatened to tip the vehicle off balance, adding to the mounting tension inside.

Autumn's knuckles stood out starkly against her pale skin, her eyes wide and fixed on the opaque veil of white that enveloped them. The world outside seemed to shrink into a claustrophobic tunnel of snow and darkness, their sense of isolation increasing with each passing moment.

"We should consider stopping until this storm eases," Rike proposed, her gaze piercing into the swirling snow that obscured their surroundings. "The visibility is deteriorating rapidly. Pull over to the side of the road."

"Did you use the snow as cover with Ada? Is that why you pulled off?" Autumn's question sliced through the howling wind, laden with an unsettling edge.

Rike whipped around to face Autumn, her eyes narrowing in bewilderment at the unexpected accusation. "What do you mean?"

Autumn's voice sliced through the tense silence, a whisper laced with hidden intent as they navigated the treacherous road. "Whispers travel fast in this forsaken hellhole," she hissed, eyes narrowed on the blizzard-obscured path ahead.

"Hellhole?" Rike felt a chill crawl down her spine at the ominous tone, her breath forming misty clouds against the frosty window. Memories of past conversations began to seep into her mind, their words now tainted with an unsettling edge that made her skin prickle. "You love–"

"I was in hell when I saw you two. Kissing. In this very vehicle."

The truck rumbled on, tires gripping the icy terrain with a sinister determination. Autumn's fingers tightened around the wheel, each turn taken with a calculated precision that sent shivers down Rike's spine. The speedometer needle climbed steadily, a silent accomplice to their escalating unease.

As Rike's gaze flickered to the increasing speed, a sense of foreboding settled over her like a heavy cloak. The metallic click of each mile passed resonated in the confined space, echoing like an ominous countdown to an unknown reckoning.

"Easy there, Autumn. Slow down," Rike cautioned, her hand gripping the dashboard for stability. Autumn's foot eased off the gas pedal, the tension palpable in the confined space.

"Did she tell you she was cold? That she wanted to go into the truck? That wouldn't surprise me. She had her eye on you from the beginning," Autumn began, her words measured and laden with a mix of envy and hurt. The silence that followed was heavy with unspoken emotions, swirling between them like a brewing storm on the horizon. "In this very truck, I saw it. The kiss," she confessed finally, her voice rife with jealousy that she couldn't conceal.

Rike's heart skipped a beat. The confession sliced through the silence, sharp and unexpected. "You saw us kiss?"

"I did." Autumn's grip tightened on the wheel once more, her voice steadier now as she continued. "And I saw you together in the hotel bar. I've been wrestling with something, Rike... I was jealous. There, I said it. Jealous of how Ada looked at you, of that night you spent together at the hotel."

"Autumn, I—" Rike started, but the words tangled in her throat.

"No, let me finish." Autumn glanced over, her eyes shining with a vulnerability Rike had rarely seen. "I love you, Rike. More than I thought possible. And seeing you with Ada—it really hurt."

Inside the truck, amidst the relentless storm outside, a whirlwind of emotions swirled between Rike and Autumn. The air crackled with emotional pain as they sat in the cocoon of warmth from the heater, yet an icy tension gripped Rike's core.

"You were spying on Ada and me?" Rike's voice cut through the howling wind like tempered steel veiled in velvet, her eyes piercing into Autumn's soul.

With a visible swallow, Autumn met Rike's gaze head-on. "Yes. I saw you two at the hotel lounge," she confessed, each word heavy with the weight of truth. "The laughter, the shared drinks—it was impossible to look away. And I followed you to the room. I was out of your sight, but you were not out of mine. It drove me out of my mind. I knew it from the start."

"What did you know?" Rike's breath formed frost on the truck window.

Autumn's words lingered heavily in the air, mingling with the falling snowflakes outside. "I knew you would end up staying with her," she confessed, her voice cutting through the silence like a sharp blade. "I waited all night in that lobby, hoping to see you come back down. But you never did." The only sounds were the haunting wind and the wipers struggling against the relentless snow, casting deep shadows of disbelief across Rike's weathered features.

"Autumn..." Rike's voice faltered, the syllables heavy with accusation. The biting wind carried Autumn's confession, her words barely audible amidst the raging storm.

"I couldn't bear it," Autumn's admission sliced through the icy air, laden with raw emotion. "The sight of you leaving her room that morning ignited a fire in me. I needed answers from Ada. Why did she have what I longed for?"

Rike's pulse thundered in her ears, each beat a sharp echo in the stillness that enveloped them. "Autumn, please," Rike implored, her voice strained with disbelief and a hint of dread.

"I passed a breakfast cart in the hotel corridor. A sharp knife caught my eye," Autumn's voice carried a sinister edge, her eyes focused straight ahead. "I pocketed it and rapped on her door. When Ada opened it..."

"Autumn, no," Rike's voice barely pierced the howling wind that whipped around them. The words twisted Rike's insides, each word a sharp blade slicing through her body.

"I attacked her, Rike. With the knife," Autumn's tone was as icy as the blizzard raging outside, devoid of any hint of remorse or emotion. "I did it for you. To keep you." The truck barrelled on through the blinding whiteout, every passing mile driving them deeper into the heart of the malevolent tempest.

Rike remained still, caught between the frigid grip of the blizzard and the chilling reality of Autumn's sinister revelation.

"Craig confessed," Rike said as she struggled to understand what was happening.

"He did, didn't he? It's very convenient. Don't you think? There is no reason to suspect I had anything to do with it. It's…It's like I will get off, scot-free." Autumn's laughter made Rike want to vomit.

In the deafening roar of the snowstorm, Rike Volk sat frozen in the passenger seat of the truck, her breath hitching as Autumn's chilling confession echoed in the confined space. The revelation of Ada's murder at Autumn's hands pierced through Rike's soul like a shard of ice, sending tremors of shock and disbelief through her very being.

As the truck pressed on through the blizzard, each passing second felt like an eternity of torment and despair for Rike. The trust she had placed in a friend now shattered, replaced by a gaping maw of betrayal and heartbreak. The stark reality of Autumn's twisted love for Rike had transformed into a deadly obsession, staining their shared history with blood and darkness.

Guilt clawed at Rike's conscience, mingling with a profound sense of loss and grief that threatened to consume her. The storm raging outside mirrored the tempest raging within her, a maelstrom of conflicting emotions that tore at her resolve and shattered her composure. She pulled her gun out of her pocket and aimed.

In the midst of the howling storm, Rike's voice sliced through the cacophony, her gaze piercing Autumn with a blend of resolve and dread. "Pull over, Autumn. This can't go on."

Autumn's face contorted with a frenzied intensity, her hands clenching the steering wheel tightly as she stared at Rike. "I won't stop, Rike. We're meant to be together. Everything I did was for us. You can't refuse."

The truck veered precariously, its tires struggling for traction on the icy road as Autumn pushed down harder on the gas pedal, escalating the peril amidst the raging elements.

Rike's grip on the gun tightened, her fingers trembling with a mix of fear and determination. "Autumn, please, don't do this," she pleaded, her voice strained with emotion.

In the tense silence that followed, Autumn's laughter filled the truck, a haunting sound that seemed to reverberate off the metal and seep into Rike's bones. "This is the only way," she declared, her eyes gleaming with an unsettling intensity. "I've waited for so long, tried so hard to earn your love. I've been by your side through it all, just like you were there for me when we first crossed paths. That Ada woman had you under her spell, but I broke it. Now you can finally love me. It's my time."

With a swift motion, Rike pulled back the hammer on the gun. "Please, just stop the truck," she implored, a hint of desperation in her voice. The icy wind whipped through the open window, carrying their tense words into the snowy landscape. "If...If you love me, you will stop immediately."

Autumn's eyes flickered with a fierce intensity, a mix of loyalty and danger swirling within them. Her grip on the wheel was firm as she steered the truck erratically, each swerve sending adrenaline coursing through Rike's veins. "You can't escape this, Rike Volk. And you will not shoot me," she declared sharply, her tone laced with a haunting determination. "I've sacrificed everything for you. I've crossed lines that can never be uncrossed."

The road stretched out endlessly before them, a treacherous path mirroring the turbulent emotions between the two women. In that moment of chaos and revelation, Rike realized that Autumn's obsession ran deeper and darker than she had ever imagined.

"P-Please. Please," Rike begged. "Pull over. Let's talk."

"We can talk later," Autumn said. "Put the gun down, Rike. I'm starting to think you don't love me." She jerked the wheel, and the truck swerved wildly. Rike gripped the dashboard to steady herself. "Do you love me, Rike?"

"This has to end," Rike said as she lowered her gun. "See? I did what you asked. I put the gun down. Let's end this now. Pull over."

"This never has to end. My love for you will never end," Autumn said. "The funny thing about your truck is, there's only one airbag. It's on the driver's side. Did you realize that? I've been in this truck. I've noticed. I thought, if I am in the passenger seat and there's an accident, I will not be saved. If we crash, I'll be okay, here in the driver's seat, but you?" She twisted the steering wheel just a little, to scare Rike. A jagged wall of granite lined the roadway, and Rike ducked as it came rushing toward her. "I'm just teasing. Geez, Rike, take it easy. I wouldn't hurt you. You could end up paralyzed. But...I guess that's one way of stopping you from wandering away from me, hmm? Like in that book? They one they made into a movie?"

Autumn hummed tunelessly just under her breath as she navigated the treacherous road. As she drove past the turnoff for Saint Berna Aux Étranger, Rike's grip tightened on the gun. A surge of adrenaline rippled through her body. She shifted in her seat, a flicker of unease crossing her face before she refocused on the threat beside her. Rike once again aimed her gun at Autumn. And fired.